SURVIVING REDEMPTION

By D.L. Roan

Published by D.L. Roan. First print edition, December 2015
Previously published as Second Nature October 2014
www.dlroan.com

ISBN-13: 978-1519331892

Cover Design by D.L. Roan
Interior eBook Design by D.L. Roan
Editing by KMS Freelance Editing Service

DEDICATIONS

Human trafficking is the largest and fastest growing form of international organized crime in the world. The slave trade exists in many forms and has no boundaries or borders. While Grant and Thalia's story is purely fiction, there are countless men, women and children who have fallen victim to those who prey on their innocence and circumstances to feed the desires of the soulless and depraved. Many have died at the hands of their captors. Some have escaped and lived to fight against them. An unimaginable number still exist within the darkness of anonymity and even more will take their place when they are gone. There are many who are ignorant of its existence, some who stand and fight for the otherwise invisible and a few who will truly never forget the lost.

To the survivors and their inexorable strength, the memories of the many lost and stolen souls, and to those who continue to fight a war that must be won to protect the innocent. My heart will never forget.

To my perfectly flawed hero husband, thank you for everything you are. I could not do this without you. To Vikki, literally the strongest woman on the planet. You are my real-life Super Woman and I love you so hard! To my fellow Indie authors who have welcomed me into the fold with open arms, it is impossible to list everyone so please know I adore you all. To the Second Nature Street Team who has promoted me beyond reason and given me the opportunity to meet so many amazing people in the Indie world. Most importantly, to my fans, thank you for your dedication and for loving my characters as much as I do. This would be impossible without you. XoXo

PREFACE

Stolen Innocence

She heard a loud pop before the car swerved and her grip tightened on the steering wheel. Her Driver's Ed teacher's words filtered through her thoughts with lightning speed as the first spike of panic laced her veins. Lifting her foot from the accelerator, she gently pressed the brake pedal and guided the car to a stop on the side of the country road.

Fine gravel shifted and crunched beneath her sneakers as she stepped around to the passenger side and got her first look at her first flat tire, on her first solo drive to school.

"Fudge." She walked down the road a bit to where the paper bag she'd hit lay torn to shreds, what was left of several green glass bottles shattered around it.

"Dad is going to kill me." Or worse, never let her drive again. How was she supposed to know it was filled with glass bottles? Okay, so she hadn't exactly swerved to miss it, but it wasn't her fault some people were jerks.

Sprinting back to her car, she thought briefly about calling her boyfriend to come change the flat. That thought lasted long enough to remember her dad's stern warning about no boys in the car. Not that they would actually be *in* the car, but she didn't need her dad giving her anymore grief about Michael. No, she might as well call the warden and get it over with. It wasn't like she took out a trec or anything.

She located his number on her cellphone and pressed send, not bothering to leave a message when the call was automatically forwarded to his voicemail. After two more tries she was about to dial Michael's number when a car she didn't recognize pulled up behind hers and stopped.

She watched nervously in her rear view mirror as a tall, lanky man got out and approached her side of the vehicle. Unsure of what to do, she was a little relieved when his lips curved into a friendly smile and he tipped the bill of his baseball cap to greet her.

"Everything okay?"

The creep factor gone, she rolled down the window and nodded. "Yeah, just a flat tire. I'm trying to reach my dad, but he's not answering."

"The glass got you, huh." He shrugged and pulled his cellphone from the back pocket of his faded blue jeans. "Let me make a quick call to my wife to let her know I'll be a little late, and then I'll change it for you."

"No, that's okay. I—"

"It's no problem. It will only take a few minutes."

Her eyes followed his movements as he held his phone to his ear and walked around to look at the tire. She couldn't sit in the car and let him do all of the work. Keys still in the ignition, her purse and book bag piled in a heap on the front seat, she opened the driver's door and stepped out onto the shoulder. Shoving her cellphone into her front pocket, she rounded the back of the car just as the man ended his call.

"You don't have to do this. My dad will be…"

The rest of her words were smothered by the hand that clamped tight over her mouth as someone behind her snaked an arm around her waist and yanked her off the ground. *Oh God!* "Help!" she tried to scream, but nothing more than a muffled cry made its way beyond the suffocating pressure. Twisting and kicking, she watched helplessly as the nice man with the baseball cap grabbed her legs and wrapped a thin length of rope around her ankles. Fear turning to sheer terror, she flailed and thrashed and clawed at anything she could grasp. When she finally managed to sink her teeth into the hand clamped over her mouth, the man holding her captive tightened his grip on her jaw until she thought it would break and she was forced to let go as he shoved her to the ground.

She tried to crawl away. Beyond words, her cries for help turned into incoherent screams as a heavy weight pressed her into the ground and her arms were pinned behind her back. The sound of tape being ripped from the roll barely registered before a long strip was slapped over her mouth, tangling in the wisps of long hair that had escaped her pony tail in the struggle. Her wrists bound tight behind her, she was wrenched from the ground and dumped into the trunk of their car. No words were spoken between the two men. No second glances or hesitations as they closed the trunk lid and the first wave of darkness swallowed her whole. It was only a shadow of the dark days to come. She would not be alone in her fate.

CHAPTER ONE

"Where's the disk?" Fire exploded behind Thalia's Brezlin's right eye as the butt of a gun crashed into the side of her skull. Random flashes of light from the bare bulb swinging above her penetrated her rapidly swelling eyelid, making either the room or her head spin out of control. Any moment now she was going to puke or pass out. She truly didn't care which came first, as long as the pain stopped. Neither option, she feared, would matter to this bastard.

"It's not a disk." Dammit, it hurt too much to talk. She could feel the fresh flow of warm blood pouring from her temple; see it dripping into her lap onto what was left of her tattered cargo pants. *My favorite pair.* Only her sick sense of sarcasm kept her from giving into her fear. A fear she knew would cripple or kill her the moment she gave it even a shred of control. If this evil creep knew how scared she truly was, how scared she'd been for so long now that she could barely remember a time without fear, he would use it to eat her alive.

Keep him talking. The pain from the metal handcuffs slicing into her wrists was nothing compared to the hell her face was going through, but she kept working. If she didn't get her hands through soon, the swelling would make it impossible. She was so close.

She'd already mapped out her escape. The chair she was handcuffed to wasn't bolted to the floor. That would be weapon number one. If it didn't splinter apart after taking out her first target, she'd use it on another. Her second choice would be to go for the metal chain she'd spotted in the corner behind the only door to her dark, mammoth-sized cell. Dammit! If only she could get her hands on the nice piece of nickel this asshole kept beating her with… *At least he hasn't shot me with it yet.*

"Don't toy with me bitch!" The sound of ripping fabric echoed past the pounding in her ears. Her body jerked against the chair with each brutal tug, cold air swirling over the sheen of sweat that covered her bared breasts. *Oh God! Oh God! Oh God!* Thalia sucked in a sharp breath as twin spikes of pain pierced her nipples and rippled down her spine. *Please don't do this!* She choked back her plea. She would not cry out and give him the satisfaction. Biting the inside of her cheek until she tasted the rusty tang of blood, she sucked in another deep breath, her nostrils flaring with her effort to control the pain. She forced herself not to look at his gun, now tucked neatly into the front waistband of his tailored suit pants. As long as both his hands were on her, the gun was fair game.

"Hamisi," she hissed through her clenched teeth, careful to mask her fear. "Were you really born on a Thursday? It is what the Hindi name means, yes?"

Hamisi kept one hand on her naked breast, tightening his vise-like grip. He threaded his other hand through her sweaty black hair and wrenched her head back, the sickening scents of peppermint and tobacco washing over her battered face. "What games are these you play? You know I will kill you if you do not tell me where it is!"

Thalia looked into Hamisi's inky black eyes, her gaze trailing over his near flawless complexion. He was an attractive man; tall and solid, his dark skin revealing his Indian heritage. Plump lips, with a hint of dryness around the edges, pressed into a snarl. He wasn't accustomed to the climate. She must have hit a nerve for Don Lalia to send his personal guard to deal with her. Killing his second in charge had been blind luck, but she'd taken it. She was quickly growing tired of running. She was tired, period. It would be nice to send another one of these bastards to hell before one of them finally killed her.

Returning her gaze to his cold, dark eyes, she knew one thing for certain. He would kill her with or without the thumb drive. His grip tightened in her hair, a fierce growl rumbled from his chest. "You will give me what I want. Or I will rip it from you one strip of skin at a time."

She didn't flinch at his biting tone or the spray of spittle that peppered her face. Her eyes slowly moved past his and focused on the rusty metal ceiling above them, ignoring the searing pain that ripped over her scalp. "I think it's a fake name," she said with a casual shrug of her shoulders, her right hand slipping silently through the cuff. "I'd have guessed you were born yesterday, and yesterday was Tuesday."

He released her hair and she turned her head just as his fist came down, glancing off her forehead. She felt nothing. Nothing but the blissfully cold nickel that soothed her palm as she wrapped her hand around the gun tucked into Hamisi's belt. *Now let's see how tough you are!*

The chair exploded into pieces over Hamisi's head, the sound of splintering wood drowned out by the staccato of gunfire. Two rounds found their targets across the room, taking out Hamisi's henchmen with practiced precision.

Before she could turn the gun on Hamisi, a suffocating silence filled the room. Arms of steel circled around her shoulders from behind, crushing her chest. "I do not die so easily, *kuttiya*," Hamisi purred in her ear, sending sickening chills racing down her spine.

Thalia struggled against his grip, holding tight to the gun as his slimy hand slithered up her shoulder. If he got his hands around her neck she was dead. "When are you guys going to learn?" she grunted through clenched teeth. "I'm nobody's bitch." Stars exploded behind her eyelids as the back of her head connected with his face, the crunch of breaking bones echoing off the steel walls of the expansive space.

She twisted from his arms, her knee finding his groin with flawless execution. Hunched over from the pain, either choking on his balls or about to puke them up, Thalia took out his knee with a swift kick, flattening him to the cold hard floor. Sweat stung the cuts on her face as she fought for each breath, her shiny, new pistol now leveled at Hamisi's bloodied face. "*I* don't die that easily, you fucking kutta." She pulled the trigger, the sound of a stale click sending shivers up her spine.

Hamisi's laughter clawed its way over her skin. "Who is the stupid dog now?"

Somewhere in the back of her mind she knew it was foolish, but she took a step closer to him, already imagining his brains slathered across the bottom of her boot. With blinding speed,

Hamisi's leg made contact and swept her off her feet, a searing hot pain slicing into her side.

Instinct had her moving before she could process the pain, clutching at his wrist. The dull light from the one bare bulb reflected off the blade extending from his clenched fist. She was no match for his brute, male strength. A scream tore its way past her bloody lips as the blade sunk into the top of her thigh. Desperate not to give into the torturous pain, she pushed away from him, the knife's blade slicing further into her flesh. Holding onto her last thread of control, her hands found his face as she blindly searched for the one thing she knew would end this.

An eerie shriek pierced the air and drowned out the other sounds of their struggle. Sticky, wet fluid coated her fingers as they found their mark. Hamisi's hands released her from his grip as he cupped his face and screamed in horror. The odd shaped eyeball, still tethered to the nerve, balanced precariously in his palm. Thalia used her arms to drag herself away from the grisly scene. Footsteps pounded from the floor above her. *Time to move.* More blood seeped from her leg and her side, leaving a sodden trail along the floor as she dragged herself closer to the door. She needed to get to her feet.

Bracing herself against a metal pole near the center of the dimly lit cargo hold, she wrapped her fingers around the hilt of the knife. *This is going to hurt like a mother.*

Sucking in one final breath, she ground her teeth together to hold back another scream clawing its way up her throat. *Son of a bitch!* The instant the blade was free, dark crimson blood rushed from the wound and began to pool under her leg. She was going to bleed to death before she could get out of this shithole, wherever that was.

Working as fast as her shaking hands allowed, she tore off a strip of what was left of her shirt and tied it around her thigh, biting back another scream. More heavy footfalls moved overhead and voices echoed through the steel hull from somewhere close.

Hamisi's screams had stopped. She guessed he'd passed out. God knows she probably would have. Nonetheless, she was thankful for the reprieve as she hobbled to the door and carefully peered around the frame. Clear in both directions, she stepped outside and was assaulted by the salty ocean air. From the familiar stench of dead fish and diesel fuel, she knew she was in a marina. What she didn't know was where. Judging the distance to the water below, the boat was a freighter of some significant size. She'd been unconscious when they brought her here. How long ago that was, she wasn't sure.

She studied the docks as she stumbled her way toward the back of the ship. The lights blurred and swayed as an icy blanket folded in around her. Her hands and feet felt like blocks of ice, dragging her to the slippery deck. She was losing too much blood. An agonized moan slipped beyond her control as she slid down a short flight of stairs, grasping the railing with her blood slicked hands.

Moving with pure adrenaline, she forced herself along the stern. *It's so dark.* If only a day had passed she should still be somewhere along the African coastline. Looking out toward the ocean, she could see the faint twinkling of a few shining lights from the nearby coastal islands. *I can swim that far.* It wasn't a question of if she could do it. She had to make it happen. It was her last conscious thought before her body hit the cold, salty water below.

CHAPTER TWO

"Son of a dickless monkey!" Grant Kendal shook out his throbbing hand. He was going to hunt down the bastard who'd sold him these cheap as shit nails and take his money back in slow, even installments of pain; one rusty nail at a time.

"Don't get your tail in a wad, Winston. I wasn't talking about you." Winston lowered his hand from his face and turned his back to Grant, arms folded over his knobby knees. Crouched on his hands and knees on top of the thatched roof, Grant hung his head and let out a frustrated growl. He knew better than to feed the damn thing. "One piece of sugar cane and I'm married to a goddamn monkey!" He pounded his fist on the bare rafter he was trying desperately to cover before the afternoon storms blew in.

He'd managed to live thirty-four years—no small feat considering his chosen profession—without falling prey to a single woman's charms. He'd never considered himself much of a ladies man. Spending most of his adult life in the shadows, hunting down the cockroaches of the human species, he hadn't had much use for the social niceties women usually expected from a relationship. Procuring a warm, willing body for a night to fulfill his baser needs didn't require a lifetime commitment of manipulation and crazy mood swings. Apparently befriending a Macaque monkey did. *Retired less than a year and I'm attached at the hip to an emotionally challenged primate with a penis!*

Twisting and shuffling his way across each beam, Grant made it to the western edge of the roof. Wiping the sweat from his eyes, he stepped down onto the top rung of the ladder. "Come down, you moody bastard. I'll fix us a drink."

Winston looked over his furry shoulder, displaying his pouty bottom lip before turning away again. "Goddamn it! I'm not apologizing! I wasn't even talking to you!" Grant moved down the ladder, but stopped only a few steps down, shaking his head. When had he become such a pussy? Solitude meant being alone, right? Not having to listen to meaningless chatter or put up with a society that had disintegrated into chaos. Or having to placate the *feelings* of a damn monkey. He would have been better off if he'd painted a face on a hand grenade and called it a day.

Nearly a year ago he'd taken a job as a favor to his mentor and friend, Daniel Gregory. For some reason it had left him feeling dead inside. Daniel's daughter Natalie had been taken and sold into the sex slave industry, and Daniel had spent the last twelve years searching for her. The cockroach who ran the U.S. side of the human trafficking ring, Hector Morganti, was now behind bars thanks to Daniel's relentless pursuit and to the testimony of Hector's daughter, Gabby. Daniel, however, never found Hector's diary of transactions he hoped would lead him to the monsters that bought his daughter. When Hector was put away, his second in command, Lucien Moretti, took over the business without a hitch, apparently using the ledger of sales as blackmail and to continue the steady supply of child slaves.

Grant and Daniel had used Lucien's obsession with Gabby to lure him into a trap, hoping to find the ledger and put him away with Hector. Their plan had failed when Lucien slipped through his fingers and he was forced to kill him before he'd killed Gabby. Putting a bullet between Lucien's eyes had felt good, even if he'd deserved a far more painful death. However much he deserved it, killing Lucien had destroyed Daniel's chances of finding his daughter. They never found the ledger. The sophisticated slave ring fell apart after Lucien's demise. It may have bought some time before some other piece of shit stepped in to fill the supply gap, but thanks to Grant, his friend may never find his daughter.

Living with that shouldn't have been a problem for Grant. Bad people did bad things to good people all the time. He was called to take out the trash and move on to the next job. No questions. No regrets. He didn't regret a single kill he'd made, but seeing the hopelessness in Daniels eyes and sweet Gabby's reaction to the monster inside him had left him feeling cold. That's when he knew he was done. For the first time in his life he hadn't liked the emotionless tool he'd become.

Setting himself up on a deserted scrub island in the middle of the Indian Ocean was supposed to give him some clarity; time to cleanse himself of the beast within and consider his next step. Ten months later, and the only thing he was sure of was that he wasn't built to mingle with the human race.

Grant banged his head against the ladder rung in front of him a few times before cursing his way back to the top. Apparently he wasn't fit to cohabitate with monkeys either. "Fine. I'm sorry. Better?" he said through his clenched teeth.

Before he could see if his half-assed attempt at placating the bratty imp had worked, the singing sound of fishing line being ripped from his reel caught his attention. Grant turned just in time to see his fishing pole fly out of the holder onto the sand and inch its way toward the water. "*Son* of a…." Winston's scolding screech had him choking back the curse as he slid down the ladder, skipping the last four rungs, and sprinting past his fire pit toward the surf. "Fish on, Winston! Fish on!"

Two days earlier he'd seen a nice sized sailfish stalking his bait from the deep channel that ran west of the island. Deciding to take up the challenge, he'd changed out his gear and reset his bait. Two whole days and not so much as a nibble. He'd obviously lost his touch if a fish could wait him out. Thanks to his newfound complacency, he was about to lose a thousand bucks worth of tackle *and* the damn fish!

Waves splashed at his feet as he made one final push off the sand before diving into the surf. His palm wrapped around the familiar corked end of his pole before another wave washed over his face, the cold salty spray stinging his eyes. Fuck all if he was going to lose this fish. Pulling the pole into his chest, his knees dug into the sand as the drag of the fish pulled him towards the deep. Digging in his heels, he set the hook, shaking the salty foam from his hair.

Snap! "Fuck!" Grant fell back into the surf, what was left of the line flapping in the wind at the tip of his pole. "Fuck, fucking godda—" The rest of his rant was cut off at the sight of the sailfish as it flew through the air with his float hanging from its bill, landing with a splash Grant could only see as a taunt. His fist pounded through the surf as he glared out at the deep, green waters. *Fucking war is what this is.*

Cold water sluiced down his face as he threaded a wet hand through his hair then pushed to his feet. He stomped through the surf toward the sandy beach, ignoring Winston's screeching cackles echoing from further down the shoreline. The damn monkey was crazy if he thought he was going to sleep inside the cabin tonight. It was supposed to rain a foot before morning. *We'll see whose laughing later, you imprudent ape!*

Grant bent and scooped up the rod holder, determined to re-rig his pole and get it back into the water. Winston's incessant screeching moved closer, and Grant looked over his shoulder to see the monkey loping towards him. When Winston saw that he'd gotten Grant's attention, he immediately switched directions, hurrying back down the beach, calling for Grant to follow him.

Waving him off, he shook his head and headed toward the pole-barn styled cabin he'd built just outside the tree line. It was only one room, but it had four walls, a roof, and a covered porch. With an added outdoor shower he'd rigged to the back, which was fed fresh, cold water by an old artesian well, it was all he needed.

Ignoring Winston's incessant protests, he leaned his pole against one of the front porch support beams and reached for his tackle box. He didn't have time for monkey business if he was going to get his bait rigged and get his roof shored up before nightfall.

A fresh spool of fishing line in hand, he turned back toward his pole and caught a glimpse of Winston from the corner of his eye. Grant paused as he watched his reluctant pet, jumping up and down and slapping at the surf as it rolled gently onshore. Shielding his eyes against the glare of the sun, he squinted toward the far end of the beach to see what had captured Winston's attention. His tackle forgotten, his feet moved with increasing speed as the object came into focus and took on an ominous form.

Grant's pulse picked up as he sprinted closer. *What the hell?* A familiar, cold calm rushed over his skin as he pushed Winston back from the pale, limp body lying face down, still half in the water. A thick curtain of black hair covered the woman's face, shielding all but a swatch of pale dead skin from his view.

It wasn't the first time he'd seen a dead body. It surely wouldn't be his last, but damn if he'd ever expected to see one here. Swiftly, Grant mentally inventoried his surroundings. He'd seen no boats milling around the island or the nearby cove lately. No one was on the island but he and Winston and a few stray vermin. Of that he was certain. Without his binoculars, he couldn't see the other nearby scrub islands well enough to scout anything out. By the waterlogged skin, he judged the body must have washed up sometime overnight. Any threat would be long gone by now. *If they had half a brain.* Of course, there could have been some sort of boating accident.

Gently he gathered the long strands of ebony hair, revealing the feminine outline of the woman's face. Preparing himself for the stench that usually came from rotting flesh, and the gore he might see from the meal the ocean's parasites had probably made of her slender form, he gingerly rolled the woman over in the sand. Letting out a sigh when the body appeared to be intact, Grant took in a cautious breath. He was relieved again to only smell the earthy scents of sea water and sand. Knowing it was futile, he placed his finger over the vein in her neck. *D.O.A. and definitely not a boating accident.*

Crouched on one knee, Grant rested his forearm across his other knee as he ran through his options. He could dig a grave and call it a day. He studied the lifeless woman before him. *Mid to late twenties*. It was difficult to tell with the swollen skin around her injuries. Her tattered shirt did nothing to hide the one inch stab wound below her left breast, or the modeled black and blue skin across her firm torso. He also recognized the bloodstains on her cargo pants as they clung to her thighs like a second skin. Someone had done a real number on her.

She had strong bone lines and manicured nails at the tips of her long, slender fingers. He gently maneuvered her arms from her sides and inspected the thin, pale skin. *No track marks.* She wore no rings or other notable jewelry. He fingered the single shock of neon blue that ran through her otherwise jet black hair as he studied her complexion. Other than the bruising and the stab wounds, she seemed too well cared for to be a homeless junkie. *Fuck!*

He'd have to call it in. Surely someone was looking for her. He had a satellite phone, but he sure as hell didn't want his tiny island crawling with local law enforcement idiots. He'd have to load her up in his boat and take her to the mainland. Tell them he fished her out of the water twenty miles or so east of his island. But not today. There was no time to secure his place and make the trip before the storms rolled in.

Resigned, Grant stood to his feet. Focused on his next task, he reached for the woman's wrist, ready to haul her over his shoulder, when he found himself staring into the ice-blue eyes of a ghost.

CHAPTER THREE

Howling wind whipped relentlessly against the bare walls of the cabin as Grant focused on the stitch he was making. It had been a long time since he'd had to tie one off. The amount of light that was cast by the two gas lamps aided little in his efforts to keep the sutures as small as possible. The entrance wound at her ribs hadn't been as deep as he thought, and it was clean compared to the jagged edges of skin he was all but cobbling together on her thigh.

Having been the recipient of a few himself, he knew a knife wound when he saw one. Someone had done a damn good job at slicing her up. In some ways it wouldn't have been so bad if whoever her assailant was had kept a sharp blade. He wouldn't be dealing with such a mess, but then she would most likely be dead. If the blade had been sharp, it would have sliced right through her artery instead of only nicking it. Tying it off had surely saved her life. That and the cold ocean water.

While removing her clothes, he'd also seen the scars on her back. Long, white lash marks baring the signature of a slave master's whip marred her delicate flesh. She was a slave, or had been at some time in her life. The raised white lines on her ankles bore the proof of her shackles. It didn't happen to all, but most slaves were tied or shackled until they were broken enough not to attempt to flee their captors. Some remained that way indefinitely. Others were caged like animals and only brought out when their owner had use for them. A select, expensive few were actually branded like cattle. Even if they were to escape their bonds, they would always bear their tormentor's mark.

It seemed odd to him at first, that he was again ensnared into the sick world of human trafficking. He shrugged it off. Slave trade was as common in this part of the world as fast food was in the

States. While the powers that be sat on their thrones and passed sweeping, meaningless legislation, then congratulated themselves on being great humanitarians, women and children were being bought and sold like horses. He would bet his favorite HK .45 that most of the slimy cocksuckers owned a few. It was all about what looked good.

Few people besides their families actually cared what happened to the thousands of women and children who were snatched from their lives and thrown into third world sex brothels every year. Hell, some mothers and fathers willingly sold their daughters into the sex trade to pay off debts, returning month after month to collect her *earnings.* It wouldn't end any time soon. There seemed to be plenty of rich men lined up to pop a child virgin, believing it would cure them of AIDS or some sick shit. *Twisted bastards.*

It was a sick mentality very few thought twice about. If they did, they'd focus more of their time and money on finding the assholes who ran the trafficking rings and cutting off their dicks, instead of spending billions of dollars on robotic squirrels and plans to control bovine flatulence. He was sure those things were important to some people, but when slapped up against this, it looked pretty damn ridiculous to him. Again he was reminded of his reasons for leaving that shitty world behind. Obviously he hadn't run far enough.

"Dammit!" Missing the loop, he carefully laid the tweezers on a roll of gauze at his knee and wiped a sterile pad across the seeping wound. Thankfully he'd re-stocked his tactical first aid kit before he'd headed out to serve his self-imposed sentence of isolation. Unconscious or not, this would hurt like a sonofabitch if he hadn't had the Lidocaine to give her.

Picking up the tweezers, his hands remained rock-steady despite his frayed nerves. He'd nearly had a heart attack when he looked down and saw her glacial eyes staring back at him from the grave. Her pulse had been so weak it was undetectable. Given the amount of blood she must have lost from her wounds, he should be sleeping next to a corpse instead of trying to patch her up like a damn quilt.

Nearly two hours later he snipped the last thread. Squeezing the tension from his aching neck, Grant leaned back and took a look at his work. He had to admit, she had a pair of legs on her. Perfectly toned, they seemed every inch of a mile long. Even in her injured state, the red-blooded male in him couldn't help but stand up and salute.

He shook off his carnal thoughts. If she survived, he was going to send her as far away from him and his island as he could get her. Knowing his luck lately, she would probably sue him instead of thanking him for saving her damn life. Not that he would expect a roll in the sheets for doing so. He looked at the swollen five inches of jagged flesh and shook his head. God only knew how many stitches he'd sewn into her perfect alabaster skin. He'd stopped counting at thirty an hour ago.

Ignoring the rivulets of water streaming in from the unfinished roof, Grant stepped around the nearly full bucket he'd placed to catch the runoff and then reached into a sack for a clean cloth. "The least you could do is empty the damn bucket," he growled as he walked past Winston and crouched back down at the woman's side. "It's your fault we're in this mess to begin with." The indifferent monkey huddled in the corner of the small hut, perched on Grant's cot, seemingly unfazed by his master's ill temper as he preened his fur.

The severe wounds tended to, Grant soaked the cloth with sterilized water and began cleaning the sand and debris from the cuts on her face. Despite looking as if she'd been hit with a battering ram, he couldn't help but notice how unusual her features were. She certainly wasn't Indian or of Middle Eastern descent. American or maybe Russian? She had high cheekbones like a runway model, accentuating her almond-shaped eyes. Deep black eyelashes feathered across her cheeks, flirting with one small freckle sitting below the corner of her right eye. Her sassy little nose looked a bit small for her face, but appeared to have escaped any damage. Her swollen upper lip drew his attention. Dabbing at the crusted blood, he was careful not to pull at the seams of the cut. *Damn, what a mess.*

His eyes roamed over her delicate chin and followed the line of her long neck to the V of her bare collarbone. His hand followed the path his eyes were gazing over, swabbing her fevered skin with the cool damp cloth. Crimson streams of water ran between his fingers as he wrung out the cloth and began again, taking notice of a few more cuts and an unusual scar at the top of her arm.

It didn't take long for him to feel his shorts tighten against his rapidly swelling cock as his gaze followed the path of her long, slender arms and then lingered on her bare breasts. He was a bastard for even thinking about her that way, but any male with blood flow to his dick would have a hell of a time keeping his mind from wandering down that path. Despite her injuries, she was strikingly beautiful.

Cursing the ache in his groin, Grant set the cloth aside and then carefully cradled her battered body against his chest. He stood and paced to his cot, laying her gently on the thin mattress, wishing he had somewhere more comfortable for her to rest. Winston scurried off to the other side of the room as Grant pulled the sheet over her naked form, careful not to snag it against her stitches.

He turned to take in the disheveled state of his once comfortable living quarters. After dumping the now overflowing bucket of rainwater, it was going to be a long night. Shrugging, he picked up the bucket and paced to the door. It had been a while since he'd slept on a hard wet floor, but it beat a hard wet rock any day.

CHAPTER FOUR

A suffocating weight pressed against Thalia's chest as she fought against the sinking feeling in her stomach. Something was terribly wrong. Sucking in a strangled breath, a hot, aching pain tore through her leg as she twisted against whatever was holding her down. Sheer panic laced her veins when she felt the bindings around her wrists tighten. No! She pulled at the ropes above her head, unable to escape the torture that was being inflicted. She could smell her burning flesh as the embers seared through her skin. Her screams were trapped in her chest, compressing the air from her lungs as she was torn in two by the demon monster that hovered above her.

Sudden silence filled her mind as blinding light eclipsed the darkness of her nightmares. Heaving in gulps of air, the room around her slowly came into focus. Thalia froze, her gaze centering in on a pair of beady, black eyes that floated in front of her face, studying her like a puzzle. *Where the hell am I?*

Afraid to move, she dragged in another labored breath as she assessed her surroundings. A shabby, palm ceiling hovered a good ten feet above her; rough cut timbers interwoven with aged two by fours. Dried frond leaves hung broken and half-hazard, a slender shaft of light beaming down from a bare spot near the center. One window, which was shuttered, and one door. Two possible escape routes, three if she could pull herself through the hole in the roof.

Pain sliced through her chest as the monkey shifted its weight. *Oh shit!* Her hands were tied above her head. She didn't know much about monkeys, but she was sure her face would be toast if she pissed it off or scared it. God only knew what or who would come through that door if it started making noise. "Nice monkey," she whispered.

As if the thing had read her thoughts, the monkey let out a cackling screech and reached to touch her face. *Ohhhh!* Thalia drew her head back as far as the pillow would allow, her chin disappearing into her neck as the monkey fingered her bottom lip. *Shit, shit, and double shit. This is not good.* She could feel her scream clawing its way from her lungs. As she'd reached her panic threshold, willing to face her captor's wrath instead of this crazy wild animal, the door opened and the monkey jerked its hand from her face.

"Get off her, Winston." The monkey chirped and scurried off the bed. Thalia's eyes darted to the new threat. Six foot two, maybe three, broad chest, corded muscles in his arms and legs, and the deadliest amber eyes she'd ever seen. *I'm screwed.* This was no tourist or zoo keeper. She knew a killer when she saw one. Judging by the amount of pain radiating through her body and the sweat soaked sheets, she was in no shape to fight him off. She'd have to be delirious to even think about it.

The sound of his boots scuffing against the floor as he approached had her muscles coiling against the pain in a fight or flight preparation. He would win, but she was determined to give him one hell of a fight.

Grant stood over her for a moment, studying her reaction to him. "Relax," he finally ordered, squatting down onto the edge of the mattress. "I'm not going to hurt you." Damn if he couldn't get lost in those eyes. They were a paler blue today than he'd seen yesterday. Almost silver and filled to the brim with a fear-laced determination he couldn't help but admire. "What's your name?" His hand paused above her leg when she flinched away from him.

"Jill," she bit out, searing him with another icy stare.

Lie number one. "Ah, she speaks English." Grant nodded. "Okay, *Jill*." He slowly lowered his hand to the sheet and lifted it away from her thigh. "I guess that makes me Jack," he mumbled as he carefully laid the back of his hand to her torn flesh. "Oddly enough, I've never been one of those."

He watched her closely as he felt for signs of heat or infection. She'd nearly knocked his lights out the night before when he'd gotten up to check her wounds. He'd had to tie her arms to the head rail on his cot to keep her from tearing out her stitches before she'd finally passed out again. Not wanting a repeat performance, he kept a wary eye on her unbound legs as he checked her stitches.

"Well, Jill." He re-covered her bare leg and reached for the top of the sheet. Ignoring her wordless protests, he peeled down the white cotton sheet, sparing only a quick glance at her plump, bare breasts as he examined the cut over her ribs. "The good news is the swelling above your eye has gone down enough so that you no longer look like a science fiction experiment. The bad news is your leg is infected. You need a doctor."

"No. No doctors. I can…"

"Yeah, I figured as much." Grant watched her struggle against her bonds. She froze when he pressed his hand to her bare chest. "I said relax. Do you want me to untie you?"

Her eyes darted up to the cord around her wrists in another wordless plea. "Well, see, I only have one problem with that." Grant smirked and pointed to the cut on his cheekbone. "Seems you have one hell of a right hook, *Jill*."

At least she had the decency to look contrite as she studied his face. He knew it was an act. She would fight balls to the wall as soon as he released her. He counted on it, in fact. "That's okay, I don't need an apology. I know you didn't mean it. You were pretty out of it last night." He reached for the knot above her head but stilled, searching out her gaze. "You won't do it again, will you?"

He almost laughed at the puppy dog eyes she gave him as she silently shook her head. *Well, here goes the neighborhood.* He took a little longer than necessary to work the knot free, watching as her muscles bunched and coiled. He could almost feel the energy rolling off her body as she prepared to strike. It was one of the things he missed about his job. Reading the people he was hunting, feeling the energy around him shift and move as the final fatal scene unfolded.

One last tug and the cord fell free. She pulled her hands down to her chest and calmly worked at the strands until they slid from her wrists. Almost teasingly, Grant shifted and turned his back to her. She certainly didn't disappoint. Striking like a cobra, she jackknifed from the mattress, looping the cord over his head and wrapping it around his throat.

With a knee in his back, she pulled hard against the cord. Grant had to admit, he'd underestimated her strength a bit. The hand he'd slipped between his neck and the cord began to lose feeling as the cord cut into his palm. He was beginning to think twice about playing games with this chick. With a twist and a shove he was out of her snare and had his hands wrapped around both her wrists. He dodged her knee as she shoved it at his groin, but he couldn't hold back the curse when she bit down on the back of his hand.

"Goddammit!" She was like a damn fossa mongoose; lean, mean, and quick as hell! Grunted curses filled the air as he hoisted her from the cot and then pushed her back into the mattress. No more games with the rabid carnivore. Her arms pinned beside her head, he straddled her hips and hooked his ankles over her shins to keep her from kneeing him in the back. "Enough," he growled as he hovered above her.

Her nostrils flared as she dragged in a series of frantic breaths. Her skin, which had been so pale and gray, was now flushed pink with excitement. He watched as her silver eyes flared with heat, her pupils dilating to encompass the hypnotizing swirls of gray. Grant was astonished. Every misconception he'd had of her being a broken victim flew right out the window. Christ, she was playing him. And she was enjoying it every bit as much as he was.

His cock, hard and aching, pressed against her pelvis as the heat from her naked body washed over him. He was suddenly aware of her bare breasts pressed against his chest and found himself wishing he'd decided to go shirtless that morning. Her pink lips parted, her warm breath washing over him as their eyes locked. He fought hard against the need to kiss those lips, to slide his tongue into her hot, wet mouth and devour the taste of pure wildness that radiated from her soul. She didn't need a snare to capture him. He felt himself being drawn in like a bee to an exotic wildflower.

His body warred with his mind as his head dipped a fraction closer. His instincts screamed for him to back away from the edge of the cliff. He knew what she was doing. It wouldn't work, but damn if he wasn't tempted to call her bluff. He could almost taste her breath on his tongue before her eyes shifted, breaking the spell as she relaxed against his hold and turned her head away. "What do you want?"

Grant blinked away the fog that had wrapped around his brain. "Your name," he said with a sigh, laboring to keep his heart rate down and his dick in his pants.

"I told you—"

"Your *real* name." Gathering his wits, he tightened his grip on her wrists. "I told you I wouldn't hurt you. It doesn't mean I'm not capable of it. I'm not going to rape you. I'm not going to hold you prisoner. You're free to stay as long as it takes for your wounds to heal, although you'll probably die soon without antibiotics, but you're also free to leave whenever you want."

When she wouldn't look at him he gathered both her wrists in one hand and turned her chin to him with the other. He could see the muscles tick in her jaw as she clenched her teeth against the forced acquiescence. "If you attack me again, I'll have no choice but to tie you to this cot and call the civil police to come get you. Is that what you want?"

He sensed her surrender the moment it happened, could see when the panic returned to her eyes. She was definitely not a fan of law enforcement. Not that he blamed her. He'd lost count of the different thugs, groups and countries that had put a bounty on his head. Lucky for him, no one knew who he was. Hell, even he couldn't remember his real name at times. He'd used so many aliases and disguises over the years that it was hard to keep track. When he'd left the States after cleaning up the mess he'd caused for Daniel, he'd decided to stick with his Grant Kendal identity. Grant had woken him up to who he'd become and he never wanted to forget that. He had a feeling she didn't quite have that kind of anonymity to hide behind.

He watched her struggle to give up that small piece of herself. There was no rush. He had all day if she needed time to work it out. Her teeth worried her bottom lip as she stared at the wall beside them and his cock twitch back to life. If she kept that shit up she might *not* have all day. Either way, he was going to have to rub one out before the day was out. *The sooner the better.* The last thing he needed was to let this fossa lead him around by his dick.

She wouldn't meet his gaze as she took in a shuddering breath and focused on the ceiling above him. "Thalia," she breathed out a sigh, her eyes then locking onto his like lasers. “Thalia Brezlin.”

Grant studied her expressions. *Almost the truth.* It was close enough. “Thalia,” he nodded. “I like it. It fits you.” He slowly released his grip and rolled to her side, crashing to the small mattress beside her, crowding her against the wall. Folding his arms behind his head, he smiled and gave her a flirty wink. “Well, Thalia. Welcome to Isle de Grant.”

CHAPTER FIVE

Christ! The past two days had cost her every shred of dignity she'd ever possessed. She'd never considered herself a vain or prideful person, but damn it all if she wouldn't rather die than let this jerk-off listen to her pee…again. It was bad enough she couldn't even stand on her own. This guy had to rub it in by watching her every handicapped move. He'd even tried to feed her soup; actually held the damn spoon to her mouth like she had the dexterity of an anteater. Now she wished she'd told him where he could put that spoon. Sweat beaded on her clammy skin, the heated ache in her leg screaming to a boil as she pushed herself from the ramshackle mess of a mattress the asshole passed off as a bed.

"I got it!" She shoved Grant's hand away as soon as she was able to shift her weight off her screwed up leg. Her teeth popped as she clenched her jaw, biting back an even more humiliating scream.

Thalia stopped to regain her balance, a long wisp of her hair billowing out from the frustrated breath she forced past her lips. God, she needed space. She didn't know which was worse–the damn monkey watching her as if she were a freak show, or the oversized baboon beside her.

"You ready to go see that doctor yet?" Grant, if that was even his real name, stood towering over her, with less than three inches between them. His arms and hands floated in the air around her, waiting for her to fall on her ass like a toddler learning to walk.

"You ask me that one more time and you're the one who's going to need a doctor." She hopped a step and dragged her injured leg along, her toe picking up splinters as it slid along the shabby wood floor. She couldn't stop the groan that billowed from the pit of her stomach.

"Fuck this," Grant cursed before he swept her off her feet. Her hands clutched at his shirt as he cradled her against his broad chest and stomped towards the open door.

"Put me down, asshole!" She kicked out her uninjured leg and twisted in his arms, gaining absolutely nothing for her efforts but a sharp sting in her side from the pull on her stitches. "I need to walk, dammit!" If she didn't push herself beyond this, it could take her weeks to recover. She didn't have weeks to waste; not when she was so close to hitting her target.

She'd pieced together enough information to know she'd already lost four days. She'd been scoping out the location where she would meet Jauhar with the thumb drive when she was jacked by that dog, Hamisi. That was Wednesday. She'd washed up onto this godforsaken island the next morning, which meant today was Sunday. She had four days to pull herself together and get to that drop.

He'd told her they were within an hour's boat ride from Madagascar. It would take her at least a day, if not more, to procure passage back to the mainland and get back to Nampula. She couldn't miss this meeting. She owed it to her uncle, and she couldn't take the chance of Hamisi finding her again. She needed to get back on her feet, literally.

"No you don't," Grant said as he marched her to the makeshift outhouse he'd constructed nearly two hundred feet from his shack. "What you need is a damn doctor." He pulled open the flap at the front of the green tarp he'd strung up around what she could only describe as a shithole.

Thalia jerked away from his hold the moment her foot touched the ground. "Why don't you go screw your monkey friend and let me pee in peace?" She hated that monkey. No, that wasn't true. That thing frightened the life out her. She'd never been an animal person. She couldn't understand why it was always staring at her. It also had this incessant habit of pounding its fists against its stomach anytime it came near her. *Talk about slapping your monkey.* And what was with the name Winston? "I'm in some *Castaway* spoof film…nightmare from hell!"

Grant backed away, his hands held up in surrender as she jerked the tarp closed. "You're all rainbows and lollipops when you wake up, huh?"

Ignoring his jibe, she turned and nearly gagged at the smell rising from the hole at her feet. Thankfully, he'd thrown together a planked bench with a space between the slats for her to sit on. She could hear him shuffling around outside the curtain as she untied the braided rope that held up the shorts he'd given her to wear. *Damn.* She knew she was being a bitch. He owed her nothing, yet he'd been nothing but kind since that first day she'd awoken…tied to his bed.

She hadn't wanted to fight him, was crazy to even try. If the last year and a half on the streets had taught her anything, it was letting someone know she wasn't an easy target. If she somehow managed to kill him, or at least escape in the process, all the better for her.

The instinctual lethality that lurked behind his golden eyes made him the scariest man she'd ever met. Hamisi was a clown compared to this guy. The only thing that scared her more was her body's reaction to him.

Locked beneath the mass of lean muscles and sun-kissed skin, his sweat fusing with hers, their heated breaths mingling as they fought for control, she felt an unfamiliar warmth rush over her skin. Her body burned to unite with his, her nipples straining to feel his bare skin. A longing ache contracted and stretched through her pelvis and thighs, sending a raw need for his touch singing through her veins.

Sex to Thalia was purely mechanical when the rare occasion warranted it. She wasn't above using sex as a tool to disarm her would-be attackers or distract an unsuspecting bystander while she lifted his car keys. And when she did indulge in a little play she was always in control. Being trapped under a man for whatever purpose, pleasure or otherwise, was suffocating. A few talented lovers had managed to get her off once or twice, but she truly hadn't been all that impressed with the results. Not enough to seek out an encore performance. A sexual relationship had never been at the top her agenda, if on the list at all. And certainly not within the last year and a half.

Never once had her body responded as it had when Grant was lying on top of her. She could sense the suffocating feeling hovering just out of reach, but the panic she usually felt with so much crushing weight had never surfaced. Her body craved more of him. That, above all else, was the scariest thing about the man standing on the other side of that curtain, listening to her pee. *How embarrassing.*

"You writing a book in there? I can always come back at lunch." Thalia rolled her eyes. Holding back a groan, she pushed to her feet and retied her shorts. She'd never wanted to hurt someone as much as she did at that very moment. Considering her past, and what drove her toward her future, that was saying a lot.

She pushed back the flap, and any thought of hurting this man was shoved right back into the shithole behind her. Grant, six feet three inches of golden god, stood before her holding out two wooden poles shaped mercifully like a pair of crutches. She clung to the dirty, green tarp as her mind swirled with confusion.

"These ought to help you some," he said and held them out for her to take. "I can cut them down if they're too long. You're pretty tall though, so I think I got it close."

She felt her stomach tighten into an angry knot. Why would he do this for her? She'd been nothing but a bitch to him. "What do you want from me?" The accusing words slipped past her lips before she could stop them. She'd learned in her first week on the run that people didn't do nice things for other people unless they wanted something. At least not for her. Not people like him.

"Helping me, stitching me up, giving me clothes, and—and food. Now this?" Thalia could see his eyes cloud over as her voice got louder. She couldn't help it. None of this made sense. "What is this supposed to get you? Who do you work for? Jauhar? Hamisi Morsai, the bastard who cut me up? What, he couldn't beat what he wanted out of me so he sent you to…to what? I don't know…somehow…"

Grant's thick fingers wrapped tight around the tops of her arms, the makeshift crutches thrown carelessly to the side. With little effort he lifted her to her toes and pulled her to his chest, his face a mere inch from hers. "I'm trying to be *nice*!" he growled, his expression fiercely twisted, his eyes blazing with the color of fire. "It's something I apparently have little understanding of and I *thought—I* would *try it—with you.*" His eyes strayed to her lips, and for the second time in two days, God help her, she thought he was going to kiss her.

Her whole body tensed in his hands, the strange, warm feeling that came with being so close to him washing over her skin. At that moment, to her absolute disbelief, she wanted him to kiss her. She wanted to kiss him back. Her eyes lingered on his lips, the masculine angles of his face. She wanted to trace the line of stubble on his jaw with the tips of her fingers, to taste the outline of his bottom lip with the tip of her tongue.

Just as she'd decided not to deny him, he uncoiled his hands, dropping her to her feet as he backed away. "I sure as hell hope you know how to swim, lady. Because if the police aren't here to collect your crazy ass by the time I get done eating dinner, I'm loading you into my boat and dropping you off at the nearest channel marker. You can wait for them or swim the forty miles to shore. Either way, you're leaving my island today."

Grant forced himself to ignore the stupefied look on her face as he turned and stomped back to his camp. *Hell if I'm putting up with that ungrateful woman one more day.* It wasn't the names she'd tossed out like familiar calling cards; names he'd long ago committed to memory as human garbage distributors. Hamisi Morsai was mid-level fish chum working for the Don of the Mumbai underworld, Kahan Lalia. Don Lalia ran real estate scams and dealt in extortion and bribery. Kafeel Jauhar represented a whole different galaxy of human bile. Drug and slave trades, espionage, terrorism, you name it. If it was high level and expensive, Jauhar was involved. *Who the hell is this chick?*

As bad as they were, Grant didn't flinch at hearing those names from her otherwise innocent looking lips. Hearing them together was a little off balance, as they ran in completely different circles. Being lumped in with them made his skin crawl a little, but no, it was the woman herself who was driving him mad.

He'd cleaned her up and cooked her food. He'd even brushed her goddamn hair! He honestly hadn't expected a thank you or even a smile, but damn if he was going to bend over and let her shove her foot up his ass just because she felt like it.

He'd tried. He truly had. Being nice wasn't his thing. And if he'd ever met anyone who was less adept at living with the rest of the human race than him, it was her. *I made her fucking crutches, for God's sake!* The floorboards of his cabin creaked and groaned beneath his feet as he stomped inside the single room. Winston screeched when he slammed the door, using the cot as a springboard to escape out the window onto the palm tree outside.

She was the most stubborn, suspicious, obstinate, guarded, powerfully compelling, beautifully resilient piece of work he'd ever seen. "Ahh!" Grant laced his fingers behind his head as he paced the one-room retreat, trying desperately not to punch something. He of all people understood why she pushed herself so hard. She was on her own, or at least he thought she was. He got that. When you have no one to pick you up after being cut down, you have to push yourself ten times harder. He'd lived by the laws of singularity for the last thirteen years. Hell, he'd thrived on them. He admired her for the strength and fortitude it took to push herself that hard.

What he didn't understand was the sudden, gnawing need driving him to help her. When he wasn't sitting on the floor beside the cot watching her sleep, he was sleeping on the floor beside her, determined to make her as comfortable as possible. He'd stayed up the night before, weaving her a makeshift belt out of some spare five-fifty cord he'd stashed away. He'd managed to fold up the length of his shorts to fit her better, but they were so big she had to hold them up around her waist to walk. She needed both hands to hold onto him for balance.

He'd added extra pepper to their soup because she'd said she liked spicy things. He was already planning a trip over to Rodrigo Island to pick her up some clothes that fit and a pair of reef shoes. Her boots would take a week to dry out, and they weren't any good for beach life.

He didn't do needy or helpful, or even *nice* for that matter. The strange part was, he liked doing those things. He wanted to do nice things for her. All evidence to the contrary, considering her reaction to his attempts, he was good at helping her.

Then there was the constant ache in his groin. That alone was enough to drive any man insane. He'd turned his jack shack into a private port-o-let for her, so he'd found himself a giant banyan tree a little farther down the beach and set up shop between two tall root walls. During the two days she'd been conscious, he'd already visited it enough times to cause suspicion if he offered any more excuses to walk to that end of the beach. It didn't help anyway. By the time he'd blown his wad and made the walk back to the cabin, all it took was one look at her bare legs and he was as hard as granite. Again.

He wasn't going to spend another infuriating second trying to understand what was going on inside his head or hers. He'd pack her torn clothes, her boots and a few staples into one of his cargo sacks and send her on her way. No matter how good she felt or how much his body was pulled to hers, he didn't need the kind of trouble she was peddling.

Resigned to cut his losses and regain some of his solidarity, he stomped to his storage trunk, turned the dial on the lock in the correct order until it opened, and reached for his sat-phone. Powering it up, he opened the cabin door and walked outside, every ounce of his resolve draining away into the sea at what he saw in Thalia's eyes as she hobbled toward him.

CHAPTER SIX

"What is it? What's wrong?" Grant strode to the edge of the woods as she stumbled out, her eyes focused behind him.

"A boat," she whispered as she picked her way across the ground, any pain or mistrust she'd felt taking a back seat to her survival instincts.

Her thoughts echoed the curse Grant grunted when he'd turned to see the small speck on the horizon. Judging by how quickly the speck grew, it was headed straight for them. And fast. "I need to get inside." She pushed past Grant, praying he wouldn't hand her over to whoever was on that boat to get rid of her.

Grant caught her arm and pulled her to the side, blocking her body from any binocular view their visitors may have. "No. It's too obvious. If they beach, and if there's more of them than I can stop, it's the first place they'll search."

Thank you. She couldn't make herself say it, but hoped he could read it in her eyes. Thalia shrugged out of his hold, casting an assessing glance behind him. With the sudden rush of adrenaline, her mind worked hastily to process her options. "There's no time. I'm not going to hide in the shithole."

"Wait over here." Her leg throbbed with the pulse of her racing heartbeat as he picked her up, moving her so the cabin was between them and the approaching vessel. He sat her on her feet before he quickly retrieved her crutches and handed them to her. "I'll be right back."

Thalia watched as he retreated to the cabin and crept along the side until he disappeared around the front corner. *What is he doing?* Every second he was gone was time she lost to get herself hidden away inside. He was right. It wasn't the best solution, but given her lack of firepower and a glaring deficiency in mobility, it was her only option.

The sound of the boat's motor came into range and Thalia decided she was out of time. She'd taken her first step towards the cabin when Grant rolled around the corner and ran towards her, a resilient confidence flashing in his eyes. A familiar calm washed over her rioting nerves as he pressed the cold steel into her palm. She looked down at the .45 in her hand, everything else disappearing around her. He was giving her a gun?

"Can you make it to that thicket?" She looked over her shoulder at the clumps of palms and sea brush about fifty feet into the woods. Speechless, she nodded and tucked the gun into her hand-made belt. "Good. Get there and don't move. No matter what you hear or see, don't give away your position. If the shit hits the fan, stay there until you can safely back away and get to the other side of the island. My boat is anchored there in a small cove. The keys are hooked to one of the life jackets stashed under the driver's seat."

"But…" She didn't have time to ask about what he was going to do before he turned and sprinted back to the cabin. Casting off the thousands of questions screaming through her mind, she pushed her way towards her target. Her pain disappeared under the rush of fresh adrenaline-laced blood flowing through her veins. The vegetation grew thin as she neared the halfway point, and she dropped to her knees, crawling the last fifteen feet so she wouldn't be spotted before reaching the thicket.

When she was sure she was hidden from view, she turned and reached for her makeshift crutches, dragging them behind the brush. She hoped like hell she wouldn't have to flee to the other side of the island, but if she did, she wouldn't be able to make it another ten feet without them.

Aware of the boat approaching the shore, Thalia spit into her hand and grabbed up some of the dark sandy soil, smearing it into her saliva. She tore off a couple of leaves from the plants in front of her and popped them into her mouth, chewing rapidly to break them down. Spitting the leaves into the mud in her palm, she swiftly swirled the darkened sludge with her finger before massaging it onto the skin on her face. She couldn't see if it was enough, but anything had to be better than her pale flesh reflecting against the dense brush.

Silent as a shark zeroing in on its prey, she watched as the boat slowed to a stop off the beach, the motor choking to a halt. One man stood behind the driver, another at the bow. Movement to her left told her Grant had exited the cabin, but she refused to take her eyes off the boat. They were thugs. No one wore black shirts and dress slacks if they were out on a Sunday fishing trip.

She hadn't spotted any weapons, but she knew it only meant they were well-hidden. The man on the bow jumped into the surf and waded towards the shore, no care for his fine dress shoes or slacks. The other two remained aboard, vigilantly watching as Grant stepped out from under the front awning of his cabin, exaggerating a yawn as he scratched his bare chest. *What is he thinking?* They exchanged a greeting and chatted back and forth, Grant shaking his head and shrugging his shoulders. The man gestured toward the cabin and Grant shook his head again.

Thalia gritted through her frustration as the two men talked. She couldn't hear a damn thing until Winston screamed from a nearby palm tree. Her blood ran cold. Would he give away her position? Her panic quickened when she saw him round the cabin and head toward the beach. *Oh shit. This can't be good.*

The man talking with Grant reached behind his back and Thalia's heart rate shot through the roof. With an ingrained instinct, her arm stretched out before her and took infallible aim at the man's head. There was a lot of distance to cover, but she was confident her bullet would hit its mark. This was it. There was no way Grant was hiding a gun in those flimsy shorts; not one that would help him in this situation. She'd have to shoot all three before they could return fire or re-start the boat.

In the time it took her to blink her eyes away from the boat to the man in front of Grant, Grant had his arm around the guy's throat, the man's gun in his hand. Thalia didn't hesitate. Two rounds left the barrel of her gun. A third shot echoed off the water as the driver flipped over the side of the boat into the surf. A red mist spewed over the boat's white hull as thug number two's neck exploded, her bullet tearing through his flesh.

Grant dropped the lifeless man in his hands into the surf and ran toward the driver who was splashing helplessly in the water. His big fist tangled in the man's hair as he heaved his head from the water and shouted something at him. The man struggled against his hold before Grant pushed him away and plugged two rounds into the back of his head.

She watched as he walked to the boat and leaned over the side, firing another round into the passenger before pulling himself aboard. Reluctantly, Thalia lowered her weapon and dragged herself to her feet. Scrambling for purchase, she reached for her crutches, her leg screaming against the little bit of weight she had to balance on it.

Scanning the water, she searched for any other crafts which might have been on lookout for the point boat. Seeing nothing suspicious, she palmed the wooden poles and pushed herself away from the safety of the brush toward the beach. Winston barked out a warning, but Thalia ignored him, focusing instead on the man lying face down in the surf. Scarlet waters churned around his torso, flowing down the sand as each wave retreated back into the ocean.

Using her toe, she pushed his hair from his face. She thought the man looked familiar, but she couldn't place him. He had the typical henchman features; steroidal muscles in his arms and chest, a neck as thick as a tree trunk with a long, deep cut across the front of it dripping with fresh blood. She wouldn't be surprised if his name was Igor, or something similarly typical of the type.

The sound of a splash pulled her attention back to the boat. The moisture in her mouth instantly evaporated and her insides began to quake. Her instincts were screaming for her to run, but she didn't. She couldn't even if she'd wanted to.

The sunlight sparkled like diamonds against the drops of water that beaded across Grant's broad chest and raced along the cuts and dips between his washboard abs. His dark blue board shorts, soaked and clinging to his equally muscled thighs, hung low on his hips. A thin trail of golden curls raced between the hard lines of his narrow hips, disappearing beneath his waistband. Only a blind woman would miss the outline of his perfectly defined erection. *Holy sin on a stick, he is packing.*

His arms and legs moved with the grace of a jungle cat stalking its prey, the tight strands of muscles bunching and stretching beneath his skin with every step. His right hand was wrapped tight around the black grip of a pistol, the thick tendons in his wrist flexing as he tightened and loosened his grip. She followed the ripple of movement to his rounded shoulder, his neck, and then up to the chiseled lines of his face. Her lungs seized with feminine lust, mixed with a healthy dose of fear as she locked eyes with the lethal beast inside him. *He's going to kill me.*

The fire in Grant's eyes blazed with a heat as tangible as the sun's rays beating relentlessly against her skin. She didn't know the first thing about this man, other than the fact that he was dangerous and locked onto her like a fast moving freight train. He hadn't hurt her yet, but that didn't mean he wouldn't kill her. Still, she couldn't make herself move or even look away. Something inside her was drawn to the beast residing within the man; to the absolute power and strength that wrecked her senses.

Paralyzed, she was powerless to resist as his hard, lean body crashed into hers, trapping her against his hot, wet skin. His hands tangled in her hair, his desperate grip holding her captive to his assault, his lips crushing against hers with frantic need.

She's incredible. Grant was so damn pissed off and turned on at the same time, he didn't know whether he wanted to kill her or fuck her. The moment his mouth landed on hers, her taste rushing over his tongue for the first time, his cock screamed for the latter. When she offered no resistance, he could feel the tight grip he kept on his control loosen a bit more than he was usually comfortable with.

Damn her for not following his orders. She could have gotten them killed. He would be a liar though if he'd said her cool-under-pressure attitude and deadly aim hadn't impressed the hell out of him. She'd nailed the driver in the lung, the other guy in the neck, from at least sixty yards away with a .45 caliber handgun for Christ's sake. Seeing her standing over that piece of shit excuse for a human being, his gun in her capable hand as she toed his head and studied his face, her own face camouflaged in dirt, Grant was done for.

His dick, well past the screaming stage, was now fully engorged and reaching critical mass levels. His hand slid from her back to her ass, pulling her tight against his groin in an attempt to feed the hungry ache in his cock. Sliding his knee between her thighs, he ground his hips hard against hers, drawing out her answering moan as she rode the top of his thigh. The feel of her hot, wet tongue sliding and tangling with his, dueling for power, sent another wave of lusty hunger rushing through his veins. He needed to be inside this woman, to taste every available inch of her. Explore whatever this carnal attraction was between them before it fucking killed him. *Just not now, dammit.*

Like never before, his body rioted against his mind's attempts at regaining control. They had a cluster of a mess to clean up before they left the island. They couldn't stay. Whenever those assholes failed to check in, whoever sent them would send three more exactly like them. He planned to be long gone by the time they figured out what happened.

Grant's mouth lingered on hers, savoring her taste a moment longer before he let reality seep back in. There would be more time to explore. He'd make sure of that. When they got this mess cleaned up and her leg looked at by a damn doctor, he was going to set them up in one of his safe houses and have a nice, long chat with Ms. Thalia. Then he was going to fuck her on every available surface until neither of them could walk.

Before he could make himself release her, Thalia broke the kiss and pushed herself away from him. Catching her breath, her hand rose to her mouth and wiped away any trace of what they'd just shared. "Sorry, uh, that…"

"Will be continued later," Grant growled. Hell would freeze over before he let her push this away like it never happened. When she looked away, he felt a prick of his earlier anger spike back to life. It only took a millisecond for his temper to flash-boil to the surface. "What the hell did you think you were doing?"

Her eyes flared bright with indignation and he could almost feel her desire to slap him. If it wasn't for the fact he needed her help to pack up, he would likely tempt her to do it so he would have an excuse to tie her to his bed again. Maybe. As her expression transformed from aroused and embarrassed to furious and lethal, he found himself second guessing that fantasy.

"I was saving your damn ass! That's what I was doing!"

"My ass didn't need saving!"

"Bullshit!" Thalia spat. "You had no chance in hell of taking out all three of them before they got off a round."

"Listen, sweetheart..." Grant liked riling her up, but he was quickly losing his patience. "You have no idea what I'm capable of. The next time I give you an order, you sure as hell better follow it! To. The. Letter."

"Like hell!" Thalia grabbed her crutches and turned to stomp away; as well as one could stomp with a bum leg and crutches.

Grant's fingers closed around her arm. Mindful of her injuries, he stepped around in front of her instead of pulling her back to him. "I haven't asked you one goddamn question. Not one! About who you are, or what the hell you're mixed up in. That stops now. I've stitched you up, fed and clothed you. They were looking for *you,* Thalia, and you didn't have the courtesy, or the balls, to give me a heads up! Now I have to dump three bodies, clear every trace of our presence from *my* island, and burn down my own fucking house. All of which could have been avoided if you'd rolled over and played dead like a good little girl!" He released her arm and grabbed her wrist, cupping her hand against his stiff-as-hell prick. "Now, if you'll excuse me, I have to trek across this island with the mother of all hard-ons to get my boat so I can feed these bastards to the sharks."

Thalia jerked her hand away. His lips curled into a smirk as he looked down at the incredulous look on her face. He couldn't help it. She was so damn adorable, her mouth gaping in shock as she fought for something to say. He finally turned and left her standing in the surf, his thoughts already turning to the list of things they had to get done before they could leave.

"As if that's my fault!" He turned to see her scrambling to catch up with him, her limp no better than it had been earlier. Her stubborn, determined strides faster than she could coordinate, the crutches were dragged along at her sides, kicking up sand in every direction. "*You* kissed *me*, you ass! I didn't ask for that!"

Grant stopped when he reached the open cabin door and turned back to see her struggling to catch up. "Woman, you've been asking for me to kiss you from the moment you opened your eyes."

"Well, you don't have to worry about that happening again, because—"

"Oh, I'm not worried, fossa. Not at all." He tucked his gun into his waistband and slipped on his boots. "It will happen again, I assure you. Now start packing up thc cabin." He turned and headed for the tree line, not bothering to look back as he tossed his final words on the matter over his shoulder. "We're leaving before sundown."

CHAPTER SEVEN

After trekking across the island to retrieve his boat, Grant had loaded the bodies into the other boat and left again to tow them to the eastern side of the island and set them adrift. Finally alone, Thalia worked herself into a sweat, which wasn't hard to do considering the on again off again fever she was trying to ignore. She'd packed everything that wasn't nailed down into the cargo sacks she'd found stuffed between the cot and cabin wall.

There wasn't much to pack. Some fishing equipment, a soup pot, and one rusty cast iron skillet with some basic spices and utensils, along with a sack of clothes and towels, and a few books. There was a locked trunk in the corner and a few full water canteens that were too heavy for her to move, so she left them where they were and piled everything else on top. She took the time to run his brush through her hair, delightfully depositing whatever lice or vermin she'd picked up from his pain in the ass monkey, before stuffing it into the bag with the remaining first aid supplies.

What the hell was I *doing?* The man was going to drive her crazy. "Here's a gun, but don't use it. Play dead like a good little girl." *Chauvinistic jerk!* She ripped the sheets from the bed. The stale odor that drifted through the air had her throwing them in the corner instead of packing them up. "Those can burn in hell with Mr. *I didn't need my ass saved.*" *Conceited prick!*

She may have the agility of a slug at the moment, but she could handle a pistol in her sleep. The sooner he learned that, the better. With a groan she sunk down onto the bare mattress in defeat. He had a point, but he was still a jerk. A jerk who had kissed her senseless, but still a jerk…who had been right. What if he'd been hurt, or shot? She could barely take care of herself, much less a two hundred pound asshat. That was *if* they hadn't taken her captive…

again. *Shit.* It galled her that she needed his help. Now he was stuck in the middle of her personal hell.

Guilt was an emotion Thalia didn't wear well. Her skin itched with the constant gnawing feeling. Up until the day her life fell apart and she woke up in hell, she hadn't done much to feel guilty about. Since then she'd had to do what she needed to survive and learned quickly that guilt only slowed you down. She should have told him. He'd been right about that, too. At least a vague warning. Telling him, or anyone else, about her problems wasn't in the cards.

Thalia didn't trust easily, if at all. The only person she'd ever trusted was Issa, and he was dead. She was getting on a boat with a complete stranger. He'd shared *nothing* about himself, other than his belt and crutch making skills, and his incredible smile and spine melting lips that could make a girl want to kiss them continually. *He's sexy, sweet, and lethal.*

Dammit! How was she supposed to resist that? How could she trust in that? She couldn't. She couldn't expect anyone to understand what she was doing, what she had to do. She certainly didn't trust the way her body reacted to his. Given half a chance, it would have her pinned beneath him, begging for everything he could give her, utterly at his mercy and totally unfocused on what had to be done. No. She definitely had to get herself as far away from Mr. Jerktastic as she possibly could.

When they got to Madagascar she'd hitch a ride to the nearest airfield and stow away on anything headed to the African coast. When the drop was made and she'd completed her ultimate mission, she would find a way to repay Grant for all the trouble she'd dumped on him. If she was still alive that is. Truth be told, she was surprised she'd survived this long.

When she pulled her crutches over and pushed herself up from the cot, she heard a muffled clunk of something falling to the floor. When she looked under the bed she saw a small iPod, the white earbud wires still tangled in the springs where it had been stashed beneath the mattress.

Curious, she scooped it up and powered it on, pushing the play button as she stuffed one of the buds into her ear. The rich, subtle tone of a cello flowed over her skin like a warm honey.

Violins played softly in the background as the strain ebbed and flowed around her. *The symphony.* She didn't know which piece it was, but she knew it was one of Issa's favorites. He used to play it every Saturday as he worked in the kitchen preparing their dinner. It was a tradition he started when she first came to live with him, and she never missed it. It was always her favorite day of the week.

She would have never, in a million years, guessed that a man like Grant would appreciate the fine arts. At least not in music. She would have pegged him as a grunge fan, or maybe even country.

The soulful sad melodies combined with the memories of her late uncle, made Thalia jerk the earbuds out and toss the player into a bag. She couldn't deny the desire to connect with something Issa was so enriched in, but she couldn't afford the distraction of getting lost in her grief. She had enough things competing for her undivided attention at the moment, including a screaming monkey.

Winston bounded through the sand and up to the cabin door as Thalia hobbled out to see what he was harping about. More comfortable with the primate than she would have ever dreamed she'd be, she didn't flinch away when it grabbed her hand and tugged her away from the cabin, or at least tried to. Stronger than she'd imagined he would be, she grabbed ahold of the porch post to keep her balance when he'd tried to drag her down the beach.

Winston let go, thank God, and Thalia regained her footing as he coaxed her to follow him. The last thing she felt like doing was taking a stroll. Actually, she felt more like downing a few shots of whisky, or ten, and sleeping until telepathy was invented. Unfortunately, she didn't have that option. The people who wanted her dead were getting closer by the day, and she was slowly losing her will to fight them. She had to push herself, and with Grant nowhere around to hover she was determined to take advantage.

"Okay. Okay. Lead the way." Pulling her crutches tight into the pits of her arms, she balanced as much weight as she could on her leg and started off after Winston. Trying to focus on something other than the searing pain, Thalia wondered what Grant was going to do about the silly monkey. He wasn't all that bad, except for being a pain in the ass. Something she was sure he'd learned from Grant. Or maybe it was the other way around. How long had Grant lived here alone, having only a monkey to converse with? Emulation was only natural after a while, right?

A little ways ahead of her, Winston left the sand and disappeared into the tree line. Not wanting to push her luck, Thalia stopped and called for him. When he didn't return she took a few more steps toward the trees, gritting her teeth against the increased throbbing in her thigh. "Winston! I need to head back!" She didn't know why she thought the thing could understand human reasoning.

A soft rustling noise grabbed her attention. "Winston?" Palming her crutches, she picked her way through the leaves and thin shrubs as she followed the noise. When Winston came into view, it took her a minute to put together the pieces of what she was seeing. When she did, she thought she would pee her pants.

It all made sense now. Nestled between two spindly, wavy roots that formed a virtual shield from the prying eye was a plethora of skin mags, opened up to various pages and centerfolds. Right in the middle of them was Winston, his fist slapping against his stomach at a fevered pace. Knowing it would be a bitch to pick herself off the ground, Thalia braced against a nearby tree as she gasped for air through her howling fits of laughter. So that's what the crazy ape had been doing every time he saw her. *Imitating his master.* Through the hysteria she could understand the poor thing's confusion. She was probably the only human female he'd ever seen.

She could picture the monkey watching Grant with rapt attention as he pumped his way to climax. A throbbing ache fluttered to life inside her womb, causing her to take a sobering gasp of air as she imagined what Winston had seen.

Thick muscles, taught and straining as Grant leaned into the tree, one sinewy arm outstretched to hold himself up, the other pumping his long, heavy shaft in a strong, steady rhythm. She could see the tendons in his neck straining tight beneath his skin, his lips pulled tight against his teeth as he chased the impending rapture. She could almost taste the pearly drops of pre-come glistening against his skin, feel the silky texture of his cock against her tongue as she peered up into his golden eyes and licked the drops away. Her clit throbbed as she heard his next breath hiss through his teeth and exhaled on a long, almost painful moan. Her scalp tingled as his fingers fisted into her hair, holding her captive as he plunged into her mouth with short, rapid strokes, deeper and deeper, crying out as he spilled his hot, salty seed down her throat. Her body shuddered with his, his grunts becoming her moans as his image faded away with his release.

Holy shit! Thalia panted as the spasms in her pussy receded, leaving behind only her thundering heartbeat and one hell of a rush. If mind-fucking him could do this to her she was in a heap of trouble. Never once had she craved to be taken in such a way. Normally she would sooner die than let a man use her like that, but there was something about him that changed her. She craved his dominance, and couldn't control or understand her need for it.

Thalia's legs shook as she pushed away from the tree and bent to gather the various pieces of paraphernalia. She had the sudden urge to run. By the time she'd reached the cabin, each breath she took seemed laced with concrete, settling into the bottom of her lungs. Her chest heaved with the effort it took to suck in a single breath. *Dammit!* Now was not the time for this to happen.

Closing the door, she slumped against the wooden panel and sunk to the floor, trying desperately to regain control of her body. *Breathe, dammit.* It had been a while since she'd had a panic attack. She hadn't had one like this since she was a teenager. After waking up in a strange place with no memory of who or where she was, they were a dime a dozen, creeping up on her seemingly without cause. Issa had understood and taught her how to center herself, how to breathe through the chaos running rampant through her body.

Since then she'd only suffered from the suffocating attacks after waking from her nightmares. Nightmares she could never remember anything of except the suffocating weight that crushed against her body and the smell of her burning flesh. Even then she could usually rein in the attacks before they got the better of her. The nightmares had stopped all together for a while, but since Issa's murder they seem to haunt her sleep with a vengeance.

Eyes closed, she sucked the stale cabin air in through her nose and pushed it out through her mouth. Focusing on a small, white dot in the darkness of her mind, she shut out every sound, every feeling, focusing only on the inner strength it would take to calm her. She was stronger than this, bigger than this. *Breathe in, breathe out.* That was all she had to do. Nothing else mattered.

Unsure exactly how long she'd been huddled on the floor, the pressure slowly lifted from her chest and her lungs filled freely with air. Her shirt was soaked in sweat, the pain in her thigh raging to test the limits of her tolerance. When she heard the sound of Grant's boat, she scrambled to stuff the magazines into one of the sacks before she hauled herself towards the cot. If she was going to pass out she sure as hell wasn't going to do it surrounded by his porn. She didn't know why she saved the crap to begin with.

When Grant entered the cabin she barely had the strength to lift her head, the room spinning with frustrating confusion. "I…" She couldn't finish the thought as she fought to keep her eyes from rolling back in her head.

"Jesus!" Grant rushed to her side. The last thing she remembered was the cool press of his hand to her forehead.

CHAPTER EIGHT

Grant ducked as a wave crashed over the bow, glancing over his shoulder to see how much water had rained down on the stubborn woman still passed out behind him. Satisfied she wasn't going to drown, he turned his attention back to navigating the traffic lane of the shipping channel.

It was busy for the pre-dawn hour. They should have been there hours ago, but tending to Thalia and uncapping the freshwater well for Winston had cost them precious time. He needed to be docked and loaded before the sun rose. He couldn't risk anyone at the marina seeing her. Or rather she couldn't. He was still trying to figure out why he gave a fuck.

The damn woman didn't know the word quit, he'd give her that. He only wished he knew what drove her to such extremes. He shook his head as he nosed the boat into an empty dock slip and quickly tied it off before jumping out and making his way to the street. As soon as he had them stashed away, he'd get every answer he needed from her, one way or another. He wasn't going to settle for bits and pieces of half-truths. If she wanted his help, and it seemed she had shit for other options, she was going to start talking.

A misty fog choked the alley and concealed his form as he leaned against the driver's door of an older model SUV. Two tries and the locks popped, the door hinge creaking as he swung the door open and climbed in. *You're getting rusty, Dusty.* Two attempts weren't bad, but he should have had it in one. A couple of sparked wires later and he was pulling up at the end of the short dock. He let out a relieved sigh when he saw Thalia lying undisturbed beneath the blanket he'd laid over her. *Why the hell does she matter so much?*

Not lending enough time to ponder that question, he shouldered the strap of the one cargo sack he hadn't let burn with the cabin then hoisted the trunk onto his other shoulder. Leaving Thalia behind grated on his nerves, but he couldn't carry everything and her as well. Leaving her unattended in the vehicle while he went back for his shit didn't sit well, either. She was safer covered up in the boat.

Depositing his cargo into the back of the SUV, he ran back to retrieve Thalia. After quickly wiping down the boat, he hoisted her over his shoulder and then threw a match into the plastic bucket he'd filled with some of the island clothes he would no longer need. By the time the bucket melted and the fire reached the disconnected fuel line, they would be long gone before the ensuing explosion destroyed his boat and any remaining traces of them.

Thalia woke with a start as he buckled her into the passenger seat. "Where are we?"

Grant smirked. He wasn't sure why, but he pressed a kiss to her fevered forehead before he closed her door, running around to jump into the driver's seat. As he pulled away from the dock he laid a hand on her neck and cursed. "You're burning up, fossa. I'm taking you to a doctor."

He grabbed her wrist when she reached for the seatbelt buckle in a panic. "You're not going to win this fight, Thalia. Your body is shutting down with or without your consent." When she tried to jerk her hand away he tightened his grip, his gaze darting between her and the narrow road as he weaved through the old marine district. "I'm taking you to someone who knows how to keep their mouth shut."

He could see how badly she wanted to fight him, to deny what was so obviously the truth. He'd never wanted to kiss her more than at that very moment. He was a little stunned when she cast her haunted eyes to her lap and relaxed against her seat without more of a fight. *What the hell is that about?* He let it go, determined to get her leg seen to so they could get to ground and he could get some damn answers.

Thalia looked down and studied her tan shorts, the tiny gray checkers in the seat cover, anything to keep from looking at Grant. She could barely hold her head up as it was. She couldn't handle the jumbled up ball of confusing need that knotted in her stomach when he looked at her with such fierce intensity. No way could she handle that kind of assault again.

Her head felt like the fluid surrounding her brain had drained away, leaving behind nothing but sticky cotton. She couldn't remember anything beyond her ill-timed panic attack back at the cabin. The ache in her leg had bloomed, spreading tendrils of pain throughout her entire body. She hated feeling helpless. It was more suffocating than the damn nightmares. She hated that Grant was right again even more. She'd have to let him help her. At least for a day or two. The moment she could put one foot in front of the other though, she was gone.

I need a phone. Even in a daze, Thalia kept a tight hold on her plan. She cringed against the inevitable. She wasn't going to make that drop. If she could get to a phone she might be able to convince Jauhar to reschedule. *He's going to kill me anyway.* She shrugged, looking down at the mangled, swollen flesh on her leg. *Death might not be so bad at this point.* No. Death was not an option. Not until Issa's death had been fully avenged. A phone and a slight adjustment in her plans was all she needed.

"Where are we?" she asked again. The one and two story sandstone slums went by in a blur as Grant plowed down the narrow streets. Hopefully they were near an airport. Mozambique was only an hour's hop from Madagascar, an hour and a half at most by plane. It would take half a day if she had to stow away on a boat.

"La Panch." Thalia braced her palm against the dash as the SUV lurched to a stop at an abandoned four-way intersection.

"La Panch? Where the hell is that? I've never heard of it." She turned her head to see what Grant was looking at out the back window.

Grant shifted into reverse, throwing his arm around the back of her seat as he backed down the street. "It's a small island near Reunion. Working class for the tourist islands."

Dammit! Reunion was about as far away from where she needed to be to get to where she was going. And it was full of elitist, high class vacation homes. No freighters coming and going around this place. "I don't suppose they have an airport, huh?" Just her luck. Tarzan had her marooned on another shitty island.

She chewed on her thumbnail as he reached a small alley they'd passed and slammed the SUV back into drive, pulling down the dark and narrow side street. "Nope. Why? You're not planning on leaving me so soon, are you?" Thalia deadpanned her expression, determined to keep him from seeing the truth in that suggestion.

"Good," Grant said when she didn't reply. He parked alongside one of the taller buildings that made up the alleyway and cut the engine. Leaning up, he wrapped his arms around the steering wheel and looked up at the pale orange sky, the first rays of the sun peeking through the darkness. An incredulous smirk pulled at the corner of his lips. "Because I'd sure miss that sweet, rosy disposition and beauty pageant smile of yours."

Thalia flipped him off, but he didn't see it. By the time her pain rattled brain caught up to his sarcasm he'd pushed open the door and rolled out of the SUV. She flinched when the driver's door slammed hard behind him. *Dammit!* There was that guilty feeling again, clawing at her insides. Even though she didn't *want* to need his help, she did. He hadn't asked one thing of her in return yet. The least she could do would be to keep her mouth shut. When he rounded the front of the car and opened her door, she couldn't bring herself to look at him, focusing instead on the suddenly interesting crushed soda can on the floor at her feet. "You're good at it, you know."

"I'm good at a lot of things, sweetheart." He unceremoniously unbuckled her seat belt and scooped her from the front seat. "I don't need you to tell me that."

She pounded her fist on his shoulder as he walked to the only visible door into the building. "I was talking about being nice!" She pushed against his hold on her but got nowhere fast, as usual. "I was trying to *be* nice, you jerk!"

Grant stopped in his tracks and peered down at her, his amber eyes searching hers. Searching for what she had no clue, but damn if that panty-melting fire in his eyes didn't cut right through the bullshit in her brain. "You think I'm good at being nice?"

Thalia forced herself to look away. "I take it back. You totally suck at being anything but an asshole!"

He studied her, a big goofy grin on his face. "I think you like me, fossa." Heat flushed her cheeks; heat having nothing to do with her infection or fever. *You should have kept your big mouth shut!*

Grant continued to the door, still holding her cradled in his arms. "You hate needing my help, but," he reached up and pounded three times on the door, then three more, "I think you like me and you don't know what to do with that."

When no one answered he carefully sat her on her feet. "Okay, Captain Psychology, what does this mean?" She elbowed him in the gut, extracting a satisfying groan.

Grant recovered and struck with the stealth of a panther. Lacing his fingers into her hair he pulled her head back, forcing her to look at him. His breath billowed out, hot and moist against the shell of her ear as he leaned in and spoke with a growl. "It means my little fossa, that as soon as I get you someplace safe and your leg is healed, I'm going to bend you over and spank that smart ass of yours."

Thalia froze, unwanted images of being naked and on display flashed through her mind. His heavy hand splayed across her ass and she could almost imagine the sharp bite of erotic pain. Grant's hot tongue slipped out and traced along the outer shell of her ear, sending a tingling blanket of electricity dancing along her skin as he sucked on her sensitive lobe.

"Then I'm going to fuck you." He turned her face and kissed along her jaw. "Long," he sighed, the tip of his tongue tickling the corner of her mouth. "And hard," he said in a low, baritone whisper before his hand tightened in her hair and he crushed his mouth to hers. Devouring her, his tongue rushed along hers in long, demanding strokes like a prophet to his promise. *Oh, damn! That feels incredible.* She could almost feel his long, hard cock tunneling through her, sliding in slowly to the hilt, filling her fully.

Thalia cursed the moan that escaped through the tattered bare threads that were left of her control. Again her instincts were screaming for her to fight against his hold. Again some insane part of her welcomed his power over her.

Three pounding knocks barely registered as she floated in Grant's arms. The reality of her situation crashed full force into the fog of erotic need that had engulfed her. She opened her eyes to see

Grant's amber irises focused on her, his lips still tasting hers. His fist pounded on the door with three more rapid knocks before his lips left hers, his other hand still clenched in her hair. "Get ready for it, fossa."

She saw the promise in his eyes. There was no escaping this. No escaping him. She wanted him. She truly wanted him. For the first time in her life, or the parts she could remember, she actually wanted sex. And he was right. She hadn't a clue what to do with that. She had a feeling she didn't need to know. Grant was going to show her exactly what she could do. What he could do *to* her. The mixture of anticipation and anxiety had her nearly gasping for breath by the time the door creaked and a petite, young woman peeked out through the small opening.

"Salina." Grant nodded and scooped her back into his arms. The woman opened the door, looking around the corner before she backed up and motioned for them to come in. "We're clear." He turned to watch as Salina closed and bolted the door behind them. "No one followed. I'll ditch the car while you're seeing to her leg."

"Who is she?" Thalia asked as Grant followed the woman down a long, narrow hallway, the scents of sandalwood and antiseptic jarring her senses. *What a disgusting mix.*

Grant scowled down at her. "You don't ask questions and neither will she."

Thalia didn't have enough strength left to wonder what the hell *that* look was for, but he did have a good point…again. The woman blew past a row of closed doors and then stopped, pulling a wad of keys from the front pocket of her pink sweater. With ease and familiarity, she plucked out a key and unlocked the door at the end of the hallway, flipping the light on as she entered.

"On the table. Strip her shorts." Thalia jerked away from Grant when he sat her on the cold, stainless steel table.

"I can manage my own clothes." *Thank you very much.* She didn't know who the hell this woman was, but the term *bitch* didn't seem that far off the mark. No greeting or introductions, nothing. Just an order to strip and sit in a snotty French accent.

The woman didn't balk at Thalia's protest as she rifled through a row of cabinets, throwing what seemed like random crap into a metal bowl. "I don't care who does it as long as you're naked from the waist down by the time I'm ready."

"She has a cut along her ribs, too." Grant shrugged when Thalia glared at him, reaching for the button on her shorts.

"The shirt will need to go as well, then." Salina whirled around and deposited the bowl full of surgical tools at the head of the table. She paused a moment, taking Thalia in as if she were inspecting a slab of beef. "You have two minutes while I ready the IV line, then I'm cutting them off you." She turned and reached into another cabinet. "Not that I would be very attached to that fashion statement."

Total bitch. Thalia couldn't stop her wince of pain or the rush of heat to her face and chest as Grant crowded around her, helping slide her shorts over the gash on her thigh. This time he didn't even try to look away from her. She didn't know why she was so embarrassed. This was nothing compared to him listening to her pee. He'd already seen her naked and beat to hell. She slapped his hand away as he reached for the hem of her shirt, biting her lip to keep from calling him another colorful name. *Be nice. He's trying to help.*

Grant braced his arms on the table, caging her in, the scruff of his almost full beard tickling her cheek as he spoke into her ear. "I have to transfer my stuff and ditch the car. Don't give her a hard time." He paused, his soft lips sliding gently along her cheek. "I'll be right back."

Thalia watched him tuck his gun into the back of his cargo pants as he disappeared down the hall, a sickening uneasiness building in her stomach. *What if he doesn't come back?* She flinched when she turned to see Salina standing in front of her with a long needle pointed right at her.

"No!" Thalia shook her head. "No drugs. Just some antibiotics."

"It's only a topical to numb the area so I can clean it out." Salina pressed forward and Thalia grabbed her wrist, keeping the needle on lockdown.

"I said no." No way in hell was she letting this bitch inject her with God knows what.

"Fine." Salina's eyes narrowed as Thalia let her go. She watched as the woman rolled up her sleeve and injected the needle into her own flesh. Thalia winced as the woman pushed the plunger in ever so slightly. "You people are all the same," she said, pulling the needle out and rubbing her fingers over the injection site. "There, see? I am not dead. This is only a numbing agent."

Thalia screamed when Salina reached out and grabbed her thigh, giving it a gentle squeeze. "Son of a bitch! Okay! Numbing agent! Numbing agent! Ahh!" *Please!* Tears clouded her vision as Salina turned and threaded another needle into the syringe.

CHAPTER NINE

As quiet as a rock, Salina worked to clean out the cut on Thalia's leg and repair some of the patchwork Grant had done. For what seemed like hours she sat in what could only be described as hell, nothing but her thoughts of Grant to keep the pain at bay. *Shouldn't he be back by now?*

"He will be back soon enough." Thalia turned her head away from the hallway where Grant had disappeared.

"I know I didn't say that out loud." Either the woman had lied and given her the good shit—which totally sucked for all the good it was doing—or the bitch was a mind reader.

Salina giggled and wiped at the stitches on her side, applying a gooey ointment before moving to the next abrasion. "No, you did not have to. Staring at the door will not make him walk through it."

Thalia relaxed a bit, hoping the uneasy feeling growing in the pit of her stomach with every minute that ticked by was caused by her fever. She watched as Salina worked above her, wondering if she and Grant had ever been an item. She was pretty enough. Auburn hair that curled around her shoulders, deep brown eyes and pouty French lips. She was also petite. Like elven tiny. Thalia hadn't always appreciated her height. Though being five foot ten had its advantages when it came to dealing with some of the people she'd come up against the past few months. But being tall next to an elf made her feel like a freak.

"What did you mean earlier?" she finally asked, hoping to pry a little information out of Tinker Bell. "We are all the same?"

Salina opened a brown bottle and poured more alcohol onto a fresh cotton swab. "CIA, Mossad, ISI, whoever you work for. You all have understandable trust issues, but it makes my job impossible to do at times."

Operative? Holy shit! Is that what he is? "How do you know him?

One of her shoulders raised in a casual shrug. "He saved my brother's life a few years ago." Salina glanced up at her through her lashes, quickly dabbing away the sting that sent Thalia's last breath hissing through her teeth. "He did not live long enough to repay his debt, but I will always honor it. I have done some of my best work on your man." Another moan escaped as Thalia's chest filled with a weird sense of pride. *My man?* She winced again as a sharp, stinging pain pinched the inside of her arm. *Dammit, that hurts!*

Salina chuckled again and sighed. "I have never seen him so attentive as he is with you. Of course," she shrugged, "I have never seen him with anyone at all before today, so what do I know? He is all bark and growl, and then gone. Until the next time. And he pays well so I do not complain."

Bark and growl. "That's my Grant," she mumbled, her lips feeling a bit tingly.

Salina's hand stopped moving, her focus fixed on Thalia's arm. A small grin pulled at the corner of her lips. "Grant?" She nodded. "I like that name much better than Silas. He never looked like a Silas to me."

"Grant, smant." Thalia waived her hands through the air, wondering why her fingers looked like fuzzy caterpillars. "I don't care what his name is. That man knoooows how to—ouch!" Thalia jumped when the woman poked at a spot near the top of her arm. Her head spun a little as she tried to focus on the trickle of blood running towards her elbow.

"Sorry." Salina prodded at the seeping hole. "This one is going to hurt a bit."

"It wasn't bleeding like that before." The room spun as she turned her head toward a loud thump which sounded from the darkened hallway. When she turned back, Salina was scowling as she dug into her arm with what looked like a wicked ice pick. She couldn't feel it, but it certainly looked like it should hurt. "What did you give me?"

"We have to go!" Grant's voice sounded hollow against the sudden ringing in her ears. "What's wrong?"

“Gr…Grant?” She tried to focus on his face but all she could see was a swirling mass of black creeping into the edges of the room. *Grant. I can’t... I need...*

“She has a tracking chip in her arm. I can’t….” Salina grunted as she made one last try for it. “There!” A thin metal sliver fell from the tweezers into her other hand.

“Fuck! That explains why the place is crawling with shitbags!” Grant bent to gather Thalia into his arms. “What the hell did you give her?”

Salina threw open a set of closet doors and grabbed a handful of clothes, pushing them at Grant. “Put those on her. I gave her a shot of ketamine. I needed her sedated once I realized what I was dealing with.” After pulling off her latex gloves she paused, brushing her hands over her face. “What the hell have you gotten me into?”

Grant ignored her, frantically pulling Thalia’s arms through the dark blue scrub top. “Grab what you can. You’ve got two minutes if you want to come with us.”

Salina grabbed a wad of gauze and taped it over the hole in Thalia’s arm as Grant pulled her shirt into place. “I will meet you outside in one minute.”

“No. We leave through the tunnels.” Salina nodded and sprinted down the hall. “Hold on, fossa. I’ve got you.” Grant hoisted her over his shoulder and marched over to the row of cabinets, throwing the doors open one by one. When he found the antibiotics he dumped the trash and raked them and a handful of other various bottles into the bag.

There was no warning before a blast rocked the building. Chunks of concrete and dust rained down onto Grant’s back as he ducked and ran from the room, Thalia unconscious over his shoulder. Bright flashes of light lit the hallway as gunfire erupted near the front of the structure. Grant followed his mental map, familiar with every turn through the maze of doors and hallways, until he reached the cellar door. It was still locked so he knew Salina hadn’t made it. With no time to search for her, he kicked in the door. Gun in hand he rushed down the stairs, stopping only to throw a steel bar across the door. He carried Thalia to the back of the small, dank room and carefully set her down against the wall.

Working in near total darkness, his hands found the edge of the hidden panel with flawless precision. With a grunt, he slid the heavy metal slab away and grabbed for Thalia, pulling her through the low opening and hauling her back over his shoulder.

As he knew it would, the short, dark tunnel led him into a maze of underground rabbit holes and eventually into the building across the street from Salina's. When he'd heard the commotion in the street and saw the group of heavily armed men signaling to another driver, it didn't take long to figure out who they were looking for. He'd quietly stashed his things into another *borrowed* vehicle and parked it behind an abandoned dumpster on the backside of the other building.

Now that the tracking device was crushed under a pile of rubble, he felt fairly certain they wouldn't be followed, but he wasn't taking any chances. After buckling Thalia into the front seat of the truck he'd procured, he reached into the back and unlocked his storage trunk, taking out his sat phone and an extra firearm. It was time to call in a chip or two.

~*~*~*~*~

Cold air swirled round Thalia, the womp, womp, womp *sound of an industrial sized fan rattling her bones. She tried to raise her head, to push herself up from the pallet of blood stained blankets, the stench of urine and feces assaulting her senses. Heavy. She felt so heavy.*

A scream filled her ears and she opened her eyes, holding her breath and wishing she could disappear. Light flooded the dim room as a door opened at the far end. A man with a gun shoved a small girl into the room ahead of him. The same man who had forced her into the room the day before.

The girl's clothes were torn and her hair hung in tangles around her face. She couldn't see her bruises or the cuts that spilled the blood running down her neck. She didn't have to see. She knew it was no different than her own beaten flesh. She watched, hovering somewhere outside herself, as the man slapped the girl, sending her body crashing to the concrete floor. He crouched over top of her and ripped the remains of her tattered clothes from her body.

She felt her screams rip through her throat. He had to be stopped. She couldn't let him! She was so little. No! Her next scream died on her lips as the man stopped, his head whipping around to pin her with his evil eyes. She tried to crawl away, to huddle against the evil she saw as he stomped toward her. Light flashed against the sharp steel blade as it was wielded at her face. Her hand flew up and batted it away, but whatever they had given her made her too weak to fight.

Adrenaline pumped through her veins and pulled Thalia from the nightmare with a jolt, her hands grasping frantically at the air around her.

"Easy, fossa. There are a lot of buttons here you don't want to push by accident." Grant's voice sounded loud in her ears, sending what felt like shards of glass ripping through her brain. Thalia ripped off the headset and cradled her throbbing head in her hands. The sudden movement, coupled with the now deafening sound of the helicopter blades and the tightening fear in her chest, caused a weird pitch and roll in her stomach, sending bile and God knows what else on a stealth flight through her esophagus straight onto the floor at her feet.

"Oh, damn. Hopper is going to kick my ass." Grant shifted and pulled out a tattered rag from his pocket and handed it to her. When she took it from his hand, he grabbed her headset and pushed it into her other hand. She snatched it back up and slipped it over her ears, squeezing her eyes closed against what she was sure was the worst headache she'd ever had.

Grabbing his own mic, he motioned for her to use hers. "You have to speak into…" Grant chuckled when she flinched and cringed back against the seat. "Okay. No talking." She nodded weakly, cradling her head again. "Just…try not to throw up again. Okay?"

Ugh. I want to die. She wiped her parched lips with the rag, but it did nothing for the vile taste in her mouth. The helicopter dipped and her stomach lurched again. *No.* She glanced at Grant. *I want to put a bullet in his knee and then die.*

Grant offered her a sheepish grin, mouthing the word *sorry*. Crap. He was being nice again. Okay, so maybe blowing out his knee was a little harsh. Even with the worst headache on record, she knew he'd saved her life. Again. There was that, and the fact that he was flying the helicopter. She ran her tongue over her teeth, her mouth so dry it stuck to the enamel. God, what she wouldn't give for a glass of water. To hell with the glass. She'd drink out of a puddle of mud if he would just land this thing within a hundred yards of one.

She cleared her throat, wincing at the sound of her own voice as it echoed through the headset. "Ahh," she coughed and tried again. "Got any water?"

Grant shook his head. "We will be landing in fourteen minutes." She could tell he was trying to keep his voice as low as possible. He was going to kill her with kindness. Her lips curled into a somewhat involuntary smile. It was something she hadn't had much use for lately. It felt almost strange.

She closed her eyes and sank back into the hard bucket seat, trying to organize her thoughts. She had a million and two questions, but nothing was going to be asked or answered until they landed. She usually didn't mind flying, but she could safely cross puking in a helicopter off her list of things to try in the future.

Grant watched her from the corner of his eye as he maneuvered the chopper into the landing zone. He hadn't known many women in his life, but the ones who came to mind resembled nothing of the tough-as-nails woman who sat quietly in the seat next to him. Other than throwing up in his friend's multi-million dollar aircraft, she'd handled waking up at thirty-five-hundred feet pretty well, all things considered.

She'd been surprising him from the minute she'd opened her eyes on that beach. Not many people could impress him these days, and she'd managed to do it at nearly every turn. He kept thinking about the look in her eyes when he'd issued that brilliant declaration back at Salina's. He could have kicked himself for being so damn thoughtless.

She'd been a slave, for fuck's sake. Most likely a sex slave. God only knew what nightmares she'd lived through. He had no right or business throwing things like spanking and bondage around so casually. The look in her eyes when he'd said it was nothing if not pure need. Aside from confusing the hell out of him, her reaction to him and his thoughtless *promise* inspired an entirely different line of questioning. He was going to have to navigate these waters very,

very carefully. First and foremost, he needed to find out who the hell she was. That, he feared, was going to be one hell of a chat.

After setting the chopper down as close to the tree line as he could, he cut the engine and unbuckled his harness. "Stay there. I'll come around to help you out." He slid his headset off and hooked it into place between the seats.

In total Thalia fashion, she unharnessed herself and was half out of her seat before he reached her. "I said to stay put," he grumbled as he ignored her protests and scooped her out of the chopper.

"What happened?" she shouted mere inches from his ear. His steps faltered as his head jerked away. "Sorry. I didn't mean to shout." Grant sat her down at the base of a nearby tree then braced his hands on his thighs as he looked her over. "What happened? I don't remember anything beyond Salina drugging me."

Grant huffed and straightened, wiping his forearm over his brow. "Stay here. I need to unload a few things from the chopper. We'll talk when we get to the compound."

Thalia moved to get up and Grant whirled around, pinning her with his fiery stare. "I. Said. Stay."

She slumped against the tree. "Can you at least tell me where we are?"

"Zimbabwe," Grant shouted over his shoulder as he turned and jogged back to the helicopter.

CHAPTER TEN

Zimbabwe. She could work with that. It was only one country away from where she needed to be. By tomorrow. *That's doable. Not.* She was so screwed if she didn't get to a phone. She was probably screwed regardless. Jauhar wasn't known for his pleasant, understanding nature. Thalia immediately began recalibrating her plan. If she could ditch Grant long enough to contact Jauhar within the next six hours and managed to get him to accept the delay, she should be able to get back to Mozambique, retrieve the thumb drive, and be in Nampula by Friday, maybe?

She looked down at her leg, realizing for the first time the clothes she was wearing. *Wonderful.* Grant obviously had to dress her. Again. She'd become a useless invalid. She carefully pressed her palm to her thigh and let out a relieved sigh when she felt the lack of heat radiating from the wound. *Blessed Salina.* Despite jacking her up on who knows what, the woman obviously knew what she was doing around a stab wound. Finally *something* was breaking her way.

Still, she had one big problem. Blowing the original drop wasn't going to win her any confidence points with Jauhar. *How did this get so out of control?* It was supposed to be simple. Both Jauhar and Don Lalia wanted that thumb drive. It had taken her the better part of six months on the run to figure out what they were after. She still didn't know why they wanted it.

Six months after Issa's murder, she'd been ready to give up and let them kill her when she stumbled upon a recorded conversation between Issa and Jauhar hidden among some of the other things Issa's estate manager had given her. The hopelessness in Issa's voice had cut her to the bone. Jauhar had threatened him. The recording was vague, but it was clear Issa owed him money, which made no sense because Issa had more money than God.

One thing on the recording was made crystal clear; Jauhar had Issa killed. Nearly every detail of Issa's murder matched the threat Jauhar had made. The revelation had given her a fresh fire in her bones; the will to not only survive, but to make sure Jauhar paid with his life for the bullet he'd put in Issa's head.

After Don Lalia's men caught up to her in Mozambique, she decided it was time to stop running. They would catch her and kill her eventually. It was only a matter of time. She couldn't let that happen before she'd extracted revenge for Issa. So she made a deal with the devil himself.

The only way she was going to get close enough to Jauhar to kill him was to demand an in person meeting to hand over the drive. People like Jauhar didn't like being given ultimatums, but apparently he was as ready to end this nightmare as she was, readily agreeing to meet her in Nampula. She had no misconceptions about his intentions to kill her. She no longer cared if she died, as long as she took him to hell with her.

Lost in her thoughts, she flinched when Grant dropped a big duffle bag onto the grass beside her. She looked up to see him studying her, a hard expression chiseled into his handsome face. Why was he helping her? In five short days she'd only managed to make his life as miserable as hers. In that moment she realized she no longer feared him, which probably made her an automatic candidate for idiot of the year, but it was true. Something inside her ached to reach out to him, to let him in and tell him everything. She knew if she gave into those feelings it would only make leaving him that much harder. And she would leave him, as soon as she was able. She was a walking dead woman with a very short expiration date. Despite her growing attraction to him, there was no sense in letting him believe they had anything more than a physical connection. Regardless of whatever else she had to deny herself, she at least wanted the chance to explore the sexual power he had over her before she said goodbye to him forever. Hopefully she would get that chance before she ran out of time.

Insisting that she be allowed to walk from the helicopter to the compound instead of letting Grant carry her was a moronic idea. By the time they reached the front door she'd nearly passed out from exhaustion. Lack of food and water, combined with the chaos her body had been through in the last week, made her capable of only two things by the time she stepped inside the industrial style flat. Taking a micro shower and finding a bed.

Thalia opened her eyes to see Grant standing in the bedroom doorway, his hands tucked into his pockets, watching her. She lay unmoving for a moment while she took in the man staring back at her. He'd shaved, the smooth skin on his sharp jawline and strong chin somehow giving him an even harder edge about him, if that was even possible. Thick veins curled under the tanned skin of his biceps as they strained against the deep green t-shirt he wore like a second skin, stretched tight across his chest. Her fingers twitched with the desire to reach out and unbutton the top button on his threadbare blue jeans. She could almost taste the fog of testosterone that emanated from him, floating effortlessly across the room as it reached out and tickled a spot deep inside her.

She closed her eyes, etching the image into her memory before she let it slip to the back of her mind. Taking a quick mental inventory, she realized her screaming headache was blessedly gone, but her stomach burned from lack of sustenance. "What time is it?" She could tell by the dim light from the window it was nearing nightfall.

"Almost six," Grant said, uncrossing his bare feet and taking the few steps needed to reach the side of her bed. "Hungry?"

Starving. "No," she said and shook her head. Flipping back the covers, she threw her legs over the side, wincing at the small ache in her thigh. "I need to make a phone call."

"Whoa there, fossa." Grant blocked her escape, caging her in with his thighs. "You're not doing anything outside of eating dinner until we have a little chit-chat."

Thalia's body temperature skyrocketed. She was practically staring at his crotch, saliva pooling around her tongue at the temptation in front of her. Her vision from the beach played in her mind like an erotic film. When Grant's fingers threaded through her hair she nearly came unraveled with the desire to touch him. A whimper spilled from her lips when he tilted her head back, giving her a glimpse of the fire raging in his eyes. There were no words needed to communicate the sudden and mutual need that filled the small space between them.

"This won't change my mind. You're not making any phone calls until we talk."

She didn't care. She wasn't playing a game or trying to seduce him into letting her go. She needed to taste him. Needed to feel his strength binding her to him. She gave a silent nod, her womb fluttering to life when his golden eyes darkened to a rich maple, his inner beast calling to her.

"Unzip my pants and take out my cock." Thalia's hands trembled with urgency as she unbuckled his belt and slipped the button through its anchor as she'd wanted to do moments earlier. The sound of his zipper raked over her skin as she drew it down, revealing his black boxers and the prominent bulge behind the thin cotton. Her fingers tingled as she cupped his shaft and ran her palm over its thick length.

"Take it out, Thalia." His gruff command sent a river of lust flowing through her veins. An aching throb unfurled inside her, flooding her with excitement. She impatiently tugged at his jeans, sliding her hands into the waistband of his boxers, quickly slipping them over his cock and down his muscled thighs. *He's gorgeous.* His swollen head bobbed free in front of her and her tongue slid over her lips with anxious anticipation. She couldn't wait to taste him. Wrapping her hand around the base, she followed the slight upward curve to the ring around his tip, the hardened silk sliding through her fingers as he drew in a ragged breath.

She raked in her own staggered breath when he threaded the fingers of his other hand into her hair, cradling her head between his hands with a commanding grip. She didn't feel trapped, but there was no question of who was in control. What she'd imagined on the beach was nothing but a watered down version of what it felt like to have him truly holding her captive to his will.

"Open your mouth." Her body tensed as his grip tightened, her scalp tingling as each strand of hair was pulled tight. His hips pressed forward, pushing the swollen head beyond her lips, his unique flavor exploding over her tongue. "*Fuck!*" Grant held her head and pushed to the back of her throat, her lips meeting her hand that still gripped his shaft. Agonizingly slow, he withdrew from her mouth, letting her taste and feel each vein and ridge with the tip of her tongue. “That’s it fossa, taste me. I’ve been dying to feel you like this.”

With the pull of her lips, she drew the seed from his slit and rolled her tongue around the smooth edge, extracting another agonized groan from his chest. “Fuck, yes!” His hips flexed again and she tensed as he pushed to the back of her throat. He waited there patiently as she steadied her breaths, the look in his eyes coaxing, demanding she relax and let him. When she did he slid past her tongue, her throat swallowing hard around his cock as she watched his mouth open on a cry.

“Christ!” His hips jerked back and he pulled from her mouth. “Stand up.” He helped her to her feet, and then pushed off his pants and boxers, kicking them away. “Are you sure this is what you want?” he asked as he bent and yanked her thin, cotton pants to the floor.

Now that she’d tasted him, tasted the power that lurked inside him, there was no turning back. As long as she kept her wits and didn’t allow anything between them to distract her from her plan, there was no reason to deny herself this one need. She nodded and stepped free of her pants, collapsing back onto the mattress when his lean, hard body crowded against her.

Hovering above her, he worked her knees apart with his and took her chin in a firm grip. “Talk to me, Thalia. I need a yes or no. Is this what you want?”

“Yes.”

“Then take off your shirt. I want to feel all of you against me.” He pulled his own shirt over his head as he watched her do the same. She cringed when she saw the brown and green swirls of bruises across her abdomen. Her arms folded over her midsection in an attempt to hide them.

“There’s no need to hide from me, fossa.” His hands landed at her sides and he pushed her back to the mattress with the weight of his body. “I’ve seen the worst of it and you’re beautiful. All of you.” He held his heavy weight suspended above her as his hot tongue traveled the length of her neck and swirled around her earlobe. His panting breaths sent a wave of heat rolling over her skin as he whispered in her ear, “This will be hard and fast, fossa. Hold on to me.”

Thalia had no sooner wrapped her arms around him when he pushed the head of his cock through her slick entrance and thrust into her to the hilt, stretching her to the point of delicious pain. "Ahh! Yes!" she cried out and rocked into him, the force of his next punishing drive sliding her further across the bed.

"Oh, fuck yes!" One arm tunneled beneath her shoulder, his hand gripping the back of her neck as the other slid beneath her ass, anchoring her to him as he thrust deeper. "Kiss me," he ordered, and she opened her mouth to him, his warm tongue sliding in to tangle against hers with an urgent demand.

The air around them swirled with the scents of their combined arousal and crackled with the electric charge that pulsed between them as each of his powerful thrusts fused them closer and closer together. His desperate grunts and ragged breaths sent wave after wave of pure lust rushing through her veins as they rocked across the bed, lost in a hard frenzy of lust. Her body tensed, the walls of her pussy tightening around his cock as the first flutters of her orgasm rushed along her spine. He tore his lips from hers in a responsive growl, the tendons in his neck stretching beneath his skin as he threw his head back on another powerful thrust. "Holy hell. That feels…*fuck…*" He moved faster, driving harder and further. She could feel his shaft swell inside her. His fingers gripped her ass so hard she knew she would have more bruises added to her already battered body, but she didn't care. She loved it. She loved the feel of his weight against her as he held her down and took what he needed from her over and over.

"Come with me." The tip of his cock nudged her womb and set off an erotic charge, igniting a wildfire that burned through her body. Her hips flexed and strained against his, the sore muscles in her legs and stomach screaming as she tightened around him, her orgasm tearing through her body as she shattered into pieces beneath him. His hoarse cry filled her ears, drowning out her own. His rhythm faltered, his cock pulsing powerfully deep inside her and filling her with a rush of his hot come. Her body still shook with her release when he collapsed against her, his warm, heavy weight trapping her against the soft mattress. Only she didn't feel trapped. She felt alive, sated, and safe for the first time since Issa's murder. *Oh, shit. I'm in so much trouble.*

All too soon, Grant pushed up onto his elbows, taking some of that feeling away from her. His hands framed her face as he dipped his head and captured her lips with a long, languid kiss. When he pulled back to look at her, something in her chest ached when she saw the concern in his eyes.

"Did I hurt you?" His thumbs drew tiny circles in her hair as he caressed her temples. It was a small thing, but to Thalia it was a gentleness she'd never experienced. She shook her head, not sure if her voice would betray the sudden emotion welling inside her.

"I know my timing is shit, but my brain, I…I lost it when I saw that look in your eyes. Please tell me you're on some type of birth control."

Still catching her breath she gave him a silent nod, not quite sure what to make of her lack of concern. She'd never once had unprotected sex, but something about holding a piece of him within her felt strangely…right. "I didn't think of it either, I….I'm clean."

"Me, too." Grant's lips curled into a grin. "I've, uh, never gone bareback before. That was…intense." He wiggled his hips and she could feel him hardening within her. "Feel like taking a shower?"

Her mind reeled with detailed visions of what he could do to her there, the hot water sluicing between their bodies. She pushed them away, forcing herself to focus on the conversation her body had hijacked. She needed to get up. Shaking her head, she pushed at his chest, but he didn't budge. "I need to make that phone call."

Grant shook his head. "You're not talking to anyone before you talk to me." He pushed himself up and slowly withdrew from her body, creating an instant emptiness she was all too familiar with. He tugged her to her feet and into his arms, cupping her bare ass and pulling her against his still stiff cock. "I've got dinner warming in the oven. Come on. We'll eat and chat," he said, giving her ass a playful tap. "After we shower."

At the mention of dinner her stomach rumbled. She ignored it and pushed from his arms then paced to the window. "You don't understand."

Grant watched her pace, her limp a little less pronounced than it had been earlier in the day. He hated the haunted look in her eyes. She was in trouble. It didn't take a rocket scientist to know it was big trouble. While he watched her sleep, he'd decided he didn't care what kind of trouble she was in. He was going to help her.

"I was supposed to meet someone tomorrow. If I don't show up, which obviously I'm not going to, I need to let them know I won't be there. Reschedule or…or something."

Grant sat on the edge of the bed and crossed his arms over his chest. He'd hoped to put this conversation off until they'd had something to eat and a nice long fuck in the shower, but it didn't appear as though it was going to happen that way. Apparently they were going to do this naked and hungry, and still horny as hell, because he wasn't about to shut her down now that she was finally talking. "And this would be a different someone than who's trying to kill you?"

Thalia shook her head. "No. I mean yes." He watched as a chill shuddered up her spine. "I'm pretty sure those were Hamisi's men at the beach, though I have no idea how they found me. The man I'm supposed to meet tomorrow will think I've played him if I don't show up. For more reasons than I can say, I can't afford for that to happen. He will kill me if I don't at least try to set up another time to meet." She shook her head and ran her hands over her arms. "He'll kill me anyway, but...."

That's what he was afraid of. In an instant he stood in front of her, his hands clamping gently around her arms. "First of all, no one is going to kill you. I won't let that happen, but you have to talk to me. What do you have that Don Lalia would send Hamisi to kill you for?"

He watched as familiar emotions of doubt and mistrust swirled in the expressions on her face, felt the surrender in her posture as she let out a long, heavy breath. "A thumb drive."

He'd prepared himself for a lie, but he could see the truth in her eyes when she spoke. "I'm guessing that's what you are supposed to deliver tomorrow?" She nodded wordlessly and, although in his gut he already knew the answer, he needed to hear it from her. "Who are you supposed to meet tomorrow, Thalia?"

"Kafeel Jauhar."

Grant closed his eyes and took a deep breath. How in the hell had she gotten mixed up with someone like Jauhar? He was literally the epitome of human waste, and the very thought of her doing any kind of business with him made the blood sizzle in his veins. Good or bad, he had to know. "You work for him?"

Thalia pulled away from him and walked to the bed, her fingers trailing over the tangled sheets. "It's complicated," she said as she sank to the edge of the mattress.

Grant clamped down on his need to shake some sense into her and paced to the window instead. "So un-complicate it for me. Because after losing my island, my boat and Salina, I'd like to think I'm at least helping the right side here." He saw the shock on her face at the mention of his contact. "That's right. Salina is dead. She was gunned down right after she took the tracking device out of your arm which, by the way, is how they found you. So tell me she didn't die helping a shit-bag like Jauhar."

"It's not like that!"

"Then tell me what it's like, Thalia!" Grant kept his distance, sure that she would bolt if he crowded her. Or worse. He was still naked after all.

"I…*shit*…" He didn't move when she pushed from the bed and began to pace like a caged animal. In a strange way she was. She may not be an operative, but they were very much alike. They had the same sense of survival and need for control. Suspicion was second nature to them both, and he could feel her struggle to give him the trust he demanded.

Against his better judgment, something inside him pushed him to comfort her. Understanding her better than she could possibly imagine, he needed her to know she could trust him. When next she pivoted away from him, his hand reached out and encircled her wrist, pulling her back to him. She wouldn't turn to face him, so he wrapped his arms around her waist and hugged her back to his chest. "You can trust me, fossa. I need to know that I can trust you."

"Oh, that's rich coming from someone who won't even tell me his real name, *Silas*." She tried to twist away from him, but he was determined not to let her push him away. "I know *nothing* about you and I'm supposed to trust you? Let me go!"

Grant carefully and tenderly tightened his grip. Not taking the chance that she wouldn't try to crack his skull open with the back of her head, he nuzzled his chin tight against her neck and whispered into her ear, "And yet you sucked my cock and let me fuck you without a condom." She tensed when he let one of his hands trail down between her thighs. A flash of lust flooded his cock and he ground it hard against her ass as he slipped his fingers through her wet folds. They glistened with the combination of her arousal and his seed as he held them up in front of her. "You enjoyed it. You can't deny this thing between us anymore than you can say that Thalia is *your* real name."

"It is my real name."

It was a nickname. Not a complete lie, or he would have pushed her further. Looking down over her shoulder, he felt her rapid heartbeat against his chest as he swirled the pearly fluids around her nipple. "It doesn't matter. I am a lot of things to a lot of different people. I'll be glad to play twenty questions with you later and give you as many answers as I can, but right now…" He lifted her breast, trailing his hand up and over the ripe swell to the long line of her neck. With his thumb he turned her head to meet his gaze and lightly pressed his lips to hers in a lingering kiss. "Right now, I am the only one who can help you. I need to know what I'm dealing with."

Her body relaxed against his, the feel of her in his arms felt better than anything he'd ever known. *God, please don't let her be on the wrong side.* He wasn't a religious man, but he would promise anything to any deity to know she wasn't one of those he'd spent his life fighting to destroy.

"Jauhar murdered the only family I had, and I plan to kill him." Her confession was made in such a quiet whisper Grant nearly missed it.

"So this is personal. Not business?" He held back the hope in his heart for a breath until she nodded, her head falling back against his shoulder as she blew out a breath of relief.

"He wants the thumb drive. He won't stop until he has it."

"So you were just going to hand it over." He could see where this was leading and he didn't like it.

"Yes." She turned in his arms and pressed her forehead to his bare chest.

"What then? You think he will just let you walk away?

"No. I don't know how, but I'll find a way to kill him once I get close enough to do it."

Grant let his head fall forward, pressing his lips into her hair as his hands idly caressed the skin on her back. "What's on the thumb drive?"

Thalia shrugged. "Shipping data, I think. None of it makes very much sense to me. It's full of codes and numbers, but I recognize some of the dates and locations." His arms instinctively tightened around her when another chill ran through her and she shivered against him. "Jauhar killed my uncle. If I have something he wants, I have to use it to get to him. He's going to kill me anyway. I want the chance to take him to hell with me."

"He's not going to kill you." He wouldn't let that happen. There was more to it, he was sure, but she'd said enough for now. He got the picture.

As his fingers played along her spine, tracing the raised lines of skin that crisscrossed in a telling pattern beneath his fingertips, he knew there was one more question he had to ask. His blood raced through his veins when he pictured her shackled and bleeding as her *uncle*, or any other man, marred her skin and tried to break her fierce spirit. He could just as easily picture himself putting a bullet between the sick bastard's eyes, whoever he was. He wasn't sure if he could handle the truth, but he forced the question out anyway. "Is your uncle the one who did this to you?" He purposefully traced his finger over the most prominent lash mark.

She drew back from his embrace, her brows furrowed in confusion. "What?"

Grant loosened his grip and let his fingers trail down her arms. "The scars on your back. You were beaten. Is he the one who took you from your family?" It was possible, would even be twistedly normal, for her to call her captor *uncle.* Some slaves were raised by their captors and beaten into respecting, or even seeing their captor's torture as love. Although, knowing what he knew of her, she didn't seem the type to remain loyal to such a person.

"A slave?" He watched as the meaning behind his question dawned. "Oh, no." She shook her head. "I wasn't a…a sex slave. Or any other kind of slave. Issa would never do that." She rested her hands on his stomach and gave him a small, sad smile. "I was in a car accident, or at least that's what Issa and the doctors told me when I woke up. I don't remember much before that."

"A car accident?" His bullshit meter was pegged into the red, but when he looked into her eyes he could see she believed what she was telling him.

"Yes. A car accident." She turned from his embrace and paced to the closet. Opening the doors, he watched as she shuffled through the miscellaneous items of clothing. "I was seventeen, I think. I woke up in a strange bed, in a strange house surrounded by strange men. Issa, my uncle, said a drunken truck driver ran my parents' car off the road into a ravine, north of Mumbai, killing them instantly. I was thrown through the windshield. I guess the glass cut me up pretty badly. Like I said, I don't remember. When I woke up I didn't remember anything except my first name." She pulled a blue and white dress from one of the hangers and held it up. "I still don't."

Seventeen. "You have no memory of your parents or your childhood?" He wasn't sure if he felt relieved or even more skeptical as he bent and scooped up his jeans from the floor. Something felt off about the timing, about the whole damn story, but he couldn't quite get a grip on it.

"No. I don't." She let the dress drop and reached up to cup her arm. "They put a tracking chip in my shoulder? Those bastards."

"Your parents, they were American?"

Thalia nodded, hissing when she pulled the bandage away from her skin. "My mother was half Indian. She was Issa's sister. We were in India on vacation to visit him."

He pushed aside the weird feeling in his gut to dissect later. Taking her hand, he pulled her toward the bathroom. "Come on. We'll take a shower, I'll change your bandage, and then we can figure out what our next step is while I feed you."

She followed him into the bathroom without argument which, when it happened, never ceased to amaze him.

CHAPTER ELEVEN

"I'm sorry about Salina." Seemed she was going to be in a perpetually apologetic state with him. She might as well get comfortable saying it. "I'm sorry about your boat and, well, everything."

Wrapped around her back, his smooth chin resting on her shoulder, she felt Grant shrug as she leaned her face into the spray and rinsed away the soap suds. "She was an asset, not a friend."

"That sounds a little harsh." She had no problems with killing someone like Jauhar or Hamisi. She may have lost some of her more delicate senses toward death, but she didn't think she would be able to compartmentalize the loss of someone who helped her like Salina had.

Grant shrugged. The heat of his tongue traveled up the side of her neck before he sucked the water from her earlobe, sending shivers racing over her skin despite the blissful heat of the water. "I don't care about anything else right now except this." The sharp edge of his teeth raked against the outer shell of her ear; she would have fallen to her knees if his thick arm hadn't been wrapped around her, holding her up.

She both hated and loved how quickly he could reduce her to a spineless puddle of lust with one look or touch. She wanted to explore *him*, find *his* weaknesses. *Surely he has one.* Resolved to keep things on an even playing field, at least for the moment, she spun away and pushed him under the spray, ignoring his grunted protests. Scooping up the soap, she lathered it into a washcloth. The muscles in his back rippled and tensed as she slowly caressed his skin, taking notice of the multitude of scars that marred his sculpted frame.

A sex slave? Grant's questions wormed their way back into her thoughts. Thalia knew one of Jauhar's biggest enterprises was human trafficking. Although she'd never met Jauhar, Issa had warned her to never allow herself to be alone with his men or trust them. She never understood why Issa would do business with someone so vile, but she never questioned his counseling. She only wished he'd taken his own advice.

"Why did my scars make you think I'd been a slave?" Hot water sluiced down his back, rinsing the soap from Grant's body, her lips laying claim to the skin on his shoulder as she ran the wash cloth down his back. "Is that something you've seen before?"

"Yes." Her fingers followed his spine then trailed along his shoulder blades and around his sides to his chest. Scraping her fingernails across his flat nipples drew a rewarding hiss from his lips before he continued. "I've seen pictures of women and children who had been branded and whipped. The marks on your back look like some of them."

The spray from the shower head hit her face when he turned in her arms. Backing her against the wall, Grant leaned down and placed a wet kiss on her forehead, then her nose.

"Branded?" she asked, trying desperately to hold on to her thoughts as his hands cupped and kneaded her breasts, gently twisting her sensitive nipples in return.

"Yeah," he breathed, sucking her earlobe into his mouth again, nipping it with his teeth. "Sometimes the slaves would have their owner's initials burned into their skin as a mark of ownership."

Thalia's blood ran cold as the hazy images from her nightmares surfaced in her thoughts and the suffocating feeling pressed down on her chest. *No. Not here. Not with him.* Grant pulled back and looked at her. His eyes, dark with need, suddenly filled with concern. Something Thalia didn't think she would ever get used to seeing. "This conversation is not working for you either, huh?" His hands slid from her breasts and framed her waist. He lowered his head and sucked on the skin between her neck and shoulder, his hips flexing to push the head of his shaft deep between her wet folds. "I say we not talk at all for a bit."

Thank heavens for the timing of her stomach. As her lungs began to seize, a loud growl echoed off the tiled walls. Grant laughed and shook his head. "Looks like I've been overruled." He reached over and cut the water, and then helped her step out of the tub before he handed her a towel. She forced herself to breathe as she dried off; trying to think of a way to get him out of there so she could pull herself together.

"Hey, are you okay?" Grant's hands cupped her neck, his thumbs tilting her chin up to him. She nodded silently and looked over her shoulder at the toilet.

"Right." He smiled and kissed the tip of her nose. "I'll, uh, give you some privacy and go check on dinner. Come to the kitchen when you're done and I'll redress your wounds before we eat."

Again she nodded, her lungs clawing for air as she forced her lips into something resembling a smile. When the door finally closed behind him, her knees hit the tile and she fell to her side, gasping for breath as a single tear trailed down her cheek and splashed onto the floor.

Car accident my ass. Grant stood outside the bathroom door and listened as Thalia fell apart. It took everything he had not to bust through the door and gather her in his arms, but he already knew her well enough to know she would only kick him right back out.

Fuck! He didn't know what had set her off, but he would damn sure find out. He threw his towel onto the bed. Forgoing his boxers, he picked up his jeans and pulled them on, then sprinted to the room at the end of the hall. Once inside, he closed and locked the door behind him. One thing about being who he was, he had access to all kinds of neat toys and contacts.

He mumbled another curse as he took a seat in front of the bank of computer screens and picked up the phone receiver in front of him. It seemed the more answers he got from her the more questions he had. Typing in a password, he accessed the system and pulled up the central departmental search engine as he dialed a number he pulled from memory.

"Diver."

"I need you to find something for me," Grant barked at the familiar voice on the other end of the line. As he spoke, he quarried Jauhar's file from three different bureaus and hit enter.

"Lieutenant! I thought you were chasing hangovers and pussy in the Caribbean. Or was it Fiji? You miss me that much?

“Get your hand off your dick and listen up.” Grant didn’t have time for social niceties. Thalia would pull herself together quick enough, and he needed to have this wrapped up when she came out.

“Shoot.”

“I want everything you can find on two unknown Americans killed in a car accident in Mumbai ten years ago. They had a daughter, seventeen, first name Thalia, last name Brezlin, or some derivative. She’s twenty-seven now, five-ten, black hair, grey eyes.”

“Okay.” He could hear Diver’s fingers flying across his keyboard in the background. “Tango-Hotel-Alpha-Lima-India-Alpha.”

“Correct. I’ll get you additional specifics when I can. And find anything you can on a tango, first name Issa, India-Sierra-Sierra-Alpha. May or may not be a relative in Mumbai. Add Mozambique and Madagascar to your search grid.”

“So you are chasing pussy.” Diver’s chuckle grated on his nerves. He was in no mood for jokes. “Okay,” Diver drew out the last syllable in feigned agitation. “Perky as usual I see, Lieutenant. I’ll dig up what I can.”

“Call me as soon as you get anything.” Grant paused before he set the receiver back in the cradle. “And Diver?”

“Yeah?”

“The Lieutenant is dead. Don’t use that name again.”

Silence weighed heavy on the line. Grant thought he’d lost connection before Diver cleared his throat. “Okay boss, but I don’t know what else to call you. Except maybe asshole.”

“Fuck off.” Grant disconnected the call. He wouldn’t hold his breath for the off chance any of her story panned out. He didn’t think she was lying. No, she believed every word of it. He had nothing to say it wasn’t true except the uneasy feeling in his gut, which he’d learned long ago to trust without fail.

On auto pilot, he dug through the desk drawers until he found a blank flash drive and popped it into the port. With a few clicks, he downloaded the files and logged out, not bothering to look at the information. He snatched a backpack from the back of the door and stuffed the drive and one of the two laptops in it before he left the room, locking the door behind him.

He could hear Thalia moving around in her bedroom as he passed by on his way to the kitchen. He understood the unyielding need to go to her, to fix whatever was wrong. And he didn't like it. For the first time in his life he cared about someone beyond himself, and a part of him knew he was fucked for it. Caring made you weak, a soft target. Ten years living with a drunk and three years in the foster system taught him that. The minute you cared about something it was gone, or worse — used against you.

Still, a bigger part of him, a deeper part which seemed nonexistent before Thalia washed up on his beach, reveled in the thought of somehow keeping her in his life. She was important.

And the sex! *Christ.* He'd literally just had the fuck of his life. She'd taken everything he had to give. Everything he'd meant to hold back but couldn't. He knew he could be dominant and a bit rough when it came to sex. Apparently more than normal with her. Knowing she had a past that was probably steeped in sexual abuse, he'd thought it best to tone down that side of himself, at least until he knew more. When she'd swallowed his dick, something inside him drove him to a madness he'd never experienced, or ever be able to explain. He would never get enough of her.

If she was a slave and she truly had no memory of it, he could be stepping into a minefield every time he touched her. He couldn't ignore it. There was no way in hell now that he'd had her that he would be able to keep his hands off her. They would have to discuss what had set her off, which would probably set her off in an entirely different, furious kind of way. His little mongoose didn't like to show her weaknesses.

He grinned as he pulled out a saucepan and grabbed the milk, butter, and a couple of limes from the fridge. He actually liked it when she went a little feral on him. Her eyes turned that wild shade if silvery blue, her chest heaving as she reined in her initial savage instincts to tear into him. The only time she was ever more magnificent was when she came apart beneath him. Something he planned to see again very soon, and very often.

A new thought splintered his attention. His dick twitched against his thigh when he thought about the fight she was going to put up when he told her she wasn't going to be making that call to

Jauhar. She was crazy if she thought he would allow her to continue with her disastrous plan for revenge.

No way in hell was he going to let that bottom feeder get within a hundred feet of her. She would have to refocus her need on something else, because it wasn't going to happen. Oh, he'd kill the mother fucker, slow and painfully, but she would be well out of reach when it happened.

He stirred a little flour into the melted butter in the pan, mixing in a little rosemary and pepper before adding in the milk and some crumbled parmesan. He loved having contacts in high places with fully stocked kitchens, especially when they owed you a favor.

"Smells good."

His well-honed reflexes had his gun drawn from his waistband and pointed mere inches from Thalia's face before he'd even blinked. "Sonofabitch, Thalia! Don't sneak up on me like that."

She froze and stared down the barrel of the gun in Grant's hand, her heart rate hitting the stratosphere. Swallowing was pointless. Her mouth instantly dry, she slowly reached for the glass of water sitting on the island bar in front of her. *Jesus.* He was like a damn ghost. She hadn't even seen him move. Between the gun and the sight of his ripped, bare abs, she thought she would choke on her tongue before she took her first sip. After spilling nearly half the water down the front of her dress, she managed to gulp down enough to satisfy a horse before carefully setting the glass back onto the counter. "I wasn't sneaking."

She watched as Grant gathered himself and tucked the gun back into the front of his blue jeans. He grabbed up a hand towel and stepped around the bar. "I didn't mean to frighten you." She stood paralyzed as he wiped the front of her dress, unsuccessfully ignoring the wave of heat that pooled between her legs when his hand lingered on her breasts.

She cleared her throat and snatched the towel from his hands. The last thing she needed was to seem more pathetic than he already thought she was. "It's okay." She dabbed at her dress as he walked back over to the stove. "I can see the calming qualities of almost having your head blown off." She threw the towel onto the counter and slid back onto one of the wooden bar stools, twining her fingers together in her lap to keep them from shaking. "You should think about marketing your approach to spas and yoga instructors." She caught his critical gaze and lifted her chin. "Besides, I think we've already established that I know my way around a gun."

"She's beautiful and funny. Whatever could she see in me?" She abandoned her quest for quick-witted reply when he plated the food and sat one in front of her, along with two white tablets and another glass of water. "Take those," he said before he turned back for his own plate.

"What are they?"

"Antibiotics." She was only marginally grateful he took the seat across from her instead of next to her. She knew she was about to be interrogated, but at least she didn't have to feel his heat so close to her skin while he was doing it. "Two twice a day for a week. And no arguments." He took the bottle from his pants pocket and set it on the counter next to her plate.

"Thanks." She popped the pills to the back of her throat and took another swig of water. When she caught his gaze over the rim of her glass she couldn't ignore his confused expression. "What?

"I didn't exactly expect you to buy into the whole no argument bit so easily."

He sat there, staring at her expectantly. "What? You want me to hack them back up and start over with a *fuck-you*?" He laughed. A big, burly, carefree kind of laugh she'd never heard from him before. Something inside her turned all warm and fuzzy knowing she'd made him let go enough to share that with her.

"No. No need to do that. I just thought I'd have to arm wrestle you into taking them." He took a drink of water, licking his lips as he set the glass back down. Another lustful shard of arousal spiked in her belly as she watched the moisture bead on his lips. When he glanced back up, his wicked grin told her she'd been busted. "So does this mean you trust me?"

She shook her head and picked up her fork. "Let's just say there is something about you that makes me want to trust you." Before she could bring the fork to her mouth he snatched it from her hand with another display of lightning speed. "Hey! I want to eat that."

"And I want you to eat it, but I need you to clear something up for me first." He set the fork down on his plate and picked up his glass again, taking another small sip before he continued. "What happened in there?" He tilted his head towards the bedroom.

She should have known he would stick around to snoop. She sat back in her seat and ran her fingertip along the edge of her plate. *What would he think if I dug in with my hands?* "I don't know what you mean."

She jumped when he set his glass down with a loud bang, water sloshing over the sides. She watched in amazement as he subtly restrained his temper and repositioned himself in his seat. "I'm not asking for the hell of it, Thalia. Did I do something that sent you into that panic attack?" The hard look on his face relaxed with concern as his arms raked down the edge of the counter and fell into his lap. "I don't know how, but I'll find a way to keep my hands to myself if that's it."

A small hiccup of laughter bubbled up from Thalia's chest at the dejected look on his face. "No," she said and shook her head, her shoulders relaxing despite the fact she'd lost the last shred of her pride. "It's not you." She found it hard to look at him so she focused on the beads of sweat running down the side of her glass instead. "I've had those for as long as I can remember. They've been worse lately, but it's not you."

"What's the trigger?" She darted a glance toward him and her heart nearly melted. How was it possible that he cared? How did she tell him that he was the only man who had ever made her crave the closeness that usually brought them on? She sure as hell wasn't going to tell him about the nightmares. Still avoiding eye contact, Thalia shrugged, as if the motion itself would toss off the weight of her embarrassment.

"Don't be embarrassed, fossa." Grant reached across the counter and tilted her chin so that she had to look at him. "I'm only asking so I don't do something that will cause it. I know I can be demanding and pushy when it comes to sex, but I can dial it back a few clicks if it's too much."

She shook her head, dislodging his grip on her chin. "No, please." More heat crept into her cheeks and she reached for the glass of water, taking a long sip before setting the glass back down. God, how could she explain something she didn't fully understand herself? "It's…I get this heavy, suffocating feeling in my chest when I'm close to someone that way. I mean, normally I can't stand for a man to be…"

"On top?"

Thalia nodded, still unable to meet his gaze, his silence as unnerving as having his gun stuck in her face. "But it's different with you. I don't know what caused it this time."

"Different how?"

Geeze, he was going to make her say it. "It just is, okay? I don't know why or how. I just want you that way. I don't want you to change anything."

"Thalia, look at me."

She straightened with the zing that ran along her spine in response to the command in his voice. She lifted her head to look at him, the gold in his eyes swirling with intent. "You will tell me if I do anything that makes you feel like that." She hesitated at first, but couldn't refuse him. She nodded and he shook his head. "Yes or no, fossa. I need to know that you understand."

"Yes."

"And you won't hide it from me again. I want to know you, Thalia, all of you, for however long this lasts. Understand?"

"Yes." She nodded. Strangely enough, she didn't feel like a child who had just been scolded. It went against her nature to give that much to him but she couldn't deny him. Despite what she'd told herself, she wanted to know him too.

"And you'll let me help you dress your wounds next time."

Her hand cupped the bandage she'd applied to her shoulder before she'd left the bathroom. "I can—"

"Yes, fossa. That's all I need to hear."

"Yes."

She scoffed when Grant cut a bite of food from his own plate and held the fork to her lips. "Indulge me."

Just like that, he shifted back into a playful, irresistible jerk, as if she hadn't had one of her darkest secrets ripped from her soul for all to see. She hesitated, wondering what kind of game he was playing, but thought *what the hell.* She could play, too. She let her eyelids droop as she leaned forward and slowly wrapped her lips around his fork. Any point to the game was lost on her when flavors she couldn't describe exploded on her tongue. "Mmm." Her jaw ached from the tangy spices and the meat was so rich and tender. "That's fantastic. What is it?"

"Zebra." Grant smiled and took a bite of his own.

Even if she'd been lost in a desert for a week without food, if someone had offered her zebra she probably would have refused it. No. Not probably. She'd eaten some pretty strange foods in India, but never once had she imagined eating a Zebra. Simple fact was, it was delicious. "I've never had zebra before."

Grant chuckled and cut another bite for her. "It's socially unacceptable in the States, and illegal. Most people think they would rather starve than to eat something like this. Then again, most of those people have never known what it's truly like to be starved. They're just talking out their asses. It's actually quite a common food here."

She'd expected him to jump right into the next interrogation phase of their evening, but it seemed he had different plans. As he continued to feed her, which she found more erotic and intimate than she ever thought it would be, he kept the conversation light. They talked about different places they'd been and their favorite foods and books. When he asked her about her musical tastes she couldn't help but tease him about what she'd found on his iPod.

"Is it so terrible that I like the symphony and classical music?" His blush surprised her. She didn't think Grant could be self-deprecating enough to be embarrassed.

"No," she laughed. "Issa listened to it all the time. He was a huge Tchaikovsky fanatic."

Grant leaned back in his chair and studied her for a moment before he picked up his glass of water and took a drink. He moved his plate to the side and leaned his elbows on the counter, his eyes turning from playful to calculating before he spoke. "Tell me about Issa."

CHAPTER TWELVE

He watched as she dabbed her plump lips with her napkin and pushed her plate away, all twelve layers of those damn iron shields she used to protect herself falling back into place. All his hard work using small talk to loosen her up swirled down the drain with a single question.

"What do you want to know?"

Grant settled back into his seat and shrugged. "Anything you want to tell me." When she didn't immediately answer he asked what seemed like the easiest questions to answer. "What did he do? What was he like?"

She shrugged, her eyes focused on a spot on the wall behind him. "He owned a transport company in Mumbai. Regional trade mostly, some international exports."

"You worked for him?"

"Yes." She closed her eyes and let out a long, slow breath. "I scheduled the loads and managed the books. All behind the scenes stuff. It was difficult, given how young I was, but Issa taught me a lot."

"Is that how you learned to shoot? Doesn't seem like there's much need for sharp shooting accountants these days."

She giggled. Honest to God giggled, and it made him want to wrap her up and keep her somewhere safe, where he could hear her laugh anytime he wanted. While it was tempting, he realized that doing so would be like trying to wrap a cactus in bubble wrap.

"No," she said on another giggle. "There isn't, but...outside the fact that I've lived on the run the past year and a half..." A mischievous smile bloomed on her lips, lighting up her entire face. "I went through a self-destructive phase during my first few years with Issa. When his bodyguard caught me trying to steal his gun, Issa thought it was a good idea to show me exactly what I was asking for. He took me out on one of his boats and let me target shoot at some offshore floats. I was hooked from that first shot. He taught me everything I know about guns and shooting. He was very strict about making sure I knew how to defend myself. Not that I minded. I loved it."

"Did he teach you how to fight, too?"

She nodded. "Yes. Well, he hired instructors for some of the more traditional martial arts like Kalari and Judo, but he's the one who taught me how to fight dirty."

Grant let out a long whistle. "Kalari, huh? That's impressive." Hell. He would have to remember to hide the brooms and mops. "So you can fight just as good with a stick as you can with a gun." She laughed again, and the sound went straight to his heart and spread to his groin. With his hand under the table, he reached down and adjusted his jeans, cursing his lack of underwear as his zipper cut into his dick.

"No. If I'm going to use lethal force it's easier to shoot someone. Besides, I didn't stay with it long enough to master it. Choreographed routines were boring. Instead I took to the streets and honed my skills in the real world."

"You ran away?" Grant didn't have a difficult time picturing her as a rebellious teenager, but he couldn't see her running from the only person she knew.

"No." She shook her head, her mischievous smile relaxing into a sad sort of grin. "I was just…unfocused, and a bit…self-destructive. I got into a lot of fights in school. Issa eventually took me out and hired private tutors. I couldn't fight at home, so I would sneak out at night or on the weekends and pick fights with the local kids. I uh…yeah." She blew out a shaky breath, nervously tucking a strand of hair behind her ear. "I gave Issa a hard time for a while. I had some things I had to figure out how to deal with. Issa understood and eventually helped me find better ways to find the answers. He helped me deal with a lot of things."

"He meant a lot to you."

Grant watched as her thoughts turned inward. Unable to defend against the need to comfort her, he reached out and laid his hand, palm up, onto the bar. She hesitated, but eventually offered a sad smile and laced her fingers with his. "He was everything to me. When I woke up after the accident I was so confused." She rested her other elbow on the edge of the bar and massaged her forehead. "You can't imagine what it's like waking up and you know your name, but you have no clue who you are."

No, he couldn't imagine. He thought *he* was having an identity crisis. Hell, she'd been just a kid. "How long were you in the hospital?"

"I don't know. I woke up in a bedroom in Issa's house." His jaw tensed as another anonymous piece of the puzzle was pulled into view. If his gut was right, and she wasn't a victim of some random car accident, they wouldn't have wanted it reported. Not that the Indian authorities would have done much either way. They weren't well known for prosecuting crimes against women.

"Do you speak Hindi?"

She shook her head. "I mean, I can get by now, but I didn't then. Issa spoke English well enough." She released his hand and reached for her glass, taking a long sip of water. "It's strange. I speak English fluently, but I can't remember learning it. I…sometimes…since Issa was killed I feel like I'm not really me, but I don't know who I should be." Grant was so focused on her expressions that he startled when she slammed the glass down onto the bar.

"I don't want to talk about this anymore. We're running out of time. I need to make that call to Jauhar and set up a new drop."

"You're not making that call." He watched as her eyes widened at first, then narrowed as that familiar fire swirled within the dark silver depths. He wasn't surprised when she rocketed from her chair and braced her hands on the counter in front of her.

"What do you mean? I've told you everything!"

It took nearly every ounce of tested discipline to keep his lips from twitching into a grin. He didn't know what it was, but seeing her like this made him want to reach out and claim the passion in her eyes; to claim her and fuck her with a ferocity that utterly unhinged him. The veins in his dick instantly filled to capacity and he had to stand up to relieve some of the pressure.

"You heard me. You aren't making that call." He scooped up the plates and glasses before turning to the sink, more in an effort to hide his expressions than to tidy up. He knew it was shitty of him to push her buttons, but he couldn't help himself.

"I don't need your permission."

Dishes clanged in the sink. Grant turned and leaned against the counter, his arms crossed over his chest. "No, you don't. But you need my phone."

"This is bullshit!" Thalia turned and stomped toward the hallway.

"If you're planning to leave then you'll also need my helicopter. Or did you forget that we're in the middle of Safari country?" When she froze in place with her back to him, he moved to where she stood and leaned his shoulder against the wall in front of her. "Where's the thumb drive?"

"Fuck you," she spat, her obvious outrage lacing her tone. Grant chuckled and pushed away from the wall.

"Been there, done that. Quite thoroughly, I believe." She dodged his hand when he reached up to caress her face, setting off a few of his own fuses. He wouldn't force her, but he wouldn't allow her to outright deny him either. "Don't push me away, fossa."

He crowded behind her and slowly ran his fingertips along the backs of her thighs, lifting her skirt when he reached the full, tender globes of her ass. "Tell me." He felt her shudder, but she didn't pull away. The need to fill her nearly overwhelming, he watched over her shoulder as her chest heaved with each labored breath. Her arms folded beneath her breasts, pushing them up until they were nearly spilling out of the top of her little sundress. Drawn to them, his hands slid up and under the bodice of her dress, peeling her arms away as the soft, bare flesh of her breasts filled his hands with perfection. "Tell me," he breathed into her ear, his tongue darting out to trace her delicate lobe.

Thalia couldn't think. His hands were so hot against her skin. Her whole body ached for his touch, his mouth, his cock. She knew she had to stand her ground, but damn she couldn't remember why. "I don't…" A flash of erotic pain zinged through her pebbled nipples when he trapped and pinched them between his splayed fingers. The muscles in her neck collapsed and her head fell back against his shoulder. "I hate that you do this to me."

Grant's baritone hum vibrated against her over-sensitized skin, sending gooseflesh racing along her arms. "You have no idea how beautiful you are when you're angry. It's impossible to keep my hands off you when you're like this."

"Why can't I just make the call?" Grant nudged her forward. Her hands shook as she reached out and braced herself against the wall. One of his hands slipped from her breasts, and she could feel it moving against her ass as he flipped open the button on his jeans.

"Because you have the upper hand right now." The sound of his zipper made her pussy flutter with need as she remembered how well he filled her. How he controlled her completely as he was controlling her now. "You have what everyone wants, Thalia. No one knows where you are." His hot breath rolled against her neck as he lifted her skirt and gripped her hip, grinding his cock between her bare cheeks. "Let them simmer a bit."

Her breath seized in her chest as he positioned the head of his cock at her entrance. He was right there. *So close.* She could almost feel the erotic burn as her flesh stretched around the overwhelming fullness of his first thrust. "We'll make them wait while we get into position."

Pushing her hips back, she clenched her teeth. *No waiting. I can't wait any longer.* She hated begging, but couldn't bite back the plea clawing its way past her lips. "Fuck me, Grant. Please."

"We'll *push* them where we want them." His shouted grunt drowned out her own cry as he pushed up and slammed into her, his body hard against her back, his cock even harder inside her. "You maintain the element of control at all times, fossa." Her nails dug into the wall, her arms no longer able to hold her up as he withdrew and slammed back in time and time again.
"Never...give...up...control."

She loved giving control to him this way. The weight of each thrust pinned her against the wall, each crushing slap of his hips pressing him deeper inside, and still it wasn't enough. "Harder! Grant, please. I need more."

Grant's arms tightened around her waist and her feet left the floor. With a growl he set her down and bent her over the kitchen bar. "Ah," she hissed when his fingers dug into her already bruised hips. His grip immediately loosened as his body tensed behind her.

"Please don't stop." God, if he stopped now she would die.

His hands traveled up her back, pulling her dress up and over her head as he slid his lips along her spine. "You kill me, fossa. I've never wanted a woman the way I want you."

"I *am* going to kill you if you don't move." She squeezed her inner muscles around his hard shaft, wordlessly begging him to take her back to that place where she felt more right than she ever had in her life.

His hips snapped forward, his thighs slapping hard against her ass, his cock penetrating deeper. "Yes!" Her climax curled in her womb as his hands clamped over her shoulders. Each violent thrust reached deeper and deeper as he used his strength to pull her against him. The edge of the counter rubbed against her clit with just enough pressure, over and over until she was nearly out of her mind with need.

Sweaty skin slapped against sweaty skin. His harsh breaths, captured and expelled with panted grunts, made her feel alive with power as he lost control and pumped inside her with abandon. One of his hands released her shoulder, slapping with a loud crack onto the counter beside her head. She watched, enraptured as the thick tendons and muscles rippled beneath his skin, his fingers flexing for purchase with every thrust. Her feet left the floor as his pace quickened. She grabbed for the edge of the counter to hold herself against him. Aching heat flooded her pussy as the first waves of her climax rippled through her.

"I'm coming. Oh, God! Don't stop." Another brutal thrust, then another. "Ahh…yes…Grant!" Her entire body quaked beneath him. A harsh growl tore from his throat and he stilled deep inside her, his cock still throbbing as her inner muscles rippled around him. Heat rolled off his body in waves when he collapsed against her back, his forehead pressed to the back of her shoulder, panting for each breath.

Time ceased as they laid there still joined together, both unable and unwilling to sever the connection between them. This. *This* is what she wanted from him. She never imagined she could feel this alive. The power he possessed over her, over everything. It was like a drug. And like a greedy addict she wanted more. Grant peppered her skin with lazy kisses as their ragged breaths finally slowed. The skin on her back stuck to his chest when he peeled himself away and carefully pulled his spent cock from inside her. Gently, he lifted her legs and helped her further onto the counter before he pushed himself up to lay beside her, spooning her tight against his chest.

"What was that about not losing control?"

Grant chuckled as something along the lines of preaching to the choir ran through his mind. Yeah, he was in big trouble. His cock should be numb, but it was already rising against the heat of her ass as she snuggled against him.

This was more than the best sex of his life. Even if he believed in forever, it was bigger than that. This was it for him. He didn't know where this was going or how long he had with her, but he knew he was living in the best moments of his life. He wasn't bullshitting himself. People like him didn't get a happily ever after, only glimpses of it; rare and small moments of goodness. He knew, at his end, this time with her would be the best of his moments.

"How sure are you? About no one knowing where I am?"

The sound of her voice pulled him from his weepy thoughts. "Hmm?"

She rolled over and playfully pinched his nipple. "Ouch!" Circling her wrist, he tugged her hand away and placed it on his cock. "If you want to squeeze something, squeeze this. Just be nice." He nearly came unglued when her hand clamped around his cock with a firm grip and pumped. "Ah, hell, you're good at that, too. Christ woman, you're going to be the death of me."

"But what a way to go, right?" She giggled, giving his dick another teasing pump before she let him go, her fingers playing along the fine hairs on his lower abdomen. "Seriously. How sure are you?"

Grant relaxed against the cool counter top and gathered her against him. "No one but us and the person who owns the house knows we're here. Why?"

"Because…" He tilted his head down to look at her when she didn't continue. She glanced up at him through her lashes, her cheeks blooming with a telling shade of red. "Your, um, suggestion to wait. It makes sense."

"Ha!" Grant laughed and turned on his side to face her. "I bet that left a pretty bitter aftertaste. Need some humble pie to wash it down?"

"Jerk! Why didn't you tell me you had a plan?"

Yeah, he had a plan. The start of one. Now he needed to figure out what to do with her when it was time to put it into action. His fingers trailed along her thigh and over her hip. "Because you're incredible when you get all worked up. I couldn't resist."

She pushed against his chest, nearly shoving him to the floor. He caught his balance and rolled on top of her, pinning her against the counter. Her giggles subsided as he lowered his head and captured her lips, taking another deep, long taste of her before he rolled back to her side and propped his head on his hand. "What's your real name?"

"You already know my name."

He grinned. He needed to know in case Diver couldn't dig up anything under the name Thalia, but he'd let slide for now. There were more important questions he needed answered. "Fine, but I will get you to tell me sooner or later. Where's the thumb drive?"

She laid her cheek against his chest, a satisfied sigh blowing across his skin. "Mozambique Island. There is an old church with a graveyard. It's where Issa is buried. I hid it in a vase that is mounted to the tombstone next to his."

"Tell me about the data on it."

"Oh no." Thalia sat up, her long hair falling over her shoulder in a mess of tangled waves, the small streak of blue peeking through the thicker strands of black. "I answered one of your questions, now you answer one of mine."

"Ah." Grant grinned. "Twenty questions time. Fine." He leaned back and pillowed his arms behind his head. "Ask away."

"What are you? What do you do?"

"Ah-ah. That's two questions." Dammit! Of course she asked the one question he couldn't fully answer. When she cocked her eyebrow he had the sudden urge to cover his dick. "Fine." He took a deep breath, fighting the urge to give her the usual rehearsed answers. "Officially, I'm a contractor. Unofficially, I'm a semi-retired beach bum. That's all I can tell you."

"So you are an operative, like Salina said."

Grant shot up onto his elbows. "She told you that?"

Thalia shrugged. "Not exactly. She thought I was your partner or something. I put the pieces together."

Grant shook his head and collapsed back onto the counter. "She knew better than to talk at all."

Thalia resettled against him and threaded her fingers through his. "So now that I know, you'll have to kill me, huh? All that secret agent code stuff?"

Grant suddenly felt dirty lying next to her. It was a metaphorical sensation, but he could almost smell the grime of the world that had touched him. If she only knew how much evil had touched him she wouldn't be so quick to joke. "Something like that," he chuckled and released her hand. When she tensed a little against him, he tilted her chin up and stole a quiet kiss. "You're safe with me, Thalia. No one will hurt you. I will make sure of that."

"I believe you." She nodded and he released her chin, rethreading his fingers with hers.

"Now. Tell me about what's on the thumb drive and what makes you think Jauhar killed Issa."

"Hey! That's two questions."

"Tit for tat, fossa. Spill it."

"But you didn't actually answer…"

He trapped her arm against his chest and poked his fingers into her side, relishing the feel of her squirming in his arms as she giggled and laughed. Oh, yeah. His little fossa was ticklish. It was sort of an odd feeling. He'd never tickled anyone before. He stilled and let her calm, but kept her trapped against him. "Spill it or I'll be forced to continue my torture to extract the information I seek."

She laughed. "Torture by tickle. You're such a badass, Mr. Kendal."

He moved in on her again and she squealed, batting his hand away. "Okay! I'll tell you everything!" He let her catch her breath and something inside him hummed when she relaxed against him. He hated that they had to sober such a playful mood with talk of dirt-bag bullshit, but he needed to keep her safe as much as he needed to hear her laugh.

"When Issa was killed…" He didn't miss how difficult it was for her each time she had to talk about her uncle's death. He didn't push her as she swallowed back her sadness. He'd never lost anyone close enough to care that much. His mom walked out long before he was old enough to remember her. His dad was nothing but an abusive drunk. A religious zealot and hypocrite who beat the hell out of him every chance he got until he was thrown into foster care at ten. He was shuffled through a dozen foster homes for three years before he finally quit going home and stayed on the streets. His adult life had shown him a few people worth his respect, but no one he would cry for when they were gone. When she wiped away a tear he wondered if he would cry for her when their time was over.

He waited quietly, unsure of how to comfort her. After a long pause she cleared her throat, her cheeks turning as red as her eyes. "Sorry. I usually don't let things get that messy."

Grant took her hand in his and brought it to his lips, kissing the tender flesh of her palm. "No need to be sorry. You loved him."

She nodded and rested her head on his chest. "Yes, yes I did. I still do. I'm not sure, but I think he was involved in something, Grant."

Grant released her hand and curled up to sit beside her, looking down into her silver eyes to see them filled with doubt. "What do you mean?"

She looked away, sucking her bottom lip between her teeth. "When his estate manager went over his will there was a lockbox full of random stuff; leather bound ledgers, discs, a few coins and unopened envelopes. I didn't even look through it at first. I dumped it in a closet at a friend's house I'd been staying at. I couldn't…I couldn't bring myself to go back to his house or go through his things. A few weeks later, Issa's house had been broken into, and then someone ran me off the road. I laid there, half unconscious as some strange guy searched through my car and my purse." Grant resisted the urge to curl her into his arms as she closed her eyes and relived what she was telling him. "I remember him saying that I wasn't worth the bullet he was about to put in my head. That Jauhar was wasting his time looking for a thumb drive when he should have just killed me and burned down the house. I…I don't know what stopped him. I heard someone shouting and then he was gone. I woke up, still in my wrecked car, a few hours later.

"I went through everything in his office, his house, in his vacation home in Madagascar. I couldn't think of anything Jauhar, or anyone else, would want bad enough to kill me for. Then I remembered the lock box. When I went through it I found the thumb drive and a digital recording of a conversation between Issa and Jauhar." She swallowed hard then raised her face to his, her eyelids slowly opening to reveal her silver eyes glistening against pools of tears. "Jauhar threatened to have him killed if Issa didn't pay him for something. Issa was scared, Grant. I could hear it in his voice."

"What did he owe Jauhar money for?"

She shook her head, her shoulders rising and falling with a helpless shrug. "I don't know. He had money. Tons of it. It doesn't make sense."

"I know this is hard for you, fossa, but I need to know." He caressed her shoulders and her arms to calm her. "How did Issa die?"

A small sob fell from her lips but she shook it off and cleared her throat before she spoke. "He, uh, he was shot in the head as he got into his car one morning."

CHAPTER THIRTEEN

She'd fallen to sleep in his arms, the likeness of which Grant had never experienced before. He was sure he would never experience anything like it again, not like how it felt with her. Lying there in the dim moonlight, staring at the outdated swirl pattern on the ceiling as he listened to her deep, steady breaths, he pushed away the things she'd told him about her uncle and thought of all the reasons he didn't deserve to feel so content.

In a way it felt like he was cheating. He'd spent the better part of the last ten years as a cold, calculated killer. In the grand scheme of things, he knew he was technically the good guy. He didn't regret his job, but it didn't matter. As the bearer of death, he didn't deserve this kind of life. The kind that made a man feel virtuous and clean, and…right. He'd thought this was the feeling he'd been searching for when he traded the world for isolation. Now that he'd found it, he knew it wasn't meant for a man like him. Like the selfish prick he was though, he had no intention of letting it go until he had to.

He hadn't remembered falling asleep when he was suddenly jolted awake by a scream. His pulse raced as he grabbed Thalia's wrists, holding her steady while she fought away an invisible force. Eventually the nightmare receded, only to repeat an hour or so later. Each time she stirred he was careful not to wake her, afraid she would pull away from him, determined to hide her weakness. She had no way of understanding that he didn't see her nightmares as a weakness. It was only another sign of how screwed up he was. She wasn't meant for this life of killing and revenge. Her subconscious, the part of her that was human and decent, rejected it wholly. He'd never been plagued by those qualities enough to give him nightmares.

Hours later, he watched her as her body slowly awakened. Her long hair splayed across the pillow like a black stallion's mane. He couldn't resist tracing the outline of her long fingers lying against the pale silky skin of her stomach. His lips soon fell prey to the same temptation, gliding along her naked torso. He peeled back the covers, revealing the delicate crease at the top of her inner thigh, his tongue tracing its path to the thin line of curls between her legs.

Damn, she smelled incredible. He couldn't believe he'd waited this long to taste her, but thank *fuck* the wait was over. Her thighs parted on a sleepy moan, and he glanced up her body to see her thick lashes rise to reveal silver eyes staring back at him. Nothing in his life had prepared him for the kind of need he felt in that one moment of connection with her.

With a swift slide, he ducked under her leg and positioned himself between her thighs. The sunlight streamed into the room, illuminating the view before him, and making his dick swell and throb with anticipation. He'd been rough with her before, unable to control his need, but he wanted nothing more than to savor her now.

A shiver danced over his scalp as her fingers slid through his hair. He turned his head and traced her inner thigh, tasting and nipping at the supple skin displayed before him. Her hips lifted from the bed in silent demand, but Grant was determined to take his time and give her the pleasure she deserved. He slid his hand around her hip and braced his forearm across the soft expanse of her lower belly, his fingers playing at the top of her pussy with teasing strokes.

"Grant, please."

He smiled against her skin, his lips trailing up her thigh. "Easy, fossa. I want to taste you."

"I want that, too. Ah…" Air hissed through her teeth as his tongue traced along the crease of her upper thigh again and slid to the edge of her wet folds. Grant could see the silky evidence of her arousal lacing her slit. It called to him, and his mouth filled with saliva.

Wicked, sadomasochistic urges pushed him to tease both of them a little further, nuzzling his nose into her slit. The combination of her scent and her mewling cry nearly sent him over the edge. He pulled back, blowing a cool stream of air over her swollen labia before moving on to give her other thigh the same treatment. Grant turned his head to glance up at her as he feasted on her sensitive skin, scraping his teeth along the inside of her knee. The impish grin on her face made him chuckle.

"You are so going to pay for this later." Her head dropped back to the pillow on another moan when he lightly pressed his finger against her clit.

"I hope so." He chuckled again and continued a slow torturous descent down her inner thigh. Her hand fisted into his hair as he nuzzled her folds again. It didn't appear as though he would be allowed to wait much longer. That was fine with him. He was more than ready when he freed her from his restraining grip, using his thumbs to spread her tender, pink lips.

Her arousal glistened against a darker patch of flesh, pushing Grant's control to the edges of his grasp. He started at the bottom with one long stroke and gathered it up with his tongue, her wild, sweet flavor erupting in his mouth as her cry rippled down his spine straight to his dick. When he looked back down at the spot he'd tasted he noticed an odd, almost purple raised mark on her skin in the shape of a slanted *V*. He tilted his head to view it from another angle, still unsure what to make of it.

"It's a birthmark." He looked up to see Thalia staring back at him, her fist clenched in the sheets. "I'm dying here!"

"So impatient." Grant smiled to hide the sudden sense of alarm that raced through his veins. *Sonofabitch, she's been branded!* Could it be only a birthmark? No. There were too many coincidences. He remembered their conversation in the shower. *Fuck! She truly doesn't remember.*

His heart pounded, pushing his anger to dick-numbing levels. He couldn't leave her like this. He didn't want to leave her, ever. Something snapped inside him. He needed to take away all the pain she'd been through. To give her pleasure and happiness and…hell, he didn't know what love was, or if it even existed, but he wanted to give it to her. Anything to take this away from her.

Closing his eyes, he shut everything out and devoured her. Feeding from her frenzied cries, he drank her in, kissing away the forgotten pain. With each loving stroke of his tongue he tried to erase her scars, hoping she would never remember anything but this. Anything but him and how she felt at this very moment, flying apart beneath him.

"Oh, God. Grant that was…I can't…"

Cradling his cheek against her thigh as she panted through her release, Grant looked up over her heaving body to watch her descend from her high. She was incredible. He was drawn to her in a way he couldn't explain. Pushing up, he crawled over her body, trailing whispered kisses up her side, under and around her breasts, and along her neck until he reached her lips.

"You heal my soul," he breathed. The tears pooling in her eyes told him she understood. He let his lips linger against hers, breathing her in before he rolled to his side and snuggled her into his arms. Capturing her wrist when she reached for his cock, he shook his head. "No, fossa. This was only for you."

"But—"

"I will take that as a promise for later." He wanted her, beyond words, but there was no way he could focus beyond the train wreck that had just happened inside his head. He would be lucky to mask his jumbled emotions until he could exercise them in private. Somewhere he could beat the life out of something without her seeing him lose it. He needed to get her out of there for a while and get himself back under control. "Let's wait until after breakfast. We've got some strategizing to do, but I need to hop in the shower, and then touch base with my friend to let him know we'll be keeping the chopper for another few days."

He fought to make himself grin at the confused look on her face. "Well, I…" She shrugged and drew her hand back from his. "Okay. If you insist. And what is this *fossa* thing you keep calling me?" He forced a chuckle past his lips as he watched her slip from the bed, her limp amazingly less pronounced.

Following her, he bent and plucked his t-shirt from the floor and handed it to her. "I do insist, and a fossa is a mongoose." Tamping down the conflicting emotions swirling inside him, he laughed when her brows shot up and her lips twisted into a distasteful expression. "Not your typical mongoose. A fossa actually looks more like a jungle cat. It's sleek, mean, and quick as lightning." He shrugged and wrapped his arms around her. "That's what you reminded me of that day at the cabin when you attacked me. It was quite impressive." His brows furrowed at her dismissive snort.

“I was pathetic,” she said as she twisted from his arms. “I haven’t been *sleek* or *quick* with anything the last week. I need to get out and walk or something. Stretch out some and get back into shape.”

Grant pulled her back into his arms, kissing her pert little nose. “I think you’re in fine shape,” he said, giving her backside a gentle squeeze. “But if you would like, there’s a ton of fruit trees out back. Maybe take a walk after breakfast and pick a bit of fruit?”

“I’ll make the coffee.” She nodded and tried to pull away but Grant held her close for a moment longer.

“I’ll finish up my calls while you’re out. Be careful and take the gun I gave you just in case. Lions love fresh fossa.”

“Eww.” She slapped at his arm and he let her go, watching her disappear into the kitchen before he turned and headed to the shower.

Grant watched Thália through the window as she moved from tree to tree, picking off the wild loquat from the low hanging limbs. The cut on his knuckles stung as he clenched and unclenched his battered fist. He wished they could put the world on hold for a week or ten. Hole up there and figure out this thing between them. He was screwed no matter what happened; he just wished he could put it off a little longer. As if the fates had heard his thoughts and rendered immediate judgment, the instant messenger icon dinged on the laptop in front of him.

He immediately closed the computer and picked up his sat phone, dialing Diver’s secured line. “About time you got your ass out of bed and answered my call,” he barked when the call was finally answered.

“Fuck you.” Grant chuckled as Diver hacked up what sounded like a piece of his lung. “It’s two in the fucking morning here.”

“Who says there’s no rest for the wicked?” Before Diver could deliver a snappy retort, Grant rattled off a list of additional things he’d learned from Thalia during the previous evening.

The feeling in his gut had only worsened as she told him about what was on the thumb drive. Issa had been transporting for both Jauhar and Don Lalia. That in and of itself didn’t bode well for her dear uncle. However, it didn’t explain *what* they were transporting. Nothing on the drive indicated the types of merchandise. No bills of lading were attached as they normally were, only alphanumerical codes entered next to each shipment.

Thalia, the crazy fossa, thought she was going to use those records to get her face to face with Jauhar. She didn't know who or what she was dealing with. He was surprised she didn't have half the goddamn continent out to kill her.

Of course Diver hadn't found anything on her or her parents. Nothing was adding up, exactly as he suspected it wouldn't. Opening up the laptop, he took another glance outside and saw that Thalia had only moved a few feet down the line of trees.

Confident he had time, Grant clicked on one of Jauhar's files and glanced over it. There was nothing there he wasn't already intimately familiar with. Drugs, human trafficking, weapons, it was all there. Picture after picture of faces he'd studied and memorized long ago. He stopped and clicked on one picture in particular.

He didn't usually like to think about his former marks. They were scum who didn't warrant any more of his time than he'd already invested in them. The dead man staring back at him on his computer screen had been worth every second. Imad Shavish, former Indian military translator turned arms dealer to the likes of Jauhar. He would probably still be alive if he'd stayed close to home, but the minute he started turning out RPG's to Al-Qaeda splinter groups his days were numbered. As soon as that number reached the top ten on the most wanted terrorist list, Grant got the call. Disgusted, he closed the file. Too bad he hadn't been called to take out the trash Shavish had been dealing to as well. People like Jauhar were the real threat. *Another bureaucratic fuck-up.*

It didn't matter. Jauhar's days were numbered now. He didn't need an assignment for that. The U.S. Government was about to get a freebie. As he reached to close the laptop, another thought occurred to him. On a hunch he opened the bureau search engine, moving in and out of servers and file folders until he found the electronic evidence file on Hector Morganti.

He'd never seen a slave brand shaped like the mark on Thalia in any of the photos he'd studied in his field research. Not that he'd seen many. Most of that type of data was overlooked as a whole since it wasn't vital to taking out the targets. His friend Daniel hadn't told him much about the case against Morganti, but he knew the bastard was the one who had taken Daniel's daughter and sold her as a sex slave. He'd also heard media reports during his trial about possible brandings. His curiosity pushed him through file after file until he found one marked as victim profiles. Clicking on the folder, more folders appeared, but each one he clicked on resulted in an *Access Denied* message.

"Dammit!" He didn't know why, but he needed to see what was in those folders. He pushed the laptop away and carded his fingers through his hair. None of the preliminary trial reports mentioned anything about branding, at least not that he could see. Was it possible the media were talking out their asses? *Most likely.*

Grant picked up his sat phone and dialed Diver again. Where there was a locked door, there was always another way in.

"I'm not going back to sleep tonight, am I?" Diver growled.

"Not justifying that with an answer, D. You should know better." Grant rattled off the server number and folder location he needed access to. Again he could hear Diver's fingers flying over his computer's keyboard and wondered if he slept with the damn thing on the pillow next to him.

"No can do, boss. That's a Federal evidence site and it's locked up tighter than my girlfriend's skinny jeans."

Grant stood and paced to the kitchen. "So are you telling me you haven't fucked your girlfriend? What's the problem?"

"I'll work on it, but I'm not promising anything on this one. They're victim profiles, so you're probably dealing with pictures of minors. That's why even we can't access them. Your best option is probably going to be filing a request for waiver, but you and I both know you won't get in that way."

"Dammit!" What good was having SCI clearance if he couldn't use it when he needed it? "Do what you can and I'll look for another way in." He sat back down in front of the laptop and clicked the files closed. "And Diver?"

"Yeah, boss?"

"Go back to bed." He heard the tail end of Diver's colorful response as he disconnected the call and dialed another number. The man could be quite creative for such an early hour.

When the familiar recorded voice came over the line, Grant entered his seven digit SCIP key and asked for a patch through to a secure line. If there was anyone who had or could gain access to those files, it would be Daniel Gregory.

"Gregory."

Grant laughed as his friend's curt voice rang in his ear. "Still the company man, I see. I thought you had retired." He chuckled again when he heard Daniel's struggle for words to respond. "I've stuck with Grant Kendal for a while. You were right. I kind of liked him too."

"Jesus, for a minute there I thought you were gonna make me guess." Grant smiled. He didn't know what it was about the old man, but he'd always liked and respected him from the first day he'd met him. He'd given up on his father a long time ago, but if he could hand pick another one it would be Daniel.

"By that country twang I gather you decided to stay on with Miss Morganti and her new clan?" He was glad Daniel had found some level of peace, practically adopting Gabby after the loss of his daughter. He chuckled. It still felt strange not to call her Claira, the name she'd used while she was still in hiding from Lucien Moretti. He'd often wondered if Daniel would stay in Montana with her and his spook friend Cade. He shook his head. In no way could he picture the suit and tie wearing former United States Marshal from Washington D.C. out riding a horse and driving cattle.

"Shit," Daniel huffed. "Is it that bad? You wouldn't believe some of the things I hear around here."

Grant laughed again when another picture of Daniel in a Stetson passed through his already overloaded brain. "How is she doing?"

"Gabby? Well, she's officially a McLendon now, and I have three outrageously overprotective son-in-laws who spoil her rotten, which is nothing less than she deserves." Grant shook his head. He would never judge, especially after all they'd been through, but he couldn't imagine himself sharing a wife with two other men. He simply wasn't built that way. A sudden and unfamiliar rush of possessiveness had him peering out the window to check on Thalia. "And I'm about eight months away from being an honorary, overall wearin' grandpa."

"Stop!" Grant held out his hand as if he could force the image away. "Stop, please. I'm going to have to eat a bullet to get rid of the ridiculous picture you're about to paint." Grant grabbed up a pencil, nervously tapping it on the desk. Now that he had Daniel on the phone he wasn't sure how to go about asking him for what he needed, or if he should. He'd been through enough and it seemed at least some of the lifelessness that plagued him since his daughter's disappearance had lifted from his spirit.

"I know better than to ask questions, Grant." A little relief washed over him when he heard the seriousness return to his friend's voice. "You wouldn't be calling if it wasn't important. I told you then I owed you one. The offer still stands."

He didn't know any other way than to come out straight with it. "I need access to the victim profile documents in Hector Morganti's evidence file. SCI clearance is apparently not enough and I can't get *need-to-know* access for what I'm not *officially* working on."

Grant could hear the air being sucked out of Daniel's lungs. He stayed quiet and gave his friend a moment to absorb the mental blow. "You found something?"

Grant shook his head and tossed the pencil across the room. "No, not on Natalie." Dammit, the last thing he wanted to do was give him some sense of false hope. This had nothing to do with Daniel except his need for access to the information. "I can't talk about it. It's probably nothing, but you know how annoying hunches can be."

Daniel blew out a breath and Grant could almost picture him running his meaty hand over his dark gray flat top. "Yeah, I do. I have copies of everything that's stored in evidence. I'll send you whatever you need."

CHAPTER FOURTEEN

Thalia closed the door behind her and turned to see Grant jump from his seat. He slammed his hand down on top of a laptop she'd never seen before, awkwardly attempting to hide it from her view. *What is it with him?*

He'd been acting strange since the moment he'd opened his eyes and rocked the hell out of her world. Then he wouldn't let her return the favor? Yeah, she could safely throw that experience into the awkward category. No one had ever made her feel so much at one single moment in time. There were no words to describe the intensity that flowed from his body into hers. He'd literally worshiped her with his mouth. It was too much.

The man was taking nice to a whole new level and it was freaking her out. *What was all of that talk about healing his soul?* She shook her head and carried the basket of fruit to the kitchen sink, leaving him to finish his call.

She'd spent the last hour and a half stretching out her sore muscles, muscles she'd forgotten she had, and trying to peel her pride from the bottom of her boot. She'd *cried* in front of him. Twice! She never cried. Stab her, shoot at her, kill her parents? No tears. Throw a hot man with a smart, talented mouth and a broad shoulder to cry on in front of her and suddenly she was an emotional train wreck.

She'd also had another nightmare. She hoped like hell he hadn't noticed. They were getting worse, and more intense. Usually she couldn't remember them, but lately there had been small, terrifying details that seemed to etch their way through the usual fog that clouded her memory of them.

Memories from the nightmares she'd had the night before were filled with images of scorpions and maggots, the feeling of being suffocated as they filled her mouth and nose and the muffled sounds of her screams as they crawled into her ears. Her skin crawled and her fingers balled into fists as she pushed the images away. *Please let him not have heard my screams.* If he had heard her at least he hadn't made her talk about them. Maybe that was why he was acting so strange.

She liked Grant a lot. Okay, *like* was a bit weak. More like one look into those lethal eyes and her ovaries imploded from overexertion. "Dammit!" Thalia hissed through her clenched teeth as she chased the dozen or so loquats that had rolled from her basket onto the floor.

She couldn't afford to get caught up in whatever this was between them. No distractions. She'd promised Issa she would finish this. She didn't care what he'd been involved in. She owed him everything, and he deserved better than dying the way he did.

Grant had a good point about waiting a few days before calling Jauhar. She was in no shape to deal with him anyway. That plan, however, didn't solve how she was supposed to gain his confidence to secure another face to face meeting with him. For the life of her she couldn't come up with anything else that might work. She was losing her focus and that had to stop.

She couldn't depend on Grant to come up with a way to get to Jauhar. She couldn't count on anyone but herself. "Uhhh!" she groaned, picking up each fruit, washing and then setting them on the counter with a little more force than was necessary. If she had to say the words *you're right* to that man one more time she would gag. Dammit, but he was right. She couldn't give up control of this. Not even to him.

"There's probably a food processor in one of these cabinets you know. It's a lot easier than beating them against the counter." Thalia jumped, splashing water down her shirt and knocking half of the cleaned fruit to the floor.

"*Sonofabitch!*" She should have known Mr. Lightning Reflexes would catch the damn fruit she'd flung at his head. "Don't sneak up on me like that."

"I wasn't sneaking." *Shit!* She wanted to kiss and then slap the sarcastic, mocking smirk off his perfectly curved lips. In that order.

Instead she left the sink and began picking up the once clean fruit. "No? Is that why you slammed the computer closed when I walked in? Because you weren't sneaking?" With the hem of her shirt pulled up to carry the fruit in, she swiveled her hips. "What were you looking at? Another porn stash?"

Shit, shit, shit. She didn't know why she was pushing his buttons. What he did was none of her business anyway. Judging by the voracious look in his eyes, it was a truly reckless idea to push him if she planned to gain back any of that control she needed.

"I was wondering when you were going to bring that up." She took a step back as he took one towards her. "Let me guess. Winston?" She was caught like a deer on a dark winding road by the white hot heat swirling in his eyes. She couldn't look away or even blink. A few more steps and she'd have no place to go. "I figured as much." His hand reached out and he pulled the hem of her shirt from her grip, the small round fruits tumbling back to the floor at their feet. "That damn monkey followed me everywhere." Her back pressed against the unforgiving surface of the wall behind her as his hands snaked under her shirt and cupped her sides, his thumbs teasing the tender undersides of her breasts as he stared at her lips. "The only thing I need to make me hard as a rock is you, Thalia."

A breath she hadn't realized she'd been holding whooshed from her lungs as his lips devoured hers, a tiny, short moan revealing the ache in her chest as her tongue slid against his. One of his hands slid from her waist, over her hip and tunneled under her shorts, clenching her ass and pulling her against the hard bulge in his jeans.

"Mmm. You taste like loquat."

And he tasted like man. Pure, hot, sexy man. Thalia squeezed her eyes shut to keep them from rolling to the back of her head. *Sexy, distracting, controlling man.* Damn, she was doing it again. Letting him pull her away from what was important. "Um, we need to stop." *Weak! That was so weak.* She pushed at his chest, but he wasn't budging, pinning her between his thick, hard body and the wall behind her.

"I know." He nibbled on her lower lip, tracing the little bite with his tongue, and sending a sharp ache ricocheting through her womb. "I wanted something sweet before we talked." He gave her lip a gentle tug, then one more brief kiss before he let her go and backed away, leaving her nearly breathless and melting against the wall. He walked to the island bar and pulled out a chair. "Have a seat. I'll get us something to drink."

"Talk?" She had a few other thoughts rattling around in her head, but apparently she was only capable of producing them one word at a time.

"Yeah, you know." Grant took out a couple of glasses and filled them with ice. "Jauhar, Hamisi, the thumb drive." The glasses full of water, he stopped and stared at her from across the room. "Earth to Thalia? Do you still want to make those plans today? Because I can think of a few other things I'd rather do, you being at the top of that list."

Her focus snapped from his wet lips to the playful look in his eyes. He knew exactly what he was doing to her. She didn't know whether to laugh or cry. There was no way she was going to win this game with him. He cupped the bottom of the water glasses in one hand and grabbed her hand with his other, pulling her past the bar stool and out of the kitchen. "I thought we were going to sit at the bar?"

"I changed my mind." When they reached the small living room, Grant set the glasses down on the coffee table and took a seat on one side of the small leather sofa, pulling her down to sit next to him. Before she could slide back and get comfortable, he reached down and carefully positioned her legs over his lap and pulled off her shoes. She cautiously relaxed against the armrest as he began masterfully massaging the arch of her foot. "Now, why were you beating the hell out of the poor, harmless fruit?"

Because I can't beat the hell out of you. Thalia released a frustrated breath and ran her fingers through her hair, resting her head in her hand as she propped her elbow on the armrest. "I'd rather talk about Jauhar."

"I see." Grant's hands paused as he watched her, those eagle eyes of his focused in on her expressions. "So it's not Jauhar who has you all worked up now."

Thalia yanked her feet from his grasp and pushed up from the sofa, pacing to the other side of the room. "It's everything. You, me, Jauhar. You say I can't give up control to anyone, but that's exactly what I'm doing! This plan of yours won't work, Grant. It buys me time, but it doesn't get me a second chance with Jauhar. How am I supposed to get him to meet with me face to face after this?"

"You don't get a second chance with a man like Jauhar." Thalia took a step back as Grant stood and stalked toward her. "Have you ever dealt with Jauhar? Do you know what he is?"

Her head shook as she watched his cautious approach. "He's a killer. I know that, but—"

"I'm a killer, Thalia. You've killed two people since I've known you. I know they weren't your first." He stalked her as he spoke, the lethality in his voice playing havoc with her resolve. Her body hummed with anticipation as his hands slowly came up and framed her face. She was powerless against his touch. "Jauhar is a capitalist, fossa. Not a suit in a high-rise raking in millions, running a legitimate business. He capitalizes on depravity. He preys on the innocent to fulfill the desires of the wicked. Drugs, weapons, sex…child slavery. He does it all without a soul and there's a reason he's at the top of that game." His eyes roamed her face, studying her carefully before they narrowed into an almost painful expression. "There is a stark difference between dangerous and evil, Thalia. I won't let that kind of wickedness touch you again."

"Please don't." She turned her head away when he leaned in to kiss her. "Don't say things like that."

"Why not? It's the truth." His breath rushed hot against her cheek and she fought against the urge to turn back to him.

"It's not true." Her chest tightened, but not in panic. She swallowed against the ache in her throat and twisted from his grip, thankful he let her go. Turning away from him, her arms hugged her stomach in a lame attempt to keep the sob that was building in her throat from spilling out. "This is all that's left of my life, Grant. I know I'm going to die doing this. I know this and…and you can't take that away from me." Her body betrayed her will and leaned back into his embrace as his strong arms folded around her, holding her gently against his chest. "You can't keep making me want…more."

It wasn't a lie. Jauhar would never touch her. She would have more than this. She may not have it with him, but he would be damned if he would let her throw it away on Jauhar. She was wrong.

He would take this away from her, but he could see that now was not the time to convince her to let him.

He turned her in his arms and dipped his head to see her face. "I don't make promises I can't keep, fossa. I will keep you safe. Hey." He tilted her chin when she tried to look away, forcing her to look at him. "I'm not taking this away from you, not yet, but you're in way over your head and it's time you stop fighting me on this. We've got one shot at Jauhar. That's it. No second chances, no room for error. We screw this up and he'll go so far underground it will be years before he comes up for air, and you'll be looking over your shoulder for the rest of your life."

"Why?" Her shoulders slumped as her head fell against his chest. "Why are you helping me?"

He gathered her back into his arms, his lips caressing her hair. "Because I know about wanting more, fossa." He kissed her forehead, her temple, trailing his lips down her cheek before nipping seductively at her chin. "Every day I'm with you I want more than I know I can have."

Intense, slow-burning heat filled his veins as she opened her mouth and his tongue slid against hers. This kiss was different than any they'd shared before. There was no urgency or frantic grappling; only a raw need to touch her, to taste her and know she was his. At least for now. The rest of the world melted away with her faint whimper of surrender and he scooped her into his arms.

Incapable of depriving his mouth the pleasure of her taste, he stumbled his way to the bedroom, setting her on her feet next to the bed. His fingers trailed over her soft skin, along the sides of her neck, over her shoulders and down her arms until he felt the hem of her t-shirt at her waist. He released her lips only long enough to pull the material over her head, letting it fall to the floor at their feet as he cupped her face between his palms and captured them again, her taste so sweet and now as familiar as his own. Never in his life had he been so consumed by a woman. The need to feel her, to taste her on his lips and wrap himself in her scent incinerated every thought, every instinct he possessed until all that was left of him was an elemental flame; a staggering carnal hunger that burned deep in his bones for her. Only for her.

She reached for the buttons on his shirt. Unwilling to let her go, he bowed his shoulders to give her room to work them loose, a heavy wave of lust crashing against his control when her hands finally met his bared chest, his nipples hardening beneath her touch. The muscles in his stomach rippled as she raked her nails over his skin to the top button of his jeans, her fingers working too slowly before popping it loose and moving on to the next.

He moved his hands from her beautiful face to fill them with her perfectly rounded breasts, her nipples stiffening deliciously against his palms, drawing out another whimper as her fingers fumbled with the last button on his jeans. At last she pushed them down his hips and freed his cock as he reached for the front of her shorts, his own fingers trembling as he made quick work of the single button and zipper, pushing them to the floor.

His tongue chased hers as he lifted her into his arms, her long legs circling his waist as if they were made for that very thing. The soft globes of her bare ass filled his hands, and he ground her hot pussy against his cock, her arousal coating his shaft as he slipped repeatedly between her folds. Whimpers slipped into moans as the head of his dick, swollen and ready, passed over her clit with each stroke, and the need to bury himself deep inside her ripped up his spine with demanding intensity.

Turning, he lowered himself to the edge of the bed, his hands skimming her sides up to her neck until he could thread his fingers into her hair. He wanted to see her take control. He needed to watch as she lost that control and flew apart above him. His fingers tightened in her hair and he pulled her lips from his, her breath falling hot against his lips as she opened her eyes.

"Ride me, Thalia." A sharp ache thrummed in his balls as he watched her silver eyes turn stormy gray. "Take me inside you." She unhooked her legs and he pulled them towards the center of the bed. His cock bobbed with anticipation as she pushed herself to her knees, his tongue snaking out to circle her nipple before she pushed him down to the mattress and straddled his hips.

Completely wrecked, his fingers trembled as they slid over her belly and clenched into the flesh at her hips. Drunk on the sight of her wrapping her hand around his cock, he held his breath as she positioned herself above him. Every muscle in his body pulled tight as she slipped over his sensitive head, the heat of her inner muscles tightening around his shaft with each inch she took. "Holy—*Fucking hell* that feels good." His last breath spilled out as a tortured groan. Sweat blistered over his skin as she finally seated herself to the hilt, rubbing her clit against his pelvic bone before she slowly pulled back up again. He watched as, inch by inch, his cock slid out and back in, over and over, as she rocked slowly against him.

He had to touch her. He loosened his grip on her hip and slid one hand between them. His thumb rolled over her clit as his fingers caressed the edge of her pussy where they joined. A raw, lustful groan rumbled past her lips as her hips canted and flexed against his hand, a rush of silk spilling over his fingers. He brought them to his mouth, licking her taste from one before bringing the other to her mouth and tracing her open lips.

"Taste yourself, fossa." He watched as her tongue snaked out and ran along her bottom lip. "Taste what I taste when you come with my mouth on you." His arms folded around her as she leaned down and invaded his mouth with her tongue, sharing even more of her flavor with him.

Any restraint he possessed frayed beyond a few bare threads, and he rolled her beneath him. She cradled him between her thighs, her hips rocking into his as he took over their rhythm, sliding inside her deeper and deeper with each long stroke. It wasn't enough. He would never get enough. Hooking his arm beneath her knee, he lifted her uninjured leg, gaining the angle he needed to feel the head of his cock tap against the end of her womb.

"Ahhh!" Hot air rushed from her lungs as her back arched beneath him.

"Open your eyes, Thalia." He had to see her, to watch as he touched the place inside her that made her such an intricate part of him. This was more than hot, sweaty sex. Something inside him burned for her. Holy hell, he was falling hard for this woman.

Folding his forearms under her shoulders, he cradled her beneath him and watched as her eyes filled with the same passion that had suddenly gripped his soul. She felt it too. He could see it; this profound connection binding them together in a way he could never comprehend. On his next inward thrust he stilled, holding himself deep inside her as an overwhelming awareness washed over him. For the first time in his life he understood what it was to make love to a woman, to feel the essence of another being as it slipped inside you and cradled your aching soul. He never believed it was possible to feel this whole, this complete. Not him. Not like this. A lone tear fell from the corner of her eye and he dipped his head, tasting the salty offering as he sipped it from her temple. Unable to remain still he moved inside her, his hips rolling slowly against hers, giving himself entirely to her with each tender stroke. He wanted her to have this. To have him in a way no other woman had.

His rhythm faltered as he felt the first subtle flutters of her climax ripple around him, sending a flash of electricity racing down his spine, straight to his balls. The blood in his veins sang with an edgy need as it rushed through his cock, the muscles in his arms and legs catching fire as he pumped into her harder and faster, each thrust pushing him closer and closer to the edge as he stared into her eyes. Her mouth opened on a silent scream, her inner walls tightening around him over and over, her nails sinking into the skin on his back as time after time he emptied himself, heart and soul, inside her. She would forever hold a part of him inside her. No matter where he went or how long he lived, a piece of him would always remain with her. Always.

Light from the afternoon sun faded into dusk as he listened to her breathing, now slow and even against his chest. Eternity wouldn't have been long enough for Grant to get used the feel of their naked and sated bodies tangled together on the sweat soaked sheets. When he knew she'd fallen fast asleep, he carefully untangled himself from her long limbs and quietly padded to the control room down the hall, grabbing his jeans from the floor along the way.

He'd never been one to count on fate to determine his next move, but he was no longer sure about his determination to investigate his suspicions about Thalia's missing past. She was perfect the way she was. If he was right, he didn't want her to relive something so vile. If he kept digging and found something, he was no longer sure he'd be able to tell her anyway. If Daniel hadn't sent those files by the time he logged in, he would send him a message to hold off…for now. They had plenty of other problems to focus on.

CHAPTER FIFTEEN

Grant stared at the single digit hovering above his inbox icon, unable to make his fingers click the button to open it. He didn't need to open it to know the message was from Daniel. He should have known better than to trust fate with anything. She could be such a fucking bitch.

He shoved the mouse away and slouched against the back of his chair. What were the odds he would find anything related to the branding mark he'd found on Thalia? Did he want to spend the next few hours combing through countless vile pictures of helpless victims that probably had absolutely nothing to do with his suspicions, instead of holding the warm, incredibly naked woman in his bed? *No.* What right did he have to go picking through her personal life, digging up things best left buried? If she didn't remember or care about it, why should he be the one to strip that away from her?

None of the answers he gave himself numbed the nagging pull in his gut that eventually made him reach up and click on the box, opening the file Daniel had sent him. Different from the agency layout, it took him a few moments to navigate the files and find the victim profiles he'd been denied access to before. After opening the folder, what seemed like an infinite scroll of files popped up, each one labeled with an alphanumeric code. *Christ, there must be hundreds.*

There was no way to tell which file contained the photos he was searching for, or if they contained any photos at all. He ran his fingers through his hair and pulled his chair in closer as he prepared to dig in. It looked as if the next few hours were going to be spent looking through these victims' own personal hell on earth while his idea of heaven was lying asleep a few feet away.

His eyes drifted off the screen to the clock hanging on the wall above the bank of computers. *Three fucking hours.* Rubbing his eyes, he ignored the faint rumble in his stomach and opened yet another anonymous file. *Three hours I've wasted combing through this filth.* He'd seen and read about more carnage than any one human should be forced to endure.

He'd been right about the press blowing smoke out of their collective asses. There wasn't one picture or mention of branding in any of the files. That didn't mean it hadn't happened, just that they hadn't yet found a victim with one. Of course, it could be Hector hadn't been into that kind of thing. Judging by some of the other shit he'd seen in the files, he was actually a bit surprised the sick bastard had stopped short of it. They would never know. Now that he was behind bars and Lucien was dead, the investigation was officially over and no one cared about finding the hundreds of kids that had fallen through the cracks. Case closed.

He blindly clicked open the next file, scrubbing his hands over his face as he leaned back in the chair and stared at the ceiling. Why was he torturing himself with this? Thalia didn't seem haunted by the things he imagined had been done to her...much. *Dammit!* His hands slapped the desk, knocking over a pile of file folders which had been stacked half-assed next to one of the computer towers. He reached to straighten the mess, the folders slipping from his fingers as his eyes locked onto the image displayed on the screen in front of him.

What the— The hair on the back of his neck stood on end and a chill raced along his arms as he reached out and touched the little freckle he knew so well. The dark, brown beauty mark rested a little lower on her cheek now, but there was no mistaking the bright, innocent, ice-blue eyes that stared back at him. Frantically clicking, Grant moved through the handful of pictures and clicked on the victim summary report…then froze. An eerie numbness slipped into his face and hands as he read the first line of information.

Victim name: Natalie Janine Gregory. His heartbeat pounded against every pulse point in his body as his eyes devoured the rest of the missing person report. In all the time he'd spent with Daniel Gregory, he'd never once seen a picture of his missing daughter. He'd never even asked, and Daniel had never offered. The only time he'd ever given her a thought was when he repaid a favor by helping him protect the daughter of the man who had taken his.

This isn't happening. How was it possible that the woman asleep not ten feet from where he stood, the woman he'd just made love to, the one woman in the world to wash up on his otherwise deserted island would be Daniel's missing daughter? *Holy fuck.*

His hands shook almost violently as he clicked through her profile and printed out each page. If this was true, and as he watched the paper feed from the printer he knew without a doubt it was, then he was right. *Son of a bitch!* He couldn't process the vile images that flashed through his thoughts of what she must have endured to have suppressed the memories of being taken and sold and…and…*sonofabitch..*

He had to get her out of there. How was he going to tell Daniel? *Jesus Christ!* He was a complete virgin to the kind of panic that ran like ice through his veins. *How am I going to tell* her*?* She was so hell bent and determined to get revenge for Issa… He froze as another wicked thought landed in front of all the others. *Did Issa buy her?*

Every detail she'd ever shared about her *uncle* replayed on fast forward as he paced the tiny room, desperate for some sort of life preserver to grab ahold of in order to keep from drowning in the sea of shit he suddenly found himself in. Everything she'd told him about the man seemed straight-up as far as him caring about her. *Why would he tell her such an elaborate lie about her family?* It didn't make sense. Was it possible she'd made it all up? *Christ! Anything is possible at this point.* But he didn't think so. He was damn good at reading people, and she practically projected her every emotion and thought for the entire world to see. If she was knowingly lying about something like that he would know it.

What a fucking mess. He gathered the printed file and rolled the papers into a tube, stuffing then into the waistband of his jeans. Too worked up to sit, he hovered over the desk as he downloaded the entire Morganti file onto another flash drive then wiped any traces from the computer before he shut it down.

Dammit. He didn't know which direction to go first. Did he try to sit Thalia down and…*wait…Thalia…Nathalia...Natalie. I'm such an idiot.* He raised his hand, pulling his punch before he slammed his fist through the control room door. The last thing he wanted to do was wake her before he had a plan in place. He wasn't actually running on all ten cylinders at the moment, and he knew he had to be in command of every molecule in his body if he was going to keep her from bolting. This wasn't going to be easy for her to swallow. Fuck, he was practically gagging on it, and other than the fact he was pretty sure he was in love with her, it had nothing to do with him.

Jauhar. It all came down to Jauhar. The odds were very much in favor of him being involved in her kidnapping, or at the very least the people who ran his trafficking organization. He had to get her as far away from that evil son of a bitch as possible. *I'll send her to Daniel's.* How much farther away could you get than Montana? Regardless of him being her father, he trusted Daniel. He and his spook friend Cade would protect her. With her safe and out of the way, he could deal with that scumbag himself without worrying about her. He shook his head and paced to the other side of the room. Getting her past customs would be easy enough with a private plane, but how the hell was he supposed to get her onto a plane to Montana without telling her what the hell was going on?

Should he tell her, or should he tell Daniel first and let him tell her? They were strangers to each other. Maybe she would remember him once she saw him. He could pull up an old photo ID of Daniel and test her memory. He shook his head. That was a bad idea. He was probably the least equipped person on the planet to deal with the mental meltdown she could have if she did suddenly remember something.

He could stay there all night and torture himself trying to figure out the right way to do this, but no matter which way he decided to go it was going to suck all the way around. He might as well wake her up. The sooner he got her the hell out of there, the sooner he could put an end to this. They had the rest of their lives to figure out what came next.

He opened the door and was headed to the bedroom when he saw the light from the kitchen shining into the other end of the hall. Had she gotten hungry and gone in search of dinner without him? He passed the bedroom door and crept toward the kitchen, an uneasy feeling churning in his gut. When he reached the end of the hall he peered around the corner. His shoulders fell as he took in the empty space. *Where the hell is she?*

"Thalia?" He turned and paced back to the bedroom, finding both it and the bathroom empty. "Thalia? Where are you?" He ran back toward the other end of the house, that unfamiliar feeling of panic thrashing through his system. "Fossa, you're scaring me. Where the…?" He stopped and turned back toward the small table where his laptop sat open. *No!* He punched a button and the screen blipped on. *Sonofabitch.* The backpack was gone, along with his sat phone. He turned to see that her boots weren't next to the back door where she'd taken them off earlier.

No, fossa. Christ, they were in the middle of safari land. She wouldn't survive until dawn out there on her own. *Shit!* He sprinted back toward the bedroom and threw open a set of metal locker doors before he reached for the landline phone. He punched the speaker button and hit redial. Grabbing another backpack, he turned back to the lockers and began tossing in the things he knew he would need.

"You know, calling me from the same number…"

"Fuck it, D. I need you to run a GPS trace on my sat phone and link the coordinates to this receiver." He grabbed another sat phone from the bank of chargers inside the locker and flipped it on. Rattling off the number, he tossed it in the pack. "Cancel the data search on the woman, but I still need everything you can get me on the tango."

"I take it you found another way into those files?" A series of beeps sounded over the line and he knew the trace had gone through. God help her if she'd made that call to Jauhar.

"I got what I needed." He spun the lock on his trunk and grabbed a case from the bottom. He'd have to leave the rest of his shit there and come back for it after he got her stashed away. The only way he was going to get her on that plane, outside of drugging her, was to spill everything and make her understand she didn't have any other options. "I need you to book a private flight from Billings to Chennai, India, and email the itinerary details to this address."

After rattling off Daniel's email address, he punched the speaker button and disconnected the call, not bothering to wait for Diver's reply. His finger paused above the call button and he looked up at the clock. This was going to be one hell of a wake-up call. He hit the speaker button again and dialed his friend. As it rang through a series of sub-secure connections he laid the case on the desk and opened it up, pulling out his sniper rifle.

"Gregory." His friend's raspy voice filled the room and Grant's greeting froze on his tongue. This was it. There was no taking this back once it was out there.

"What's going on? Did you get the file?"

He sunk into the chair as he stared at the phone, wishing there was an easier way to say it. There wasn't, so he let the words slip past his lips. "I found her." Silence rang loud through their connection and he could almost hear the doubt buzzing in his friend's thoughts. "Daniel, did you hear me? I don't have a lot of time. I found Natalie."

"Is—" Daniel cleared his throat, surprise and disbelief echoing in his voice. "Is she alive?"

"Yes." Grant nodded as he loaded a full mag into his rifle and grabbed the extra magazines from the case. "Yes, she's alive."

"I want to talk to her. Where is she?"

He stuffed the magazines in his pack and stood, throwing the rifle sling over his shoulder. "It's complicated." He let the pack drop to the floor as he picked up the receiver and held it to his ear. "She doesn't remember anything, Daniel. She has no idea who she is. There's a lot going on and she's in a lot of trouble. I need you to get on a plane and get the hell over here. It's not a good idea to go into too much detail on this line. I've already booked a private flight out of Billings. The travel details should already be in your inbox."

Grant waited as another long moment of silence passed. "Daniel, snap the fuck out of it. Do you understand? I need you to get on that plane if you want to see her again." He understood Daniel's shock, but he didn't have time for him to piece it together. She was out there in the dark on foot, surrounded by some of the most dangerous creatures on earth. No matter how good she was with a gun, she didn't have enough bullets to stop even the smallest of them. *Stubborn, foolish woman.*

"Is she there with you?"

"No," Grant barked and held back the groan of frustration that clawed at his insides. "But I know where she's going. Daniel, I have to go!"

"I'm on my way," Daniel snapped into the phone before the line went dead.

Thank fuck! Grant slammed the receiver down and swiped up the backpack. He made a short detour to the bedroom for a shirt and his boots before digging out the sat phone. Judging by her location, she had about a two hour head start. Shoving his pistol into his waistband, he rushed through the back door and slammed it closed behind him. He should be able to cut that time in half and hopefully get to her before she became a fresh meal for some other predator. *Her ass is damn sure going to be mincemeat when I get my hands on her again.*

CHAPTER SIXTEEN

The crisp *snap* of another twig sent Thalia crouching to the ground, her last breath seizing in her lungs as she listened through the darkness. Despite the cooler night air, beads of sweat ran down her neck and trickled between her breasts, the thin cloth of her shirt sticking to her back. She ignored the ache her position caused to her still sore thigh and peered into the pitch black expanse where the noise had come from. Something was stalking her.

The moon had been hanging high and bright in the sky when she snuck out of the compound hours ago, calming her anxiety over not being able to find a flashlight. Thick clouds had settled in and now she was lucky to see her hand in front of her face. *Shit.* Her head snapped around, her fingers tightening around the gun in her hand at the sound of the leaves rustling behind her. *Make that two somethings.*

She didn't know how far she'd traveled. At this rate she would reach the service road she'd seen on the map she'd pulled up on Grant's computer sometime near her thirtieth birthday…if she lived that long. Her skin prickled under the heavy weight of the eyes that were watching her. For the last half hour she'd felt them zeroing in on her, stalking her like the prey she knew she'd become.

She'd foolishly thought that facing whatever predators lurked in the darkness would be easier than facing the one that was stalking her heart. She lowered her hand and searched the ground around her feet for a rock, her eyes still focused in the direction of the sounds in front of her. Her stomach tightened as an almost claustrophobic feeling swirled around her. Was this what a gazelle felt like before a lioness pounced? That final moment when they raised their head from grazing to have a four hundred pound beast lunging for their jugular?

I should have stayed with him. She couldn't. She knew what was happening between them. The way he looked at her earlier, she recognized the emotion swirling in his eyes. Gone was the dominant, controlling killer who took command of her mind and body to fulfill a mutual sexual need. In his place was a caring, tender lover who was intent on reaching her heart. He'd watched her face and her expressions, determined to make her feel what he was feeling, and she'd felt it. It frightened her to her core. He demanded everything. She could give him nothing. *It isn't fair.* There was nothing left of herself to give. She'd already promised her life to Issa. She owed him that. Grant was going to take that away from her. He may not outright deny her revenge, but making her want more than that would garner the same result. Now that she was staring down the dark path to certain death, she wasn't so sure she'd made the right choice.

Thoughts of her time with him floated through her mind as her fist clenched around the rock in her hand. She could see his golden eyes, narrowing in on her thoughts as if he could pick them right out of her head. And the fire that blazed in those eyes as he hovered above her, possessing her body with his. She almost giggled as she pictured the goofy grin on his lips when she paid him a compliment, as if he'd never had one before and didn't quite know what to do with it.

I'm such a fool. Her entire life had consisted of nothing but one bad decision after another since Issa had died. *No! He didn't die. He was murdered, and Jauhar deserves to pay for that.* She repeated the familiar mantra in her head, but she could feel her resolve weakening as the faint whisper of Grant's voice rolled through her memories – *You heal my soul.*

She swallowed back the lump in her throat as she slowly raised her arm above her head and prepared to throw the rock in the opposite direction of where she would run. She didn't know if whatever was stalking her would come after her or go for the rock. She readied her gun and prepared to sprint as fast and hard as she could, praying she would find somewhere to hide until the sun came up. Hopefully, if her plan didn't totally work, only one of them would follow her. Her magazine was full, but it was hard to aim when you couldn't see what you were shooting at. Her legs tensed, her feet shifting inside her shoes as she prepared to run. Another twig broke in front of her as she took in a few deep breaths and cocked her arm back as far as she could.

"Thalia, don't move."

Grant's deep voice filled her ears and blazed through her body like a violent bolt of lightning. A loud, high-pitched growl sang through the night air. Less than a second later, a bright burst of muzzle-flash exploded into the darkness behind her, a deafening boom rattling her bones as she was pushed to the ground by an unseen force. A scream lodged in her throat and she pushed against the weight of the animal, unable to free herself from its heavy weight.

"Get it off me!" Her heels dug into the dirt and pushed her backwards as Grant peeled the smelly beast from her body. Her fingers grasped and clawed for purchase before she grabbed onto Grant as he lifted her into his arms. "Oh, shit. Oh, shit." She panted for breath as her head spun to look into the darkness around them. "There was another one. Where'd it go?"

"Shh. I've got you." She felt the coolness seep into her backside as he set her down on a nearby boulder. "There was only one."

She shook her head, but before the protest could pass her lips, understanding flooded her fear soaked brain. "It was you?" She squinted and held her hand up to shield her eyes from the bright, blessed beam that shone from the flashlight he pulled from his backpack. "You were following me this whole damn time?"

She didn't need to see his face to know she'd unleashed another lethal beast. She could feel his anger rolling over her like an ominous fog. "You do *not* want to have this conversation right now," he spat through his clenched teeth.

His hands never stopped moving over her body as he glared at her. It was making her already frantic heartbeat do funny things. She tried to swat his hands away, but he grabbed her arms, giving her a gentle shake to get her attention. "Are you hurt anywhere, in any way?" He crouched down and cupped his big hands around her face, forcing her to look at him. "And so help me *God*, Thalia, you better not lie to me." She paused a moment and took a mental inventory of her condition, then shook her head in a silent reply.

The last threads of his sanity snapped and Grant was on her in an instant, feeling her rapid breaths of life against his skin. "You scared the shit out of me." Her heartbeat pounded beneath his lips as he buried his face into the crook of her neck and breathed her in. *She's alive. She's okay.* The words in his head, repeating in a constant loop, did nothing to sooth him. His hunger for her was beyond his control, and his hands moved with reckless abandon, the sound of ripping fabric barely audible through the pounding of his own heartbeat against his eardrums. *Fucking hell!* Seeing that leopard stalking her every clumsy move through the brush had nearly been his end. If he'd caught up to her even a minute later…

He squeezed his eyes closed against a barrage of horrid mental images. Her shirt lying in tatters on the ground, he filled his hands with her soft, warm flesh. Driven by a fear he'd never known, nothing else existed beyond his need to feel her, alive and thriving around him. The salty tang of her sweat burst over his taste buds as he flicked his tongue along the slender column of her neck, over her bare collarbone to the soft swell of her breasts. A sudden euphoric sense of belonging and possession washed over him.

"Ahh!" She hissed as he forcefully peeled away any remaining barriers of clothing between them and crushed his body to hers. Each of her muted cries drove him closer to some undefined edge of an abyss he knew without a doubt he would never return from. His teeth scraped over her nipple as he ground his aching cock against her, pressing her into the unforgiving rock and drawing out another string of hisses and moans.

"Why did you leave?" He wrapped her bare legs around his hips, then fisted his cock and slid it between her slickened folds.

"Grant, I…oh God, please."

"Tell me!" He held himself there, pressed against her but not allowing her to feel him inside her. He was a selfish bastard for making her say it, but something inside him was breaking under the weight of his need to hear the words from her lips. Somewhere deep down in his soul he could sense their world unraveling, and he needed to have this one thing from her before it all fell apart. Gathering her wrists in his other hand, he held them above her head as he devoured her mouth with a punishing kiss, allowing his tongue the pleasure his cock had been momentarily denied.

She writhed beneath him, struggling against his hold. Her hips canted and bucked, her legs tightening around him as she tried to pull him into her. "Tell me," he growled as he fought against her attempts, his cock throbbing in his fist as he held himself at bay. "Tell me why you ran."

"You know why!" She released a whimpering sob into his mouth and he pulled back to see the faint glow from the discarded flashlight reflect off the unshed tears in her eyes.

"Say it, Thalia."

He watched as she shook her head and blinked back her tears, her chest heaving beneath him. "Being in love with you changes nothing. I'm still going to die…*ahh…*"

Grant's body bowed against hers as he released his cock and entered her in one long hard thrust, sending sparks dancing along his spine that made his toes curl inside his boots. *"Fuuuuck!"* This wasn't about making love. Every molecule in his body raced to claim her. *Mine!* Every stroke was made with the determination to erase all who had come before him and lay claim to what was now and would forever be his. *All…fucking…mine!*

"Grant....I…oh, God…ahh…don't stop!" He couldn't even if she had begged him. His cock swelled inside her as thrust after thrust, her body coiled tighter and tighter around him. His scalp tingled as his muscles began to burn. Every tendon in his arms and legs strained against his skin as he fought to hold out for one more thrust, then another until everything seized with one last drive, flinging him over the edge as he came deep inside her, filling her over and over as the sound of his own primal cry filled the night air surrounding them. *All. Fucking. Mine!*

I don't deserve her. Wrapping her in his arms, he rested his forehead against her shoulder and tried to come to terms with his new reality as she continued to tremble and pant beneath him. She loved him. He had no idea what to do with that concept, or the fact that he was so far gone for her he would never be the same.

There was one thing he knew for sure. He lifted his head and tilted her face toward his. "You're wrong, Thalia," he breathed against her lips. "It changes everything."

They lay there panting, their breaths mingling together as he traced the contours of her face with his fingertips, soaking in the similarities to the innocent child he'd seen in that folder full of tragedies. No matter what had happen to her, she'd won. She'd beat them at their own game and would never be broken in his eyes.

"Grant," she breathed against his lips. He closed his eyes as her fingers trembled over his brow. "I'm so sorry."

He pushed himself up and pulled her into his arms, the fear he'd felt for her still fresh and raw, lying just beneath his skin. "Don't ever run from me again, fossa." He'd been hell bent on nothing but reddening her ass when he found her, but he was unprepared for the rush of fear and relief he'd felt when he'd finally gotten his hands on her. "So help me woman, if you ever do that again…"

Her arms tightened around him. They stood there together in the silent darkness as his body caught up to the knowledge that she was okay. He wasn't sure he'd satisfied his need to hold her when he felt a shiver run through her thin frame. "Christ, woman. You're freezing."

He was such an idiot. Seeing the tattered remains of her shirt on the ground behind her, he pulled his own shirt over his head and handed it to her. "Put that on." He pulled up his own damn pants and retrieved hers from the ground, shaking them out before he handed them to her. "I'll collect your boots." Hell, he'd been in such a frenzy he didn't even remember removing them. He handed them to her then collected the flashlight and his backpack, reaching into hers to retrieve his sat phone.

Flipping it off standby, he scrolled through the call log and bit back a curse when he saw the last dialed number. "You called Jauhar."

She bit her thumbnail and nodded. "But I didn't talk to him. One of his men picked up and I…I couldn't do it. I hung up without saying anything."

"Fuck!" Grant pulled up his pant leg and drew the knife from his boot, ignoring the flash of panic that washed over her face when she saw it. "Well, at least you only have half a death wish." He stepped over to the dead leopard and sat the two backpacks down in the dirt next to the animal.

"What are you going to do?"

Ignoring her for the moment, he grabbed ahold of one of the big cat's front legs and rolled it onto its back. With the point of his knife he made a long slit in its skin, straight up the middle of its belly, careful not to cut past the flesh and fur. He pulled the skin away and emptied the carcass of its inner contents. He took the sat phone apart and removed the memory stick which held all the tracking data and then stuffed it and the phone inside the animal.

"Grant, why…?"

He turned and motioned toward his backpack. "There's a bottle of water in the outer pocket. Get it and open it up for me." He held out his hands as she poured the water over them, washing off the traces of the animal's blood. "If we're lucky, something bigger then she is will eat the phone whole, and Jauhar's men will be chasing their asses out here long enough to give us time to get the hell out of here."

"What?" She looked at the cat and then back to him. Even in the darkness he could see her confusion. "How would they know where to find it?"

He reached into his backpack and pulled out the other satellite phone, keying up the GPS locator application. "Same way I found you." He handed the phone to her and grabbed the bottle of water from her hands. Wiping down his knife, he nodded to the slain leopard. "We need to get moving. The smell of that blood will have this place crawling with scavengers before dawn."

He slipped the knife back into its sheath and slung his rifle over his shoulder. Grabbing up his backpack, he handed hers to her and kissed the tip of her nose. The look of shock on her face was almost as entertaining as when she was angry. Almost. "You got your gun?"

Thalia nodded and took the backpack from his hand. He laughed and shook his head. Yeah, speechless was a damn good look for her. If they weren't mired in the middle of a shit storm, he might take a few moments to enjoy it. As it was, they'd be lucky to get through the next day alive.

He took her hand and pulled her past the leopard, further into the brush, holding back a disgruntled groan as she pulled against his hand. "Where are we going? The compound is the other way."

"Can't go back there." He'd thought about it, but it wasn't a smart idea. "It's the only structure within forty miles in any direction. This close to the satellite signal, it won't take them long to put two and two together and hit the compound."

He hated leaving the chopper behind. It would be a hell of a lot quicker and safer than trudging through the brush, but he couldn't chance that Jauhar hadn't already closed in on the place. Players like him had men everywhere, forces that could be mobilized and deployed in minutes to almost any location. If they'd been anywhere but out in the middle of nowhere he wouldn't chance moving out at all, calling in for a pick up instead. As the first bright rays of the sun pierced the early dawn sky, he could already see the buzzards gathering overhead. He might need to do that anyway. Telling her about her father would have to wait.

CHAPTER SEVENTEEN

As she waited in the stolen, dilapidated jeep for Grant to return, Thalia reached up and scratched her scalp. Her entire body itched, and the funk wafting from her dirty clothes was nothing less than disgusting. She'd never craved for a shower so badly in her life. She didn't once question her sanity as she imagined herself wrestling the crocodiles out of her way if they by chance passed a decent stream before they found a place to crash.

Her eyes closed against the hot sun which had sliced its way across the sky and now teetered on the edge of the horizon, mocking her undeniable thirst and withered skin. She would have wandered around in that godforsaken brush for a month before eventually dying of dehydration at best if Grant hadn't followed her. *Stupid! Stupid! Stupid!* Depressingly, yet again, he'd been right. The decision to leave was reckless on so many levels, but she had panicked and wasn't thinking straight at all. Aside from her complete lack of wilderness survival training, he'd also pointed out that several of her wounds were still fresh enough to attract a predator's attention from a mile away. *Thank you once again, Captain Obvious-To-Everyone-But-Me.*

The terrain they'd hiked through to get to anything even resembling a road was nothing like what she'd imagined when she map searched it on Grant's computer. The brush was eight feet tall in some places with huge muddy ponds surrounded by animals she'd only seen in pictures. It was a wonder anything could smell their scent over the wild animal stench that permeated the open air, but Grant was careful to lead them in a wide circle around the gathering animals, which seemed to make their trek through the wilderness a never ending venture. She'd been a nervous wreck when they passed the first pond, scared to even breathe. Of course, almost passing out from lack of oxygen every ten steps hadn't worked too well either. She didn't think she would ever miss that crazy monkey, but by the time they passed the third group of rhinos and Grant had pointed out a lion pacing in the not too distant brush, she craved Winston's silliness and hint of domestication.

Voices in the distance caught her attention, and she opened her eyes to see Grant approaching the car from the ramshackle roadside market, a man who she presumed to be the owner waving him off. Her eyes were drawn to Grant's wide shoulders and thick chest. She studied how stealthily he moved. Even walking next to him in the brush, she'd rarely heard him make a sound. How was that possible?

She lowered her gaze to her lap and shook her head at her own clumsiness and naivety. For the last year and a half she'd known what it was like to be hunted and stalked by Jauhar and Hamisi. Even compared to the leopard they were amateurs. When measured against Grant, they were more like schoolyard bullies. If she'd ever had a doubt, it was now buried with what was left of her long lost pride. Whatever target Grant set his sights on wouldn't stand a chance, not even her.

When he opened the driver's side door and slid into the tattered seat beside her, she turned her face back to the window. She could feel the heat bloom in her cheeks when the still vivid memory of the night before skittered into her thoughts. Had she admitted to being in love with him? What did that even mean for her… for them? They had barely spoken at all since that moment. He'd been too focused on getting them to safety, and all of her concentration had been on not screwing up and attracting another carnivorous beast. Now that they were crammed inside a small tin can together with no radio or any other distractions, she could feel the awkwardness of it all creeping between them.

She didn't know the first thing about being in *love*. The only thing she knew for sure was that if she lived beyond killing Jauhar, she would never be the same without Grant. Is that what it meant to him? She'd thought that was what she had seen in his eyes, what had sent her running, yet he hadn't said it back. What if he'd been expecting something different than what she'd confessed? Was his silence something more than simple determination to get them to safety? Dammit! This kind of confusion was exactly why she needed to push him away. She simply couldn't find the will to do it any longer.

"Drink up."

Grant's commanding voice snapped her out of her thoughts, giving her a temporary reprieve from her emerging doubts. Greedily she reached for the canteen in his hand as her long forgotten thirst came roaring back to life. They had exhausted their meager supplies earlier that morning. She'd successfully pushed the need for more to the back of her mind, ignoring the scratchy itch at the back of her throat and the raw, chapped skin along the edges of her lips. It did no good to complain about what they didn't have. Now her mouth was suddenly on fire.

"It's not bottled water, but it's clean." She was so thirsty she wouldn't have cared if it had been filtered through a rotten sock. Tilting her head back, she slowly poured the clear, cool contents over her face. Her dusty, parched skin tingled back to life as it drizzled down her neck, beneath the shirt Grant had given her, and trickled between her breasts. She opened her mouth to quench her fiery thirst as she reached up and lifted her hair off her shoulders, clearing a path for the water to run down her back.

Far too soon the canteen ran empty. She lowered it to her lap as she licked the remaining drops from her lips, savoring every one as if it were her last. Wiping her mouth with the back of her hand, she paused. Feeling the sudden weight of Grant's silence, she opened her eyes and turned to see him staring at her, his fists clenched in a white-knuckled grip on the steering wheel, his eyes languid pools of heated…something. Was he still angry with her?

"What?" She shrugged. When he glanced at the canteen in her hand, then back to her, she cringed. "Oh, crap. Sorry. Did you want some?"

Did he want some? Holy hell, he wanted it all! The water, her, all of it; just like that. Forget the canteen. He'd lick what he needed right off her skin…and…and…*fuck!* He shifted in his seat to relieve the building pressure in his pants. Jesus! His dick had been hard for what felt like an eternity. It was certainly on board with the idea of fucking her right there in the front seat. Hell, he could almost hear it screaming in protest as common sense flooded his veins and worked its way to his brain. *Right question, shit timing, fossa.* He wavered for a moment between his carnal need for her and his instincts demanding he get her hidden away from the two parasites who were hunting her. He had to get them to that goddamn thumb drive, then on a plane to Chennai to meet Daniel. They were going to be a day late as it was.

He shook his head and turned the key, surprised when the hunk of junk turned over on the first crank. "There are a few packs of crackers and another canteen in my pack if you want them. I'm sure the crackers are a few years past their expiration date, but it was either that or a rusted can of sardines."

He'd garnered enough information from the roadside merchant, if you could truly call the pile of shit he was pedaling merchandise, to know they had surfaced near the A-5 about five kilometers south of Kadoma. He couldn't take the chance of being seen in the larger cities like Harare. They would have to stick to the secondary roads which would add several hours to the otherwise twenty hour drive to Mozambique to retrieve the thumb drive.

They were both exhausted and in dire need of a shower and food, but he needed to get at least twelve hours of the drive behind them before he could even think about stopping. He would call Daniel from wherever they crashed and fill him in on the delay. Hopefully somewhere between here and there he'd find a way to talk to her about her father. He took one more wistful glance in her direction before pulling onto the empty road. Damn, he wished like hell they'd had one more day at the compound.

Nearly twenty-four hours later, the last five or six of them spent in blissful sleep, Thalia stood at the open window of their musty hotel room. Dressed only in a bath robe, she looked down onto the overcrowded street below and ran her fingers through her wet hair as she breathed in the smells of the food being offered up by the street venders. It seemed the locals were holding some sort of week-long celebration. This particular evening's festivities began with a parade that slowly wound down the narrow road they'd followed into the small town. Her empty stomach rumbled with the expectation that Grant would return soon with something that smelled as good as what was wafting on the gentle breeze flowing through the window.

Leaning against the battered window frame, she watched as natives in full tribal dress filed by. She couldn't help but be mesmerized by the colorful peacock feathers adorning their head dresses. Towering several feet above their heads, the teal and gold hues reflected beautifully off the setting sun in the distance and the bright flashes of fire that streamed through the air as they waved the heavy torches they carried in a rhythmic, synchronized dance the men were performing. It was a wonder the feathers didn't catch fire, coming precariously close to the flames of the other marchers as they dipped and swayed in unison.

When the loud cracking sound of a whip echoed through the night air, she startled and took a step back, her eyes drawn to the next set of men marching toward her. Barefoot, they were dressed only in bright yellow loin cloths and wore black hooded masks that concealed their faces from the unruly crowd of onlookers. Against the darkness that surrounded them, she could barely make out the slits cut into the fabric for them to see through, transforming them into soulless demons as they wielded their long, leathery whips toward the crowd around them. Another crack filled the air, then another. Her hand lifted from her side to pull the curtain closed, but paused when one of the hooded men turned his face up from the crowd. His black, soulless eyes stared straight at her as he marched slowly by her window, another loud crack snapping at her nerves with an effortless yet purposeful flick of his wrist. She couldn't contain the involuntary shudder that ran through her body and she jumped away from the window, pulling the curtain closed. Caressing the sudden unexpected chill from her arms, she stared blankly at the billowing curtain. *Maybe this wasn't such a good idea.*

Mutare wasn't the small village Grant had been hoping for. He certainly hadn't been keen on the idea of staying in the middle of town where so many people had gathered, but after thirteen hours of muddy dirt roads riddled with pot holes, they simply couldn't go any further. The clerk at the front desk had been distracted by the mid-morning festivities and hadn't asked for any identification. Paying with a wad of cash he pulled from his backpack, Grant scribbled an *X* on the piece of paper and quickly shuttled them to the room, locking the door behind them and shoving a chair beneath the door handle.

Despite their wariness, hunger, and the cramped space, they'd made love in the shower before they collapsed into the dilapidated bed and slept tangled together until the noise from the street party below had roused them. She glanced at the bedside clock, wondering what was taking Grant so long, an uneasy feeling tingling its way up her spine.

He'd pulled on his clothes, shouldered his backpack, and dashed out the door for food, telling her to keep her gun ready and not to open the door for anyone but him as if she was the airhead in a B-rated slasher flick. In a way she felt like she was exactly that. Since she'd met Grant, she'd become wholly dependent upon him. Not only did her body melt every time he looked at her, it seemed as if her IQ had dropped a few points as well. She'd had a plan, dammit! How could she have let things get this far out of her control?

Both hungry and exhausted, she slumped down onto the bed and pulled her knees into her chest. *Think, Thalia. What would Issa tell you to do?* As if in a paranormal answer, a knock at the door had her reaching for her gun. She stood, barely daring to breathe as she waited for Grant to let her know it was safe to open the door. Nothing came but another set of forceful taps on the frail thin door. *Shit!* She'd forgotten to put the chair under the doorknob after Grant had left. As she glanced at the chair, considering if she had time to move it back into place, the knob rattled with force as a heavy wave of pounding began.

"It's Gregory! Open this damn door! Is she in there?"

Gregory? Who the hell is Gregory? Thalia threw open her bath robe. Gun in hand, she silently poured herself back into her crusty shirt and pants, pulling her wet hair back into a pony tail. Whoever he was, he was after her. She needed to get the hell out of there. *Now!*

Sitting in the window sill, she tucked the gun into her pants and studied the side of the building. The distance to the street from the third floor window was too far to jump from, but to her left was a ledge barely wide enough to grab on to. Beyond the ledge was a second floor balcony. If she could reach it, she could hang from the bottom and drop the shorter distance to the street below. The noise from the crowd on the street drowned out the banging on the door but, as she leaned out to test the distance to the ledge, she heard a woman's voice calling from inside the room behind her.

"Natalie, don't jump!"

Hanging on by her fingertips, she clawed her way across the side of the building to the railing surrounding the balcony. Her knees and bare feet scraped along the wall as she dropped to the balcony platform, the cut on her thigh pulling against the stitches as she landed in a heap. A familiar burning sensation washed over her leg as a dark red splotch bloomed on her pant leg, confirming she'd reopened the wound on her thigh. Without a look back, she flung herself over the railing, the rusty bars cutting into her palms as she looked over her shoulder to the ground below. The fall wasn't going to do her leg any favors, but she didn't have a choice. Before she could talk herself out of it, she relaxed her grip and fell the rest of the way to the street. Shards of splintering pain exploded in her left ankle, barely cushioning the blow to her already butchered right leg as she crumbled against the broken pavement.

The crowd swirled around her, laughing and shouting as the parade finale floated by, oblivious to her awkward arrival or any attempts she made to stand. She could barely hear her own screams of pain as her hand was crushed beneath the heel of someone's shoe. She pushed against a prison of legs and limbs surrounding her. Her efforts to free her hand were meaningless against the crushing crowd as they stumbled over her, drunk and ignorant of her pain until her entire body had been kicked or crushed beneath the throng of partygoers.

Three loud gunshots rang out in the distance, the laughs and shouts turning into screams as the crowd around her peeled away and a pair of meaty hands wrenched her from the jagged gravel street. What little breath she had left was punched from her lungs as she was thrown over someone's shoulder, her ribs caving in against each jarring blow as she was hauled away from the crowd. The last thing she saw before her blood rushed to her head and a deep blackness overtook her vision was the soles of the stranger's worn and tattered boots as they beat against the pavement at a frantic pace.

CHAPTER EIGHTEEN

"Sonofabitch!" Grant held back a knowing grin and concentrated on Thalia as Daniel rubbed the ache from his jaw. His girl was a survivor and he was damn proud of it, even if she'd busted herself up pretty badly and unknowingly slugged her own father. Repeatedly.

"She has one hell of a right hook." His cheek still bore the remains of her last unconscious battle with him. He couldn't believe less than two weeks had passed since he lifted her lifeless body from his beach. Capturing her wrists in his hands to keep her from striking out at him again when she finally came to, he carefully caressed the raw scuff marks marring her knuckles. "I would have warned you if I knew you were coming." He turned his head to glare at his friend. "What the hell are you doing here, Daniel? I left clear orders to meet us in Chennai."

He could barely hold back the growl of frustration that clawed at his chest. By not following those simple instructions they had not only nearly gotten Thalia killed, but now the local rag-tag guerilla security forces were chasing them. God only knew what kind of bullshit he'd have to wade through if they didn't get this damn plane off the ground before they caught up to them. "How the hell did you find us?"

Daniel cupped the back of his neck and paced the length of the otherwise empty cabin. Empty except for his female friend Grant had yet to be introduced to. He'd quickly dismissed the leggy redhead as a non-threat. Considering her conservative business suit and dry no-nonsense attitude, she was definitely another department lackey he'd just as soon not know. Probably a Fed. What the hell had

Daniel been thinking bringing someone else into this nightmare? The last thing Thalia needed was a damn audience as her life was ripped to shreds…again.

“I don’t give two shits what your orders were!” Daniel shouted over the jet engines as they fired to life. “That’s my goddamn daughter!”

Grant’s patience was wearing fatally thin. With the determined vipers they were hiding from still out for Thalia’s blood, he couldn’t afford any leaks. He needed to know who compromised their position, and he needed to know right fucking now! “Who the hell told you where to find us?”

“I had your man on the ground redirect the flight through DC instead of Newark to pick up Rebecca. He was rattled enough to give you up. Hell, I had to threaten to tie his ass to his shiny new sports car to keep him from boarding the damn plane. He was more than willing to update the flight plan to intercept you here.” Daniel stopped pacing and came to stand in front of him, a crimson flush firing beneath the aged skin on his face and creeping beneath the collar of his casual button-up. He looked anything but casual. “I’ve fought too damn hard to find her, Grant. I wasn’t about to let her slip through my fingers again, and I don’t give a *damn* if that pisses you off.”

Grant’s teeth popped as he ground them together to keep his temper in check. He didn’t blame Daniel. Diver had given up their position after one frantic phone call. Sure, he’d been a little crazed when he’d called him, but everyone is entitled to at least one meltdown in their life. Right?

His gaze drifted back to Thalia as she stirred in his arms. He would deal with Diver and the rest of this bullshit later. Right now his hands were literally full of the woman he loved, and he needed to tend to her injuries in private. The last thing she needed was to wake up inside a plane full of strangers before he could stop her bleeding and clear this clusterfuck up for her. He should have told her everything the minute they found their way back to civilization. He simply couldn’t find the words.

His attention focused on the unconscious woman in his arms, he waved Daniel and his guest away. “Take a hike to the back while I wake her up and get her injuries taken care of.”

“She’s my daughter, Grant. I’m not—”

“I told you, she doesn’t remember you!” Grant held tight to the last vestiges of his control, trying to remember that Daniel held more of a claim to her than he did. That fact hadn’t escaped him. Maybe he was making decisions based on emotion like Daniel had been, but his friend would have to kill him before he’d let anyone else get near her. Not now. Not until he knew she was okay.

Daniel held his stare, his silence speaking volumes as he quietly assessed Grant’s protective posture. He watched as a kaleidoscope of emotions colored his friend’s face. Hurt and confusion sparked to life in his eyes, and Grant could see him fighting to deny it. Finally understanding filtered its way in, and Grant could feel the man’s disbelief as it rolled off him in an electrifying wave. *Yeah, I’m in love with your daughter. Shocks the hell out me too.*

Thank fuck they were spared the impending conversational disaster by the pilot’s announcement to secure the cabin and buckle up for departure. Daniel’s friend took him by the arm and dragged him toward the back of the plane while Grant laid Thalia across the front row of leather seats and began the task of tending to her injuries. The sedative he’d raked into the bag along with her antibiotics at Salina’s clinic had come in handy when she’d regained consciousness on the way to Daniel’s vehicle and began kicking the living shit out of everything within reach. The last thing he wanted was to knock her out again, but she’d become lost to her rage and fear, causing a scene and attracting the kind of attention they were running from.

“Wake up, fossa.” He cupped the top of her head in his palm, his thumb rubbing soothing circles on her forehead, waiting for her ghostly gray eyes to appear from behind her twitching eyelids as she fought her way back to consciousness. She was going to be in one hell of a mood waking up in mid-air again. A secret smile pulled at his heart from somewhere deep inside him at that thought. He truly loved this woman, even when she was spitting mad. Especially when she was spitting mad.

As he was beginning to fuss with the buttons on her pants to take a look at her busted stitches, the redheaded woman stepped up and held out what appeared to be a fresh change of clothes.

“I brought these in case she needed them. I’m Rebecca Danes, International Organized Crime Intel.” A familiar, bitter taste soiled his taste buds as he heard the title roll off her tongue in the usual arrogant tenor of a Fed. It was nice to know his sixth sense about people hadn’t taken a hike with his common sense. Without so much as a nod, he took the clothes from her outstretched arms and went back to work removing Thalia’s blood drenched ones. When the persistent redhead didn’t retreat from her post next to the row of seats she was perched against, he paused and turned his lethal, *what-the-fuck-do-you-want* stare her way, a not so subtle warning to either spill what she came to say or move on. To her credit she didn’t seem to scare easily.

“I’m not a spectator, Mr. Kendal.” She crossed her arms over her chest and Grant noticed how that one confident move seemed to add at least three inches to her five foot six frame. He met her challenge and popped to his feet, enjoying the way her face drained of color as the blood rushed toward her rapidly increasing heartbeat. He wouldn’t hurt the woman, but he sure as hell wasn’t going to let her bully her way into interrogating Thalia before she’d even had a chance to process what had happened to her.

He knew how the game was played. She needed information. Thalia was nothing but a new source, an untapped well of information she needed to access to make her next big move up the departmental bullshit ladder. She and her career could go to hell. One lean closer and he could smell her fear as she tried to swallow it back.

“Mm…” She cleared her throat, and Grant would have been amused if Thalia wasn’t lying unconscious and bleeding on the seat behind him while this woman was wasting his fucking time. Grant watched as she quickly gathered herself back together and was mildly shocked when she opened her mouth to speak instead of turning on her prim three inch heels and running for her life.

“Mr. Gregory asked me to come along because I’m also a victim’s advocate. I’ve helped many other girls, uh, women like Natalie. I’ve personally worked her case for the last five years, Mr. Kendal. I’ve given my life’s blood to find the evil psychopaths who did this to her and I won’t stop until I see them either castrated and locked away in a sweat box in the middle of a South American jungle or dead. Preferably both."

Grant considered her for a moment as they locked stares in an unspoken challenge. There was more fire in her green eyes than he gave her credit for. Maybe his sixth sense had taken that hike off a cliff after all. When she refused to look away he shrugged and gave her a smirk. "Both is good." He nodded and turned back to Thalia, resuming his inspection of her wounds as the woman turned and gifted them their privacy.

She stopped a few steps down the narrow aisle and looked back over her shoulder at him. "If you need my help explaining this to Natalie...I mean, she might need a woman's perspective to see this clearly." He nodded wordlessly and watched her retreat the rest of the way down the aisle before settling in next to his friend.

Would he ever get used to calling her Natalie? Would she ever forgive him for not telling her sooner? Damn, this was going to be hard. A part of him, a small, selfish part, didn't want her to remember. Not for him. He hated the idea of awakening such morbid memories she'd so successfully locked away. To him, she would be better off not remembering, even if that meant forgetting some of the good things too. He would give anything to be able to forget his past. He couldn't take that choice away from her though. No matter how horrid, they were her memories to command. He only hoped he still had a place in them when this was all over.

Nearly thirty minutes after they had taken off from the small private airstrip outside Mutare, Grant tied off the last of the few stitches Thalia had ruptured in her thigh. The wound had looked far worse than it was, but her ankle was a different story. She moaned when he pushed on the swollen flesh to see if anything was broken, and he quickly moved up to see if he could rouse her.

"Wake up for me, Thalia," he crooned into her ear as he peppered her face with gentle kisses. Reading her movements, he gathered her wrists back into his hands, anticipating her fight or flight reaction in time to keep her from bolting up from the makeshift bed he'd nestled her into. "Easy, fossa. You're safe. I've got you."

"Grant?" He watched as her brows furrowed in confusion and her sleepy, glazed eyes cleared of the drug induced fog.

"Yeah, it's me. You've had one hell of a night." He coaxed her back into a prone position and pulled the blanket further up her naked body.

"Ugh, tell me about it. I had a terrible nightmare." She closed her eyes and he could feel her muscles coil beneath his palms as her memories broke through the haze from the sedative. He braced himself as she shot up again and began to fight his hold on her. "Oh shit! It wasn't a dream! Where the hell am I? Who were those people?"

"Shh, fossa. Don't get up yet." He waited patiently as she marginally relaxed back into the seat, her eyes wild as she tried to catch up. "We're on a plane to Mozambique. Can you tell me if anything other than your thigh or ankle hurts?" Her eyes squinted shut as she rotated her ankle, a muted moan escaping her lips. "I don't think it's broken, but you won't be running anywhere for a few days."

"Grant, they knew my name." He pulled the shirt from the pile of clothes Rebecca had given him and gathered the hem in his hands as he moved to help her put it on. "I can do that." He smirked as she snatched it from his grip and feebly maneuvered it over her head and worked her arms through. *That's my girl.* "Did you hear me?" She pulled the shirt over her bare breasts and then pushed herself up to lean against the seatback. "Ugh, why does my head hurt so badly?"

Careful not to snag her ankle, he worked her legs halfway through the soft material of the slacks, effectively trapping them from kicking out at him before he answered her. He was sure he was going to need all the advantage he could get. "Yeah, about that," he sighed. Unable to procrastinate further he stood, resting his hands on his hips, every molecule in his body preparing for the coming fight. "That would be the sedative I gave you."

He flinched when she moved, his hands rushing out to catch thin air instead of her flying fists as she lethargically pushed further up into the seat and shuffled the slacks over her hips. Christ, had he overdosed her? He expected her to at least throw something at him.

"The rounds I fired off attracted too much attention. And the way you were fighting Daniel..." He crouched in front of her and pushed her tangled hair behind her ears. The look in her eyes held more fear and confusion than anger. He hated seeing her like that. He'd never been one for apologies, but he'd beg her forgiveness if that's what it took to rid her of that look. "I thought I'd lose my mind when I saw you drop from that balcony. I'm sorry, but you were frantic when Daniel finally got to you, and I had to—"

"Who's Daniel?" Her voice wavered with the same fear he'd seen in her eyes. "Who is Daniel, Grant? How did those people know my real name? I haven't even told you."

His heart froze inside his chest as every word in his vocabulary evacuated his brain. Dammit, what had he done? He wasn't ready for this. He'd thought of nothing else during the long drive to Mutare but how to tell her. For a man who had been trained to plan for every contingency possible, this was a complete fail. How could he even begin to explain that her entire life had been a lie? That she'd been kidnapped from a loving family and sold into a world in which one would rather die than endure? He knew what had been done to her. He wasn't naïve enough to think she'd escaped being raped and beaten. Her body bore the scars of her forgotten nightmare. Truth was, it didn't matter. Not to him. She'd survived and that was all that was important to him. She was strong and beautiful, inside and out. She was perfect in ways he would never deserve.

He swallowed back the bile that had gathered in the back of his throat and tried again to say the words. They twisted in his gut, clawing their way up his throat until he nearly gagged in another mute attempt to spit them out. He couldn't do it. Four simple words and he couldn't say them.

"Grant you're scaring me. What the hell is happening?" With limited grace, she pushed out of her seat, stumbling with the first bit of weight she tested on her ankle.

"Thalia, please. You're going to make it worse. Sit back down and I'll try to explain!" His arm snaked around her waist and locked her against him, her hands frantically working to pry herself loose from his hold.

"Natalie?" Her head snapped up at the raspy voice calling her name, halting her struggle as she took in the stranger who stared back at her from a few feet away. "Natty, honey?"

Her hands fell away to her sides, her body shifting lifelessly in Grant's arms as she stared at Daniel in confusion. His heart ached for her, for both of them. He couldn't let them suffer in silence any longer. The words that had been impossible to say flew from his thoughts, rolling off his tongue with such little effort it shocked even him when they were uttered next to her ear.

"Daniel is my friend, fossa." He turned her in his arms and tucked her into his chest, resting his chin on top of her head as he looked over at Daniel. "He's also you're father, Thalia. He's been looking for you for a very long time."

CHAPTER NINETEEN

"You should eat something." Thalia reached for the tablets Grant handed her, numb to his touch as his fingers lingered on her hand before he hesitantly let them fall away. She closed her eyes, shutting out the pity she saw in his worried expression. She threw back her head and popped the antibiotics to the back of her throat, ignoring the sharp sting as they slid like razors into her empty stomach. She didn't care. It was an inconsequential pain compared to the breathtaking ache that filled her chest and threatened to tear her in two.

Periods of heavy silence filled the too cozy hotel room, everyone watching her every move each time she dared take a deep breath, making the tangled web of voices in her head scream louder against the quiet darkness invading her thoughts. Voices she barely knew mingled with the haunting ones of her past, of people she thought she knew. People she'd trusted. How could Issa lie to her...about everything?

"I don't understand." Her fingers twined together so tightly she could feel the icy sting when the lack of circulation began to takes its toll. "My family died in a car accident when I was seventeen. Issa told me…they…but…why would he lie?" Relaxing her cold, numb fingers, she reached out and traced the edge of one of the photographs lying on the table in front of her. It was a photo of her, standing in an outdated kitchen, her silver eyes crossed in a funny pose, her tongue sticking out as she licked peanut butter from a piece of toast. Behind her was this man, Daniel, holding a cup of water over her as if he were about to pour it over her head, a devious, quirky smile on his much younger face. She looked like the girl in that kitchen. She searched inside herself for any recognition, but felt nothing. Nothing that would tell her she deserved to feel as happy as the girl in that photo looked. She found nothing that said she'd ever owned that life.

"That's not what happened, Natalie." She flinched away when a warm hand caressed her shoulder and Rebecca slowly slid into the space next to her, pulling her further away from the perfect scene in the picture. "You grew up in Maryland. Daniel raised you after your mother left. You had just turned sixteen and gotten your driver's license when you disappeared. Daniel had let you drive to school and…you never came home. Another girl who had gone missing managed to escape. She couldn't identify the men who took her, but she remembered you. She picked out your photo, along with four other girls who had been held with her. We don't know who Issa is or why he would lie to you, Natalie. Maybe if you told us a little about him we could figure it out."

Tell them about Issa? Where did she start? How would hearing about him teaching her how to cook or playing Romeo against her horrible rendition of Juliet when she was having trouble staying focused on her studies help them understand why he'd lied to her? Or the time he took her to France and visited every cheesy tourist trap with her when she finally graduated? Or all the times he helped her focus and breathe after her lungs seized in one unexplainable panic attack after another when she first awoke in Mumbai to a world she didn't recognize. He always made time for her, even when she was acting bratty and spoiled.

A hard lump she couldn't swallow formed in her throat when one of her most treasured memories of him floated into the chaos of tattered thoughts in her mind. Her favorite time with Issa was when he was on one of his boats, large or small. His smile beamed with pride and freedom, his nearly white hair ruffled by the heavy sea breeze that always kept the costal air cooler and cleaner than the stuffy smog in the overcrowded cities. The memory was so clear her fingers twitched with the desire to reach out and trace the fine lines that formed at the corners of his eyes as he laughed, throwing out orders to his men to get underway. He loved the smell of the sea and the sounds of the birds as they flocked the loading docks. He was like a small boy with a shiny new toy each time he bought a new ship. She could feel the tug on her hand as he raced up to the bridge, dragging her behind, excited to show her how everything worked. All the new bells and whistles his other ships lacked. He never kept secrets from her. Anything she ever asked him, any question or interest, he was always ready with an answer or instruction. How would knowing about any of that help them understand why he'd lied to her?

She could feel the hurricane of emotions brewing inside her, confusion controlling its path of destruction. She stared at the pictures, dozens of them, of her with this man Daniel. None of them made sense. Surely if he was her father she would remember *something* about him. The weathered burly man standing on the other side of the large hotel room, now engaged in what looked like a silent argument with Grant, looked nothing like the pictures of the man Issa had told her was her father; the father who had died with her mother in India in a car crash that had apparently never happened.

The images of her life, of what she thought she knew to be true, were now blurred with lies and irrevocably twisted with the images of a stranger and a man she loved like a father she never knew she had. It was beyond confusing. Everything spun together and played on a never ending loop in her mind until nothing but white noise filled her senses. Another wave of nausea crashed against her soul, making her wish she could run away from it all and never look back. Out of sheer desperation she tried again to stand, but it was useless. Her ankle was braced but still had no chance of holding her weight. She was back to being weak and useless again, completely dependent on Grant.

Grant. She closed her tired eyes. Again, she was assaulted with his haunted expression as they stood on that plane and he told her she was someone she wasn't. The things he'd said about the scars on her back came rushing back, bringing with it a violent reality that challenged everything both familiar and new in her life. If any of it were true, how could Issa ever love her? How could Grant still want her? Why would he? He looked at her differently now, a sad sort of sympathy in his eyes every time they hesitantly met hers. *Dammit!* She didn't need his goddamn pity! *None of it happened! None of it!*

Digging the heels of her palms into her eyes, she tried to force some sort of order into the chaos waging war on her mind. She wanted to scream at them all that it wasn't true! They were all liars. She couldn't accept that Issa would make her believe such a lie. Why? What purpose did it serve? He wasn't the monster they were trying to make him out to be. She would know, dammit, if he was! He never, *not once*, touched her or asked her to do anything that was…was...

Her shaking hand flew to her stomach as burning bile churned in another nauseating wave. Even thinking about Issa as a man capable of such horrid things was impossible. *He was my father.* The only father she could remember having. He was a good man. He loved her when she had no one left to love. How could she ever doubt him? Blinking back the burning sting of threatening tears, her blurry gaze caught again on the pile of photos lying on the coffee table, mocking her memories. The evidence in front of her was irrefutable. *How can I not doubt him*?

Overcome with shock, she'd barely cried when she found Issa slumped over the center console of his car at his Mumbai mansion, the driver's door glass shattered around his lifeless bloody body from the single bullet that had pierced his skull. Even days later, after flying his body home to Mozambique Island, her tears were stubbornly absent at his funeral. She'd been too scared out of her mind for the first year to mourn him, too set on revenge for the last six months to allow herself to feel the pain of his loss. The closest she'd come was the first night she'd told Grant about him.

Time and place ceased to exist as the pain clawed at her chest, no longer willing to be denied. The once impenetrable wall she'd built around her heart weakened and crumbled, falling in jagged pieces to the ground at her feet, and her insides began to quake with uncontrollable sobs. *Issa!* In an instant her weary mind took her back to that fateful day, kneeling in the broken glass as she cradled Issa's cold, dead body to her chest. *No! Oh God. Issa, no! No! You can't die! You can't!* Forbidden tears fell unchecked from her eyes in wistful streams of overpowering sorrow. Calming numbness surrendered to a searing burn, like a thousand tiny flames dancing beneath her flesh as her mouth opened on a silent cry, her lungs unable to release the scream of injustice she so desperately wanted the world to hear. *You can't leave me, not like this! Issa, please! Please don't leave me!* The room began to spin around her, her body clinging helplessly to the strong arms that carried her into the darkness.

Grant felt the moment her body succumbed to her exhaustive sobs and she fell into a fitful sleep. Careful not to disturb her, he peeled his arm from around her waist and propped up onto his elbow to watch her breathe. She'd been inconsolable. Seeing her like that had wrecked him. Shifted his entire foundation. He'd never allowed himself to get close enough to anyone to actually feel their pain. That kind of pain, her pain, was something he never wanted to feel again. Yet he would trade places with her in a blink of an eye if he could. If nothing else, so she would never have to remember.

They'd spent the last four hours battling against the lies she'd been told. The sheer number of emotions she'd processed in that small window of time was staggering. She was three days past exhausted and he was shocked she hadn't broken sooner. He'd been ready to snap at more than one point himself, and kick his friend's ass over the constant barrage of Q and A they were throwing at her. She was clearly not ready for any of it. His rage was in check now, barely, but he could feel it simmering beneath his skin as he watched her chest rise and fall with each labored breath she took. He wanted more than anything to rip that Issa from his grave and demand answers.

Thalia and Rebecca both seemed confused about her *uncle's* role in Thalia's abduction, but he had no problem seeing him for what he was. If nothing else, Grant was a professional liar. He'd spent his life perfecting that tradecraft, sharpening it into one of the deadliest tools of his profession. He knew skilled deception when he saw it, and this Issa bastard had played a master's hand. If it was the last thing he did, Grant was determined to find the piece of shit that was ultimately responsible for taking the innocence from the child inside the beautiful, strong woman in his arms. It was time to pull his aces, find out who the key players were and end their game for good. Before they could destroy another beautiful living soul.

Without a sound he rolled from the bed and crept from the darkness, his bare feet quiet against the plush carpet beneath him. Carefully, he latched the heavy door closed securely behind him when he entered the adjoining hotel suite. His skin crawled with uneasiness as he took in the skyline beyond the twentieth floor balcony. Either the Bureau was paying the redhead well enough to fork over the cash for this palatial palace or she had someone by the balls. Either way, it was a foolish move to be holed up in the penthouse in the middle of town. He needed to get his hands on that thumb drive and get them the hell out of there.

"Is she going to be okay?" Daniel paced to the closed door, his hand resting on the doorknob.

"Don't." Grant threw the warning over his shoulder as he walked past Daniel to the other side of the room and pulled the curtains closed. "She's done in. Let her rest."

"She's stronger than you think if she's survived this long," Rebecca said, her elbows resting on her knees as she studied the screen on the laptop in front of her. "It may not seem like it, but it was good for her to release her grief. Give her some time to process."

Gritting his teeth against the rage that flowed through his veins, Grant marched over to her laptop and slammed the lid closed. "What you *don't* know about her and this situation is going to get us all killed."

Rebecca didn't flinch. She straightened her spine and slid back onto the sofa cushion. "Then tell us, Mr. Kendal. What do we need to know to get the bastard who did this to her?"

"I don't give a damn about that right now." Daniel paced to the polished hardwood curio and poured himself a glass of what looked like expensive bourbon, his lips twisting in protest as the spicy fire burned its way down his throat. "I only want my daughter back."

"She's not the same little girl you lost, Daniel. We've talked about that." Rebecca stood, running her palms down her prim slacks, tossing her long red hair over her shoulder before she walked over to a black briefcase sitting on the floor by the front door. Hoisting it up and sitting it on top of the bar in front of Daniel, she opened it and pulled out a well-worn file stuffed to bursting with dog-eared pages. "She's safe, Daniel," she said, pausing to rest her free hand on top of Daniel's. "I have a job to do now. That's why you brought me here. We have to strike now to get these bastards."

The thin thread left of Grant's patience snapped free from his grasp. Shattered pieces of Rebecca's laptop littered the marble floor in the small foyer at the front door before he could think twice about the loud crash waking Thalia. These fucking people didn't get it.

"Both of you shut the hell up and listen to me." His nostrils flared, each labored breath working against his rising heart rate to calm his temper. He wasn't accustomed to losing it, and he sure as hell wasn't going to now. Instead, he carefully focused his rage on those who deserved it and turned his attention to the only two people who could help him get Thalia the hell out of there. It was time they were educated on exactly who they were dealing with and what needed to be done.

CHAPTER TWENTY

Dusk fell like a blanket across the quiet marina, the humid air making the newspaper in Grant's hands curl and sag against its weight. He sat on a sailboat docked across from the graveyard where Thalia's uncle was buried. His legs were stretched out, his back propped against the tall mast as he pretended to read. Judging by the amount of shale build-up on the hull, the boat's owner hadn't been around in while. That played perfectly into his plans as he sat comfortably and watched the comings and goings of a three block radius from his inconspicuous, uninhabited perch.

He casually turned the page, peering over the top of the paper as a woman and small child walked along the broken sidewalk, turning left into the spacious graveyard. The bill on his ball cap shielded his watchful eyes as the woman released the child's hand and rolled open a paper bag, carefully laying three dried rice balls on a modest looking headstone before wiping away a tear and turning to leave. A relatively outdated custom he couldn't have cared less about, but he did find it a little odd that she hadn't lingered. The suspicious thought strayed as he pictured Thalia kneeling there, the sobs he'd witnessed hours earlier wracking her normally strong frame as she mourned her uncle.

He'd never spoken the words *I love you* to another human being. He'd never wanted to speak them more than he did to her as she cried herself to sleep in his arms. It wasn't fair to add that emotion to an already overwhelming tide of confusion, pain, and grief. They had time. As soon as he took care of Jauhar, Don Lalia, and Hamisi she would be safe and he would go to her. Tell her that he wanted forever with her. He needed forever with her.

He'd been looking for something when he marooned himself on that island. He didn't know it then, but there had always been an emptiness inside him he longed to understand. In the past he filled that void with the rush of his job, always moving from one target to the next, never looking back to see what he might have missed along the way. He'd been good at simply existing, thriving on solitude, but he'd missed something; something he never knew he wanted. He'd been looking for her. He wasn't sure if she would have him. He sure as hell didn't deserve her, but living without her was no longer an option.

After explaining what she was up against to Daniel and that rabid redheaded bulldog he'd brought with him, he was confident everyone was finally on the same page. The only important thing was getting Thalia out of Jauhar's reach. He'd secure the thumb drive, and by the time he got back to the room they would have everything arranged. One flight to Montana. One to Mumbai. Once Thalia was safely hidden away he would make his play on Jauhar, take out the threat on her life, and then make his way home to her.

After two hours of surveillance, he saw no suspicious movement in or out of the surrounding buildings or boats. Positive the gravesite wasn't being watched, he folded the newspaper, letting it drop over the side of the boat as he hopped to his feet. With a casual stretch of his arms, he scooped up his backpack, hoisted it over his shoulder and stepped off the boat. His free hand rested nimbly on the gun tucked neatly in his waistband beneath his dark-blue windbreaker as he wandered at a leisurely pace down the dock and up the steps leading to the street. A few moments later he was strolling through the middle of the graveyard, counting the rows of headstones to mark his target before he approached.

Snagging a single rose from an unknown tomb, he stepped up to the grave marker Thalia had described. Taking one last unnoticeable glance to check his six, he bent to change out the flowers, palming the plastic bag containing the thumb drive as he placed the stolen rose into the vase. It was there, like she'd said it would be.

He stood and stared at the unimportant name on the headstone, his fingers playing along the contours of the thumb drive now stashed securely in his pocket. Like the woman and child, a quick departure could raise suspicion. After a few solemn moments, his well-honed senses felt no prying eyes upon him. He allowed himself to entertain the curiosity burning in his gut. He simply couldn't ignore it. His calculating eyes roamed the rows of headstones, counting the appropriate number until they rested on the object of that curiosity. He was drawn to it like a moth to a flame.

Issa's memorial stone stood a head taller than the other stones in that section of the buried dead. Unable to harness his need to know, his feet moved swiftly over the grass toward the domineering monument that marked the grave of the man who held Thalia's undeserved affection. His pace slowed as he approached, the chiseled letters of the tribute coming into focus along with a framed photo embedded into the top of the intricately carved marble.

His heart leapt in his chest when Thalia's silver, sparkling eyes stared back at him from the picture, full of life and fire, almost daring him to love her. She looked different now, hardened and more aware of the evil in the world. Her powerful yet innocent smile beamed back a happiness he'd never seen her express in the short time he'd known her. He knew it would be difficult, but standing there alone in the middle of so much death he made a silent promise to bring that happiness back to her.

His eyes flickered to the image of the older looking man in her arms, the man she'd vowed to avenge. The hair on the back of his neck suddenly prickled to life with disbelief. There, staring back at him, were eyes of a man that reflected too much knowledge of his own wickedness. A man he was far too familiar with to believe for one moment he'd had nothing to do with Thalia's abduction. A man he'd studied and watched. He knew every nuance, every habit, and every movement this bastard made in the last few days of his despicable life. Staring back at him with a mocking smile was a man who knew he'd just extracted his own twisted, fated revenge. In the grave beneath his feet rested the body of the last man Grant had killed in service to his country.

His blood turned to ice as he read the name on the headstone again before looking back at the man in the picture. *Issa was Imad Shavish.* The man who had been at the top of the food chain for dealing arms to the Al Qaeda terror organization; the only person in the world Thalia had ever loved, and he'd killed him with a single bullet. *Son of a bitch.*

Sweat laced his palms. A chill flushed beneath his skin as fiery bile burned its way to the back of his throat. The crash of his heartbeat drumming in his ears drowned out any sounds of the violent retching that instantly wracked his entire body. Forearms braced against a nearby tree, he doubled over in fierce, involuntary spasms. His soul was ripped away as wave after wave of sickening images of blood and death he'd never before allowed to haunt him, now plowed over and destroyed any happiness he'd allowed himself to believe in. He knew. He'd known all along he was never meant to know the kind of life he dared allow himself to imagine with Thalia. He would never be anything more than a mindless killer.

I killed Issa. A twisted laugh mingled with his hoarse cries of self-loathing and gut-wrenching loss as another wave of bile spewed from his mouth. It was ironic how fate would bring her to him and then snatch her away just as he understood that losing her would all but destroy him. He deserved it.

Begging for forgiveness was pointless. She would never understand. She would never see Issa as the man he knew. A man who never thought twice about the multitude of deaths he facilitated in a quest for money and greatness. The man was a plague to the human race. There would be no forgiveness for something he couldn't bring himself to regret. It was a righteous kill. But that would make him a monster in her eyes. He could imagine her beautiful face; see it twist in vile disgust as the soulless creature inside him was revealed to her. He would never be anything more than a murderer to her.

He didn't think he could stomach the cold hatred he knew would fill her damning eyes when she discovered the truth. He was the authentic target of the revenge she sought for Issa's murder. He could feel his rage at the injustice of it all bubbling to the surface as he labored for each calming breath. Jauhar may be innocent of the crime she sought to kill him for, but he would still die a merciless death at his hands, if only to secure her future safety. It would be, no doubt now, a future without him.

Swiping the back of his hand across his numb lips, he straightened and embraced the increasing weight of the returning emptiness that had once been his closest companion. He was a killer. Nothing would ever change that. Not now. Not ever. In his pocket he held the key to reaching his next target. Once more he would stalk his prey. Once more he would feel the soul drain from another worthless life as he condemned it to the pits of hell where it belonged.

Another wave of bone chilling awareness splintered like shards of ice beneath his skin as his trembling fingers wrapped around the thumb drive tucked deep inside his pocket. No one knew what was on it. It was obviously damning enough to have both Jauhar and Don Lalia foaming at the mouth and willing to kill for it. If Imad Shavish's empire was somehow linked to Jauhar's, and Jauhar was now in business with Don Lalia…the NSA, shit, an entire alphabet soup of agencies would ass-fuck each other on a national stage to get their hands on it.

His years of self-discipline kicked in to overtake his grief as he processed each outcome with lightning speed. The minute those political leeches got their hands on the thumb drive Jauhar would be off limits. He would be untouchable, protected as an asset until the powers that be had crawled up his ass and combed through every possible source they could squeeze out of him. Only then, once he was of no further use, would someone like him be called in to eliminate the waste left behind after their plundering. That could take years. Countless other lives could be destroyed under the false flag of national security as different international agencies sat passively by and watched in hopes of gaining a fresher source to do their bidding.

No. His head shook as he rapidly denied that outcome. He wouldn't let that happen. He understood the game. He'd played his part flawlessly in the past, but this was personal. He couldn't play by their rules on this one. He owed Thalia her freedom. She deserved a life free of the monsters that had ruled over her for so long. Free of the monster inside him. There was only one way to guarantee Thalia's life would be her own once again: Jauhar had to die.

His stomach void of anything but the acidic pain of regret for what he was about to do, he shouldered his backpack and made his way out of the now darkened graveyard. He told himself it was what was best for Thalia, but in truth he was a selfish coward. He couldn't face her. He wanted her memory to remain unspoiled for the many lonely years he would face without her.

Following the twisting alleyways, he came to an abandoned rail station on the far side of the small tourist village. A lone phone booth stood adjacent to the closed ticket office. Grant marched purposefully across the platform and picked up the receiver, dialing the operator for a connection to the hotel suite. He would be long gone before anyone came looking for him. When they did come for him, as he knew they would, his trail would end here. No satellite traces, no signal triangulation. He would be off the grid for the next seventy two hours. Maybe forever.

~*~*~*~*~

A small whimper echoed in the darkness as the coarse concrete bit into the bare skin of her knees. She tried to breath past the pain, but kept gagging on the dirty cotton rag they had stuffed to the back of her throat. Her matted hair stuck to the spit and sweat that coated her face. Lose strands had tangled in the piece of cloth they'd used to gag her and tickled her nose as she fought to dislodge the material. Her wrists burned from the rough fibers of the rope binding them behind her back so tight that her shoulders screamed in agony each time she moved even a fraction.

She could hear others crying, some openly sobbing in the darkness around her. Her own pain and shame faded a little as she wondered if they too were naked. If they had been stripped of their clothes in broad daylight and tossed from man to man, their hands roaming and inspecting places on their bodies no other had touched before. She didn't wish it upon them, but believing she wasn't alone helped calm the panic inside. She believed she would wake up, that it was all a nightmare, but as the hours turned into days of nothing but darkness and pain she knew, deep inside, she was going to die here.

The room she was in had been sectioned off into make-shift stalls with sheets hung from wires strung from the weathered, pot-marked ceiling. It reminded her of an emergency room, but with no sterile equipment or busy nurses running from patient to patient. The floors were bare concrete, the walls painted a putrid green and peeling from years of neglect. Her stall had a stained and smelly mattress for her to lie on and nothing else. She was kept naked and bound in total darkness. Except when, every few hours, a man they called Stu would open the door to their room. Blinding light from the rows of overhead florescent bulbs would flood her senses, making her head throb and her eyes sting. She could not see anything beyond the tattered sheets surrounding her stall, but she could hear the screams of each girl as they were taken from the room, one by one. Darkness would once again cocoon them as the door was slammed closed, the click of the lock sealing her fate until it was her time to go.

Voices, loud and angry, shouting beyond the door shook her from her thoughts of the other girls. Fear, cold and violent, raced through her veins as the door opened again and more blinding light flooded the room. She could hear the scuffling of shoes as they approached her, a few wicked chuckles echoing around her like ghosts. Her lungs filled with acid as breath after breath she fought not to gag or scream. Maybe if she was quiet enough they would forget about her.

"I told you. She wasn't to be kept with the others." *A harsh accent she couldn't place sounded beyond the curtain before it was yanked away.*

Instinctively her body flinched, turning away from the large man who stood looming over her, his arms above his head as his fingers hung from the wire above. Through her light-deprived eyes she could only make out a gauzy shadow as he released the wire and moved closer. When she tried to move away she fell from her kneeling position, and her cheekbone slapped against the cold, gritty concrete, sending more waves of pain through her skull.

"Now, now. Can't have you scarring up that pretty face." *She tried to fight him off, but was helpless against the ropes that bound her as his hands wrapped around her aching arms and yanked her to her feet like a lifeless doll.* "Having fun yet?"

She squeezed her eyes shut and turned her head away from the foul smell of his breath. He'd been drinking. His smelly body was pressed against her naked skin, his fists clenched in her hair. "When someone asks you a question, you answer it like a good little bitch."

She shook her head, unsure of what the question even was. The only thing she could think about was getting away from him. Please, please, please. *Her thoughts begged and screamed the words her mouth couldn't.*

"That's a good little princess." *His fists fell from her hair and she was released from his hold. His fingers framed her chin and turned her head, his thumb caressing the burning scratch on her cheek.* "We've only just begun, little girl. Mind your manners and this will be a lot easier for you."

As he turned to usher her from the room a deafening, blood-chilling scream filled the hallway beyond the door. Her battered legs froze in place, unwilling and unable to take another step toward the door that so many others had disappeared through. The man pushed her forward and she stumbled back another step. No! Please! I can't go with you! Please don't make me! Please!

"Please! I'm begging you! Let me go!"

"Natalie!" Frantic, Daniel rushed into the bedroom. "Natty, honey. It's just a dream. You're safe, honey."

Drenched in sweat, Thalia kicked out, her legs flailing against the sheets as she sat up in the bed and scrambled away from the man looming over her. *Daniel Gregory.* Her chest burned, each breath harder to take in as her memory of the last few hours pushed its way through the panic.

"Breathe, Natty. It's okay. I won't hurt you." Daniel stayed at the foot of the bed, his hands held out to her.

She didn't know those hands. She shut her eyes and bit back a scream of frustration. If she didn't get control now, she would lose her mind forever. Closing out the world around her, she forced herself to focus. Breath after breath, she allowed the space inside her mind to expand a little further until finally she was able to open her eyes.

"What happened in your dream?"

The redhead's voice filled the space in the room where Daniel had been. He was gone, but Thalia could hear someone shuffling about in the next room. "I never remember." She shrugged and looked away. A shiver of residual fear fluttered beneath her skin. It wasn't an entirely true statement anymore, but whoever this woman was, she didn't need to know. "Where's Grant?"

"You don't have to talk about it, but it might help if you did."

"Trust me." Thalia flung the covers away and slid from the bed, her ankle protesting the weight, but was surprisingly less swollen than it had been earlier. "If I remembered I'd tell you all about it, because you're *such* a close friend, right?" She pulled her shirt up and over her head, enjoying the embarrassment and shock on the woman's face as she limped into the adjoining bathroom. "That's what best friends do, right? Tell each other their deepest, darkest secrets."

The sound of the spray hitting the shower floor drowned out whatever reply the woman may have had. *Just what I need, someone else to hover.* Thalia allowed the hot, steamy water to wash the sweat and grime from her body. Too bad it couldn't wash the last year and a half from her mind as easily. God, she wanted more than anything for Grant to come in and join her, to make love to her aching body and take her away from all of the relentless questions that were demanding answers she didn't have.

When she exited the shower, a fresh change of clothes lay on the opulent counter top, mocking her foul mood. *Damn her.* She closed her eyes and tried to massage away the nagging ache growing in her temples. She hated being a bitch. They seemed like nice people, but all she wanted to do was scream at them to leave her the hell alone and get back to finding a way to Jauhar. She didn't know why Issa had lied to her, but it didn't keep her from loving him. Jauhar still had to pay for his murder.

She pulled on the fresh blue jeans and tank top before fingering the larger tangles from her hair and pulling it back with a rubber band she found around a clump of other toiletries sitting beside the sink. Her mouth watered when she spotted the fresh toothbrush and toothpaste packaged neatly beside the sink. It had been a while since she'd felt this clean. She wasn't sure if her heart could take another look of pity from Grant, but at least now she felt strong enough to set him straight. *Shit! Shit! Shit!* Missing a step, her swollen ankle collided with the cabinet. "Ouch." As long as she didn't have to run anywhere she should be able to hold her own.

CHAPTER TWENTY-ONE

What do you mean he's gone? Thalia could hear herself asking that question over and over in her mind as she sat crammed like a sardine into an aisle seat on a jumbo jet bound for the U.S. The flight attendants made their way down the aisle, pushing and shoving the bags into the overhead compartments as the last few passengers boarded and they prepared for takeoff.

He'd left her, taking the thumb drive and what was left of her heart with him. He'd stolen the only chance she had at revenging Issa's murder and left her with nothing. Not even him. She'd been right. He no longer wanted her. She'd seen it in his eyes, the passion and fire that once called her to him was replaced by nothing but pity and disappointment.

"Natalie."

Ignoring Daniel, she shifted restlessly in her seat, desperate to be somewhere, anywhere, other than where she was.

"Natalie, I know he cared for you. He's just…"

Fuck Grant! The urge to hit something grew stronger with each claustrophobic second that ticked by. She could feel the raging scream building in her chest as she wavered constantly between anger and anguish over losing a piece of her soul to a man she knew better than to trust. *God, I trusted him.* How could she have been so foolish?

He'd lied to her. She'd been utterly stunned when Daniel told her Grant had left and was never coming back. Was he only after the thumb drive all along? He'd left no reason as to why he'd done it. Only clear instructions for her to leave with Daniel and Rebecca and never come back. No goodbye. Nothing. No reason for her to believe what they had was anything but a lie. Now she was supposed to follow along and let go of everything? Give up on seeing justice done for Issa? Let go of what she'd thought she'd seen in Grant's eyes when they last made love in that ramshackle hotel room in Mutare? All because Daniel was his so called friend she was supposed to trust him now?

She turned and studied the man sitting next her; really looked at him. He was a nice man with a kind heart. She didn't fear him and honestly believed he meant her no harm. The simple truth was that she didn't know him. Even if all they had told her was true, it didn't change anything. She wasn't that little girl in those pictures anymore. She wasn't the damaged person who had supposedly been beaten and raped and sold into a life of slavery either. She was just a woman who had no memory of being a girl, seeking justice for the only person who had ever loved her.

Her fingers trailed down her neck as she fought against the suffocating noose of confusion that threatened to strangle the life out of her each time she thought about those pictures. She couldn't allow herself to slip into another panic attack. Not now. She had to think, dammit!

The only thing she knew for sure? Issa had lied to her, but he was still the only father she'd ever known. Not the man sitting next to her. What was left of her life, as dismal as it was, was in India. She didn't need Grant or these other people. She hadn't asked for any of this. She couldn't allow them to distract her from achieving justice for Issa. She had one goal, one purpose, and blindly following them away from that purpose was not, and had never been, part of the plan. *I have to get off this plane.*

Decision made, adrenaline rushed through her veins as she quietly flipped the latch open on her seatbelt and let the ends slide behind her back. Her legs and arms tingled with anticipation as she waited. An oncoming passenger pushed his way down the aisle, his overstuffed carry-on bumping against her seat on his way by. She saw her one and only chance and took it, darting from her seat, rushing to the front of the plane. Shoving past a frantic flight attendant, she ignored the sharp pain in her ankle and sprinted up the jet way, then back through the gate. A horde of security guards gave chase, their voices growing closer as they closed the small amount of distance the element of surprise had given her.

Her borrowed shoes, half a size too big, squeaked on the industrial linoleum floor as stride after stride she pushed her way through the throngs of people disembarking from their flights. The terminal narrowed and the crowd thickened as she neared the main security checkpoint. Crashing into bystander after bystander, she didn't bother looking back or apologizing. All she could see through the tunnel vision created by her frantic state and determination to escape was the wall of glass doors at the end of the terminal that would lead to her freedom. Until she hit what could only be described as brick wall.

Her legs pumped frantically but found no purchase as she was lifted from the ground, her head still spinning form the collision. Everything happened so quickly. The room spun. Her heart pounded relentlessly in her chest. Shouting voices in the distance were drowned out by grunts and curses in a language she didn't understand. She couldn't right herself or focus on anything but the blurred faces that whirled by as she was dragged away into a darkened hallway.

She screamed for help, or at least she thought she did. Her arms and legs were moving but connected with nothing as she fought for distance from her captors. Hot, damp air filled her lungs as she was dragged through a series of doors and then outside the air conditioned building. She'd lost her shoes in her struggle to escape and the scorching, rough concrete bit into the soles of her feet with each staggered step she took. A dark sedan sat beyond the doorway, surrounded by three more men she didn't recognize and one man she would never forget. The black patch he wore over his right eye didn't mask the satisfied expression behind it. Hamisi's evil grin was the last thing she saw. Fire exploded behind her left eye and everything around her went dark and blissfully quiet.

~*~*~*~*~

"Here you go, sir." Grant smiled his irresistible delivery guy smile and took the clipboard from the nice looking receptionist, giving her a flirty wink as he handed her the package marked as *urgent delivery*. He turned and left through the front doors of the posh, seaside apartment building, throwing her a final glance over his shoulder on his way out. Security in these places was usually a joke at best, but this one had a few extra layers to wade through. High class pussy demanded high class protection he guessed, but none of it made a difference to him.

Thanks to the quick work of Miss Efficient at the front desk and the idiot who came up with the brilliant idea of labeling the valet tickets by the resident's floor number, fifteen minutes later he had the exact location of Jauhar's mistress' apartment and a security key fob that granted him access to her floor.

He'd spent the last three days running intel and watching Jauhar's ocean front compound. It was nothing less than he'd expected. Guards posted in random shifts both inside and out. No set pattern of ground sweeps, so there was little chance of sneaking in undetected. Unlike most, he seemed to run a heavier guard presence at night. Getting in under the cover of darkness alone was unlikely.

Based on the satellite photos and security system plans Diver had been able to dig up after they'd had a fuck-all chat about his role in their little partnership, his chances of storming the compound, killing Jauhar, and getting out undetected were slim at best.

If he managed to scale the fifteen foot high concrete security wall and slip past the team of lackeys on the outside, it would be next to impossible to penetrate the building undetected with the amount of technology inside. Motion and infrared sensors built into the walls, bulletproof glass shutters that activated on voice command and covered every entry and exit point. There was a panic room in the east wing situated between what he was sure was Jauhar's bedroom and office. It wasn't listed on any of the plans, but his gut told him there was an escape tunnel that led from the panic room away from the compound. He'd thought briefly about going in through the tunnel, but it would take too long to find the entry point if there was one. No. If he was going in it would have to be through the front door.

After the initial shock of what he'd learned at Issa's grave had worn off, he'd been able to see things much more clearly and had scrapped his initial plan. Now that he knew who the key players were, there were some things about the hit on Issa that didn't quite add up. If his suspicions were correct, all of the intel he'd gathered might be useless anyway. There was a fifty-fifty chance Jauhar might not even be there. He hadn't seen him step foot outside the compound since the day before, but he also didn't have eyes in the back of his head or time to wait around for additional visual confirmation. The heavy guard presence told him he was there, and that's all he needed to know for now.

During his three days of recon, it had only taken him one day to nail down the one weakness in Jauhar's security. The raven-haired bombshell that had Jauhar by his balls was a royal pain in his security team's collective ass. In the two and a half hours he'd shadowed her from Jauhar's compound on Juhu Beach, he'd seen her break protocol no less than twenty times. The gorillas guarding her didn't even bother getting out of the car to walk her to her apartment after she'd finished massaging her driver's tonsils with her tongue. After the day they'd had they would run, not walk, when they saw her car pulling back into Jauhar's compound. Now was the time to strike and she would be his ticket in.

The one thing he hadn't counted on when he entered the luxury flat was the innocent face of the small, dark haired boy who greeted him at the door after a single knock. A shriek of terror erupted from the woman on the far side of the room as he pushed his way in and scooped the little boy under one arm, the other skillfully and calmly taking aim at her with the silenced throw-away piece he'd acquired the day before.

"Not one word." He motioned with the gun for her to take a seat on the white leather sofa. *Fuck.* He hadn't come here to screw up a kid's head, but he had no choice. There was no backing out. He was now fully committed. "Is there anyone else in the apartment?"

The woman shook her head as she dropped to the sofa, pleading sobs muffling any reply she tried to give. "Don't move." Keeping the gun trained on his target, he shouldered the partially opened bedroom door and peered inside. Quickly and silently he cleared the other two small rooms before returning to the main parlor where the mistress sat, a pleading look of shock and horror marring her unusual beauty.

"Is he Jauhar's?" When she shook her head no, he lowered the crying boy to the floor and knelt down to comfort him. "Hey, little guy. What's your name?"

"He does not speak English," the mistress cried, perched anxiously on the edge of the cushion, her arms outstretched, pleading for the boy. "Please. He is my sister's son."

Shit. This could be a problem. "When will she be back?" There was no room in his plan for a four year old, and he couldn't leave him there by himself.

"She is on holiday with her husband."

"You have a babysitter, yes? Someone who watched him while you were fu…servicing Jauhar earlier?" Jesus, he was going to hell already. What difference did it make if he cursed in front of the child?

"Nadia, yes." She nodded frantically, her eyes darting continuously between him, the gun in his hand, and her nephew.

He scooped up the boy, ignoring the woman's escalated pleas as he walked to the hall table and grabbed her designer purse. Forgoing what he knew would be a time consuming, blind and fruitless search, he dumped the contents onto the table and grabbed the cellphone from the pile of other useless shit women seemed to carry with them. He scrolled through her contacts, found Nadia's name and tapped the call button before tossing the phone to her. "It's ringing. Tell her you need her to take the boy for the night." He tucked his gun under his arm and reached up to caress the little boy's tears away, never taking his eyes from her. "Let's make sure she doesn't ask any questions, got it?" He didn't have the stomach to hurt the kid, but she didn't need to know that. She understood his warning loud and clear.

He had to hand it to her. Mistress of The Year was smooth under pressure. She had quite the acting ability, which played perfectly into his plan as they approached the gated entrance to Jauhar's compound. "Remember," he said as he pulled the driver's cap down to better shield his eyes and turned into the drive. "One misstep and your sister will be coming home to plan her son's funeral."

"You do not need to remind me," she said, her tone dripping with venom and disdain. She held Grant's stare in the rearview mirror a moment longer than he was comfortable with before she turned her head and stared silently out the passenger window into the surrounding darkness.

As was customary through his earlier observations, she sat behind him in the back of the dark sedan. Normally he would have her sitting next to him where he could keep his eyes on her. That would have been too risky even considering her rebellious behavior. He needed everything to appear annoyingly normal for this to work, and that meant she sat behind him as he played the dutiful servant driver.

Clearing her car of anything that could be used as a weapon and stripping her of all her clothes except for a scarlet red, silk robe he'd found lying across her bed only lowered his apprehension level a fraction of an inch. If she chose to try to escape or alert the guards he would have very little recourse to stop her. Other than her belief that he would kill the boy, he held very few other cards in this deadly game he was playing with her. It was the weakest part of his plan, and the sooner this phase was completed the better.

As he'd expected, two of the three security guards ran from the guard shack and disappeared into the darkness as he approached. The third man tried desperately to mask his irritation and disbelief that he'd been abandoned by his comrades. Grant had to work hard not to smirk at how predictable the whole scene was. Leaving the car in drive, he stopped and rolled down the rear window, silently praying to a God he wasn't sure existed that he wasn't about to make a huge mistake.

The young security guard pasted on a fake smile and confidently approached the rear of the car. Grant held his breath, his face hidden from view by the dark tinted windows. "Miss Nadal. How nice to see you again this evening. What brings you here at such an unexpected hour?"

"As usual it is none of your business, Nigel. Now please let me through."

"Miss Nadal, you cannot be here unannounced at this hour. Mr. Jauhar is not...."

"Stuff it, Nigel." She waved him off and casually pulled a mirrored compact from the small clutch he'd allowed her bring along, convincingly unconcerned as she checked her flawless lipstick. "Call him if you must, but it will ruin the surprise. And I am sure he will be unprepared to hear how you inappropriately ogled me after you ordered me to disrobe."

Grant nearly blew his own cover as he watched her from the rear view mirror. She reluctantly lowered her shoulder, her silk robe falling to her waist, exposing her more than ample, naked breasts for all to see. The Oscar moment came when she cast a pleading, embarrassed glance toward the security camera mounted above Nigel's head. The idiot looked as if he was about to forfeit what little dinner he may have had as he tripped over himself to open the ten foot tall iron security gate.

"Well played." Grant smirked as he slowly passed through the entrance and navigated the narrow, dimly lit drive to the main house.

"You do not get to be in my position with a man like Kafeel Jauhar without possessing some elevated level of acting ability." She shrugged back into her robe and flicked the compact into her small clutch. "It does not matter. We are both dead the minute we walk through that door. I only hope my sister will forgive me."

Grant cut the lights as he approached the front of the main house and slowed to a stop under the architecturally overstated arched portico. He felt little pity for the woman. She knew what kind of man Kafeel Jauhar was, yet she still shared his bed for a small piece of his ill-gotten gains.

"*We* are not walking through that door, Miss Nadal." He turned in his seat and raised his silenced pistol, taking precise aim as he began the next phase of his lethal plan. "I am."

CHAPTER TWENTY-TWO

"What in bloody hell…?" The middle-aged butler met them at the top of the short flight of stairs that led up to the front door.

"Help, she's been shot." Grant shoved the bleeding but conscious brunette into the confused doorman's arms before knocking him out cold with the butt of his gun. Swiftly and silently he moved down the hall toward the security command post where he knew the other ill-prepared guards on duty would be scrambling to get their shit together.

A group of shadows preceded the muffled sounds of scuffling feet moving in Grant's direction from an adjacent room at the end of the long hall. He darted into the nearest open door before they spilled into the hallway. The house had gone quiet, something that didn't quite sit right in his gut.

Crouched out of sight, he could make out three distinct sets of movements as they approached. One man on point as the other two followed a few steps behind. They didn't pause to check the darkened rooms they passed before they moved beyond the doorway where Grant was hidden and turned towards the front entrance. *Clumsy bastards.*

He closed his eyes, letting everything else fall away and counted the seconds, listening to their heavy footfalls as they moved away. *One. Two. Three. Four.* His blood raced through his veins with explosive velocity, giving him a taste of the high he once craved. The power of a calculated kill. It wasn't something he'd ever been proud of, but he understood it. He harnessed the energy and used it to his advantage, the ability to do so making him one of the best in his field. This was his true nature, coming back to him with lethal ease. He could so easily let it take him over and kill everything with a pulse, but he kept the leash tight. He was in complete control as he rose from his position and stepped soundlessly into the hall. Three calm breaths later, two of the guards lay dead at his feet. The third wordlessly pleaded for his life as Grant dragged him back into the control room, the razor-sharp and bloody blade in his hand resting against the man's throat with enough pressure to break the skin.

"Enter the code."

The guard gave a quick shake of his head in protest. A desperate groan hissed through his clenched teeth, the blade slicing deeper into his skin. With his free hand, Grant reached into the man's pocket and withdrew his wallet. Holding it up, he flipped it open to reveal the guard's identification and address, along with some other useful pictures. "You're going to die tonight. Whether or not they join you is entirely up to you." He stuffed the worn, leather wallet into his coat pocket and shoved the guard into the metal chair in front of the bank of computers. "You have three seconds to cut the surveillance and motion sensors."

The guard's nervous fingers flew over the keyboard in front of him. Grant watched as monitor after monitor blipped to blank screens until nothing was visible from the central control room. "Ple-please." The guard swallowed and Grant could smell the blood as it ran red down the man's neck, mixing with the mingled scents of sweat and fear that permeated the air inside the small room. "Please don't kill me. I won't—"

"The backup drive. Wipe it." The guard wasted no time complying as Grant stood at his back, his hand steady at the guard's throat. Within moments he'd disabled Jauhar's entire security command. No one would be able to place him there.

"How many are left?" The guard shrugged and Grant lunged at the man with viper speed. He didn't have the time or the patience to deal with this kind of bullshit. The asswipe may not value his life, but he'd damn sure mourn the loss of his balls before he died. With a flick of his wrist the sharp point of the knife sliced through the crotch of the man's pants. "How many guards are left?"

"Fo-four! There are four left!"

"Four all together? Inside and out?"

The guard nodded frantically, his body strained against the back of the chair watching in horror as a trickle of his own blood pooled in the seat beneath him.

There were only four guards left. Counting this loser and the two he'd taken out, it was less than half the total number he'd counted on duty the three nights before. If three of them were the fuck-ups from the front gate, that meant there was only one other man on post inside the house. *Sonofabitch!* He'd been right. Jauhar had been tipped off.

"If you live through the night you're going to need a new job to feed those twins. Choose your next employer with caution." Grant slammed his face into the top of the desk, breaking his nose and knocking him out cold. Satisfied the guard would no longer be a problem, he tossed the leather wallet onto the desk and left the room.

Moving through the mammoth hallways, his footsteps silent against the plush carpet, he found his way to the servant's staircase and swiftly moved through the second floor. His gut instinct screamed at him to pull back, every one of his senses set to maximum sensitivity levels. The whole thing reeked of a setup. Why else would Jauhar have cut his security forces by half? The other half was probably waiting for him behind one of the closed doors in front of him.

"Mr. Jauhar is not here, I'm afraid."

Grant froze, his back glued to the wall outside what was supposed to be Jauhar's office as the unfamiliar voice raced down his spine. Cold sweat peppered his forehead as dread and regret churned in his gut. A twisted chuckle echoed through the opened door from inside the room, confirming the worst possible outcome.

"Come in, Mr. Kendal. There's no use in prolonging the inevitable."

Fuck-fuck-fuck. He'd been made. His eyes closed on a steadying breath. *Dammit! Shit!* He'd had called him by his alias. Only a hand full of people knew him as Grant Kendal, and this dickwad, whoever he was, shouldn't be one of them unless he'd seriously screwed up somewhere along the line. *Dammit!*

He was right. There was no sense dicking around with this guy. If they knew he was coming, Jauhar would be long gone. He might as well get as much intel as he could before he killed this fucker, because no way in hell was he giving up. He'd dog Jauhar to the ends of the earth if that's what it took to make sure Thalia was safe.

With a grunt, he pushed away from the wall and stepped through the darkened doorway, his pistol aimed at the looming shadow before him when a blinding light suddenly flooded the room. Squinting through the glare, he found himself surrounded by nothing but unoccupied office furniture and old books as he faced the still unfamiliar threat.

"Please, have a seat."

Grant sized the man up. Six-two, one-ninety, maybe two hundred pounds. It was difficult to tell with the traditional, white sarong he was wearing covering most of his features. He looked like a native Indian, but spoke English with a cultured British accent. His stance and tone screamed basic asshole with a god complex, but something in his cold, black eyes told him not to underestimate this man.

"No thanks." Gun in hand, he inched his way to the right side of the room. If he was about to be ambushed by a team of guards he was going to have the wall at his back and go down shooting. He'd be damned if he wasn't going to take at least a few down with him. "Who are you? Where's Jauhar?"

"I would like to thank you for taking care of a few...*personnel* problems I've been putting off for far too long. You cannot just fire people in this business. They see too much." An incredulous chuckle bubbled past the man's lips and he ruefully shook his head. "I venture to say Mr. Jauhar will not be as pleased to hear the news of Nadal's accident. She may have been a pain in my arse, but he seemed to be quite fond of her specific talents."

So this loser was Jauhar's head of security. Grant tensed as the man reached for a box sitting atop the obnoxiously oversized executive desk. When he raised his gun the man paused, his steady hand hovering over the box's varnished lid. "Cigar?"

"Stop fucking with me and tell me what you were left here to tell me." The man casually shrugged and began to sink into the plush oversized chair behind the desk. "I don't think so." Grant motioned for him to move from behind the desk. "Over there. Keep your hands where I can see them."

"I am unarmed," the man chuckled and held out his hands, palms up for Grant to see. "I believe we can dispense with the threats and discuss our business like civilized humans, can we not?"

"I said move!" Grant was one second away from making dog food out of this guy's frontal lobe.

The man leaned forward, resting his palms on top of the desk, his fingers splayed wide. "It is not I who you should be concerned with, Mr. Kendal." He pinned Grant with a deadly stare. Ice filled his veins as the corner of the man's mouth pulled into a wicked, knowing grin. "Over your left shoulder is a television monitor. If you want answers, Mr. Kendal, I would advise you to turn it on. I believe you will find the answers to everything you wish to know."

Keeping the gun trained on his target, Grant backed away until he could easily reach the giant monitor. Sliding his finger along the bottom edge, he pushed the button and the screen blipped to life. He studied the crude, greenish image on the screen, an eerie feeling churning to life in the pit of his stomach as the night vision camera zoomed out. He could see the outline of a woman's body lying on a table in the dark room; her arms stretched high above her head, the top half of her face covered by some sort of cloth or blindfold. Her mouth parted on a silent cry, her head turning frantically back and forth as a bulky, male figure moved into the picture, partially blocking the woman from view as the sound of ripping fabric filled his ears. A familiar whimper of fear leaked through the speakers as the woman twisted away, trying desperately to free her arms. *Jesus Christ! No!*

"Hand over the thumb drive and you can walk out of this house and disappear back into whatever cave you live in. No questions asked." Grant watched in horror as the sick fuck on the screen touched Thalia, rubbing his slimy hands over her beautiful skin. "Or we can watch together as he takes her apart, inch by inch."

Fuck, no. This was not happening. It had to be a trick. She was supposed to be on a plane with Daniel two days ago! Before he could convince himself it was a lie, Thalia's voice rang unmistakably clear through the speakers. The sound of defeat in her tone nearly brought him to his knees as she pleaded with her captor.

Fire raced through his veins, his lungs tightening in his chest as they filled over and over with panicked breath after panicked breath. A thick hand clamped over his shoulder and he flinched, barely able to contain the raging fire inside that pushed him to the edge of his sanity. "Don't think your Thalia gave you up without a fight, my friend. Jauhar can be quite persuasive with the women."

His well-defined and tightly leashed control snapped. He shrugged the man off and pushed him away, a wildly thrown punch finding nothing but air as Jauhar's henchman calmly stepped away untouched. The gun in his hand felt larger than life and every ounce of his focus was drawn to it. One bullet and this piece of shit would never utter her name again. His normally calm hand shook almost violently as his finger tightened against the trigger. Panic fueled his rage; a deadly cocktail of emotions he knew could be his end if he didn't rein it in. And fast. He wanted to kill this mother fucker; rip him apart limb by limb and put a bullet between his eyes for even thinking of touching her, but it would solve nothing. He fought every ounce of training and instinct he'd ever possessed not to pull the trigger. He needed to think goddammit!

Time. He needed time and information. Most of all, he needed to make that bastard touching Thalia pay! Forcing himself to keep his eyes on his target and not on the screen, his mind raced to come up with a plan. Fear paralyzed his instincts. He couldn't function like this!

"I don't have it," he spat, fighting like mad to tune out the desperate cries for help blaring from the screen behind him.

The parasite laughed. Actually laughed! He was wrong. Grant made a silent promise right then and there. If he got out of there alive, this man would never see the mercy of a bullet. If it was with his last dying breath he would see this man die screaming.

"Mr. Jauhar thought you would say that." The man turned and paced back to the desk. He took an expensive looking cigar from the box and lit it. The acrid stench filled the air as he took his time to savor the taste before he exhaled the putrid smoke and continued. "I'm sure Jauhar will be able to find a brothel somewhere in Cambodia that could make a profit from her flesh. While light skinned girls such as your girl can be very lucrative, I'm not sure how attractive she will look once Hamisi is finished with her."

His insides twisted as images of those evil, filthy places littered his thoughts, threatening the limited amount of control he'd been able to gather. They were nothing but slaughter houses for the young and innocent where children and women were drugged, beaten, raped and discarded over and over by sick, rich men who thought they were entitled. Bile rose in his throat and he swallowed it back. *Turn it off.* His teeth ground together, his jaw aching with the force of his efforts to close that door. The harder he tried to tune it out the closer the unfamiliar terror came to consuming him. He couldn't afford to lose it now. If she was still alive... No! She was alive. He had to believe that. She needed him. He was no good to her like this. He. Would. Not. Fail. Her.

Digging in, he channeled his training, something he hadn't had to do in a decade. From a dark place deep inside, a violent tempest of anger and resentment was born. Severing any ties to the useless, crippling feelings of love and sympathy he'd only recently discovered, he shut down every other emotion he possessed one by one. He embraced the rage that tore its way to freedom and locked on to the trained killer he'd spent the last year and a half trying to destroy. Every nerve ending, every cell hummed to life in perfect unison. He felt the moment it happened, the moment when everything else fell away and nothing else mattered but the mission; the moment when the beast inside him surfaced from a deep sleep and took its first breath in over a year. He welcomed it, giving it full rein and control. It was like an alcoholic tasting a fine whiskey after years of abstention. A warm calm fell around him, bringing with it a lethal clarity he was shocked to discover that he'd missed.

He filtered the last ten minutes through fresh new eyes, and Grant laughed as he saw the many flaws in this idiot's demand. If Jauhar knew he was coming then he also knew he no longer had the thumb drive. This douchebag had been left behind to rot and he didn't even know it. A new plan unfolded before him, his thoughts firing with a sharp intensity he hadn't had in months. It felt good. He laughed again, not because there was anything funny, but because he couldn't believe they actually thought him to be that careless. And because he felt fucking incredible!

"She could already be dead for all I know." He forced himself to look at the screen. Nothing but vengeance filled his soul as he watched Thalia flail like a fish on that goddamn table, her clothes being cut from her body piece by piece. "Take me to her. Let me see that she's still alive." He turned his venomous glare away from the horrid scene playing out in front of him and focused it on Jauhar's hired hand. "And if she walks away with so much as a single scratch, so help me God, the contents of that thumb drive will be front page news in every newspaper on the face of this planet. Jauhar will have every agency known to man crawling up his ass to—"

"Maybe you didn't hear me, Mr. Kendal."

The blast of three consecutive gunshots filled the room, plastic from the bullet-riddled monitor ricocheting off the hand-carved book cases to pepper the marble floor beneath his feet. Grant walked over to the desk and picked the bastard up from the floor, shoving him into the leather chair before he put a bullet in his left kneecap, the right one already blown to smithereens. "Call me Lieutenant."

CHAPTER TWENTY-THREE

This asshole may have thought he knew who he was dealing with, but he'd pissed off the wrong damn assassin. Not a single tremor was evident in Grant's outstretched hand as he held the gun to the loser's head. The calm, smug expression on his face had shifted a bit. If Grant was a betting man, he'd call odds that he'd pissed his sarong. It was actually refreshing to watch as shock gave way to understanding and reality finally set in, the first hint of alarm blooming in his eyes as he realized who he was dealing with. *That's right you piece of human garbage. You're going to die today.*

"Until I see her with my own eyes I'm under the impression that I hold the only important card in this game you're playing. You got that? She dies, no drive. She doesn't walk away under her own volition, no drive." He took a slight step in the asshole's direction, taking aim at his throat. "One shot and I sever your head from your spine. Make the call, Mr…?"

"Hinjal."

"Mr. Hinjal." Grant nodded and pulled the phone to the edge of the desk and punched the speaker button, the sound of a dial tone filling the room. "Make the call to Jauhar. Explain your new circumstances and arrange for transport or I kill you where you stand and find her myself."

He watched the dead man dial the number, under no misconception he was gambling with Thalia's life. These bastards had her. If they hadn't already killed her they would. The only way to win was to not play their game. He was playing his own game now. His rules.

After a series of beeps connected the call, a voice Grant recognized immediately resonated over the line with a curt greeting. *Don Lalia.*

"Jauhar…please." Hinjal's pleading voice quaked, his eyes darting nervously between Grant and the phone. So Don Lalia was Jauhar's new bitch. Grant masked his reaction to the revelation, careful not to reveal that he knew exactly who had answered the call. Considering what Thalia had told him, he wasn't surprised to confirm his suspicions that they were working together.

"Did you kill him?"

Grant pushed the muzzle of the gun deeper into Hinjal's jugular and kicked his dangling lower leg with the toe of his boot. Hinjal swallowed back a scream, his bloody hands grasping the edge of the desk for purchase. "Jauhar! Ahh, dammit! Get Jauhar on the bloody phone!"

A few moments passed, only the melodic sounds of Hinjal's pain-filled breaths hissing through his clenched teeth filling the room before Jauhar's voice came over the open line.

"Good evening, Lieutenant. I trust you have made yourself at home. How do you American's say it? Mi casa, es su casa?"

"That's Spanish you dumb fuck."

"You knew?" Hinjal growled into the phone. "You fucking knew who he was and you set me up!"

Jauhar chuckled. "You are not the only one cleaning up loose ends, Hinjal." The connection grew eerily silent, his tone reflecting no such humor when he continued. "You have failed me for the last time, my friend. I have no further need of your services. Oh, and thank you, Lieutenant, for returning my property to me. You have been quite useful. I am very grateful for the opportunity to reacquaint myself with her."

Grant lunged for the phone when he heard the click, Jauhar disconnecting the call. *No!* He pushed Hinjal from behind the desk, dumping the worthless pile of garbage onto the floor. He picked up the receiver and punched in Diver's number, what seemed like a lifetime screaming by as he waited for a secure connection to go through. "Come on, come on, *come on*! Pick the fuck up!"

"Where the hell have you been? I've got sixteen different kinds of hot shit piling up here. Fuck me six ways to Sunday if—"

"You've got fifteen seconds to run a trace on the last number called from this phone or you won't have a dick to fuck with come Sunday." Grant pulled drawer after drawer from the desk as he barked orders at Diver, dumping the contents of each one until he found the gun he knew Hinjal had been counting on using. "I want an eye in the sky and real time updates on that location sent to this number." He walked over to Hinjal, pulling a cellphone from his front pocket and flipping it on to give Diver the number.

"I can't get clearance for a UAV, boss. This is off the books, remember?"

"Isn't everything we do off the damn books?" *Shit!* "Contact Deputy Director Keller and get him to authorize it. And make it happen yesterday, Diver!"

"We've got a lock on the girl, if that's what this is about."

Grant's spine stiffened, his fingers tightening around the receiver until the plastic cracked. "What? Where? Why the hell didn't you say you had her?"

"As I said. I've been waiting on you to check in." Grant pulled the receiver from his ear and looked at it, his blood pressure rising to critical levels. He wished desperately that he could reach through the damn phone and squeeze the idiot's throat until his eyes bled. "I've got it. The call was routed by a cellular tower thirteen miles southwest of your location near downtown Mumbai. Give me two more seconds and I'll tap the GPS."

"The girl, dammit! What's her location and how the hell did you find her?" Grant pinched the bridge of his nose and tried to take a deep breath.

"The redhead. The clothes she gave the girl had a tracking device sewn in. Director Keller is already on the ground in Navi. No visual confirmation, but his whole team is about to move in."

Navi? That's almost forty kilometers from Mumbai. Grant turned and stared at what was left of the video monitor, his mind racing to pick apart the details of what he'd seen. The bastard on the screen had removed her clothes. Shredded them. If he hadn't killed her, Jauhar wouldn't leave her there. So why the hell were he *and* Don Lalia forty kilometers away in Mumbai? *What kind of game are you playing?* Had Thalia been moved to a different location? Or had they already killed her?

His fingers tightened around the receiver again, his other hand scrubbing over the rough stubble on his jaw. *Christ!* With the help of his Washington partners, Jauhar had been calling his every goddamn move. Would he have anticipated the call trace and was trying to lead him away from her? Or had they found the tracker in Thalia's clothes, moved out, and left Keller's team to walk blindly into an ambush? He could feel the seconds bleeding away as he tried to figure it out. If Thalia was still alive, they were seconds he knew she didn't have.

"Warn the team it could be a setup and get me that location in Mumbai." Grant couldn't take the chance that he was missing something and have Keller's team pull out. If she was still in Navi, he wanted her out yesterday. He'd cover the Mumbai location on his own until they could make a visual confirmation.

"Shit! You think so?"

"I wouldn't have said so if I didn't think it was important. Christ, Diver. Get your head out of your ass and get me that address!"

Diver blew out a frustrated breath and Grant bit back another curse. All he wanted was that damn address. "I just sent the digits to the cellular number you gave me. It's an apartment building on the lower eastside." Grant opened the message and entered the location into the mapping app already loaded on Hinjal's phone. "If we can't get a bird in the air, I've tapped what few traffic cams are posted nearby. I'll let you know if anything moves in or out. Give me some time and I'll see if I can get a visual inside."

Thank fuck! That was the best piece of news Grant had heard in weeks. "If the team pulls a dry run in Navi, get them to Mumbai. I'm on my way there now."

Not one to break a promise, even to himself, he turned to the pile of human trash lying on the floor, blood and urine staining his once pristine white sarong. Unmoved by the pleading look on the coward's face, he crouched down next to his lower legs and admired his work, the gun he'd found in the desk leveled steadily at Hinjal's forehead.

"I don't have much time." He glanced at the clock on the wall then back to the dead man breathing. "Seconds, actually. Unfortunately for me I'm going to have to make this quick." He reached out with his gloved hand and grabbed a handful of the shattered bone protruding from Hinjal's knee, shoving his thumb beneath what was left of his kneecap. His grip tightening as the man squealed and flailed on the floor like the trapped pig he was, he glanced back at the clock. The seconds tick by as Hinjal's screams filled the room, Grant's patience running thin as he watched Thalia's time tick away. Without one second of remorse, his finger tightened on the trigger, his deadly gaze conveying his message loud and clear. *Die screaming, mother fucker.*

~*~*~*~*~

She'd suspected Grant's motives were less than noble when she first learned he'd taken the thumb drive and abandoned her, but Thalia's heart wouldn't allow her to fully accept the traitorous thoughts. Deep down she still believed he wouldn't betray her. She'd been so wrong.

After she was stripped of her clothes, was led into another room, stumbling repeatedly with her injured ankle and her hands bound tightly in front of her. Once the blindfold was removed she got her first look at her worst nightmare. Hamisi's evil chuckle sent a chill down her spine as he brutally yanked her arms above her head and hooked them to one of the many chains dangling ominously from the low ceiling above. *Oh shit.*

As she thought he was about to rearrange her face the same way she had his, a sharp order was barked from the opposite side of the room. Hamisi growled in frustration, but turned away immediately as an imposing figure stepped confidently from the shadows.

"Jauhar," he spat through his teeth, giving him a curt nod of respect.

Jauhar. Hatred boiled in Thalia's veins, her body lunging toward him despite her restraints. Her shoulders alighted with fire when the chain was pulled tighter above her head to halt her advance. *One step closer, you murdering bastard.* He didn't seem affected by her savage response to his presence. If anything, he appeared amused. His tall, thick frame relaxed as he approached, his hands lazily resting inside the pockets of his crisp dress slacks. His beige shirt looked almost white against his dark skin as he passed beneath the overhead spotlights, his dark eyes dancing with laughter as she hung there seething with desperation and rage.

"Some things never change I see." His lips curled into a grin and Thalia wanted nothing more than to blow his damn head off. "Your Issa was a fool to spoil you as his own." She bit back a curse, watching his every move as he stalked a wide circle around her naked body, stopping short of kicking distance. "We will address his error later, my pet. Right now I have a few questions about your friend." Holding out his hand, he took the stack of papers Hamisi handed him, his cold, calculating eyes never leaving hers. "I believe the ankle cuffs are in order, Ham. I would not want her to cause herself any more trouble than she already has."

Despite her suspicion of betrayal, she covered for Grant as long as she could. When Hamisi and Jauhar demanded she hand over the thumb drive she denied having it, telling them nothing of him. She refused to acknowledge his involvement, even when they showed her a few dark and grainy pictures of him carrying her limp, feverish body from his boat. Another of him leaning in to kiss her forehead after he tucked her into the passenger seat of the vehicle he'd stolen. She remembered nothing of that moment. Her heart ached at how far he'd gone in his ruse, even when he didn't need to act the part. *Why would he kiss me if he didn't have to?*

A loud crack of a whip snapped her attention from the confusing thought. "I don't know who he is. I woke up in a clinic and ran when *Ham's* men blew it up."

Hamisi lunged toward her, Jauhar stopping him with a single, clipped rebuke. Jauhar's previously forgiving expression hardened to one of impatience as he stepped closer to her, so close she could nearly taste his breath when he spoke. "You and I have quite a few things to settle, pet." His warm finger trailed delicately along her hairline, his touch sending bile rushing to the back of her throat. She swallowed it back as he continued his sick game, caressing her cheek before curling his finger under her chin, forcing her to look him in the eyes. "But you must first understand you have choices to make." She strained to meet his gaze. He stood there silent as he studied her for a moment longer, his expression shifting once more. A deep crease appeared between his eyes, his hand tightening on her lower jaw until she'd had no choice but to open her mouth. A bitter taste coated her tongue before he released her jaw. Whatever it was had dissolved before she could spit it out. "Until the day you choose not to lie to me, pet, we will have to use a bit of persuasion to get to the truth."

They had given her some sort of drug. When Jauhar and Hamisi returned ten minutes later, she felt a little funny, but nowhere near inebriated enough to tell them anything. That was until Jauhar had asked her once more about Grant. She spilled everything. Every moment they had spent together, every word of every conversation, every kiss and touch. She knew she was doing it, but she couldn't stop herself. It was like having an out of body experience. As if she was looking down on herself, dangling naked and afraid from a chain as she shared the most intimate details about the man she loved. The one man she hated most in the world was soaking in every syllable. She tried to stop herself, an inner voice screaming over the words she spoke aloud, but nothing she tried kept the words from spilling from her lips. What the hell had they given her?

She didn't know how long she'd blabbered on, but sometime later a man she hadn't seen before entered the room and handed Jauhar a wireless tablet. Even as she was trying to bite her tongue off to keep the words from leaving her head, she told Jauhar he looked like an angel against the glow cast off from the tablet's light. *Shut. The. Hell. Up!*

His head whipped up, a sultry grin pulling at his lips as he closed the distance between them, the feel of his clothes against her bare skin sending an unwanted chill racing down her spine. Jauhar felt her shiver, his regretful expression telling her he knew it was not one of pleasure. "Soon my pet, you will shiver with anticipation for me."

"Never." Her head shook frantically. *Yes! Finally!* It was about damn time she got to tell him off. "You're a murdering pig! I will never want you the way I want Grant."

"Ahh." Jauhar grinned, his lips grazing her ear, his hot breath flowing down her neck. "But you have already confessed to loving a murderous pig, my pet. You see?" He held up the tablet for her to see. She didn't feel dizzy, but everything was out of focus. She had trouble seeing the image on the screen. She shook her head, trying desperately to dislodge the cotton in her brain. When it did finally come into focus, her heart shuddered inside her chest, burning tears welling in her eyes to blur the image again.

"No! It's not possible!" *No! No! No!* "That's not him. He didn't even know me when Issa was murdered." She shook her head, refusing to play into Jauhar's evil hand. "You killed Issa. You killed him in cold blood and I swear I will kill you for it!"

She turned her head away, determined not to believe what she'd seen. Jauhar gripped her chin and forced her to look at him again. His head tilted to the side, his eyes searching hers with focused intent. "You truly do not remember me, do you?"

Remember him? Why the hell would she remember him? She'd never met him until he'd walked into the room shortly after Hamisi's men had stripped her. A second later Jauhar released his grip on her chin and took a step back, amusement dancing in his eyes as his gaze raked over her outstretched body. "I think I am going to like getting reacquainting with you, my pet. But first you must pay the price for that lie you told me when we first began our little chat. And my friend here would like a little word with you regarding a spat you two had a few weeks ago. Oh, do not fret," he chuckled when her eyes widened in panic. "I will not always be so lenient, but today no permanent harm will be a part of your punishment."

He turned away and marched toward the door, tossing the tablet to Hamisi on his way out. "No penetration and no permanent scars." His head turned, tossing a wicked grin in her direction as a mixture of panic and adrenaline burned away any lingering effects of the drug he'd given her. The bastard winked at her before turning back to Hamisi with a nod. "She is yours until midnight."

She'd long ago lost track of the time she'd spent inside the small, dark box Hamisi's men had stuffed her into. Another bone jarring chill wracked Thalia's naked frame, her muscles seizing until she thought her spine would snap in two. It could have been hours, or days, for all she knew. Her only connection to the world outside the box was the sound of Hamisi's bellowing laughter bleeding through the thick walls each time she screamed.

The more she struggled the hotter the inside the box became, the small amount of oxygen inside turning stifling and heavy, disappearing rapidly with each struggling movement until she could feel the fine edge of unconsciousness begin to take its hold. When she thought she would take her last breath, a powerful blast of ice-cold air would explode over her sweaty skin, shocking her back to awareness. It was like being thrown into a frozen pond after soaking in a hot bath, her lungs seizing inside her chest from the sharp sting of the cold air. She was unable to process the fresh wave of oxygen that came with the beginning of each new cycle of torment.

More hours had passed. Lying on her side, the sharp plastic band binding her wrists behind her back sliced deep into her skin, making it feel as if her hands were being severed from her body each time she tried to pull them free. Her throat was raw from screaming, her skin now coated in a dirty sheen of sweat, her hair matted and sticking to the side of her face. She didn't think she would ever know the day when she would beg for Jauhar's mercy, but she was approaching her breaking point with Hamisi's depraved torture.

Eventually she gave up and stopped struggling altogether, unable to do anything but shiver or sweat. She was uncertain if the numbness in her hands and feet was caused from lack of circulation or the extreme cold from the last blast of frigid air, but an entirely different type of pain had spread like fire over a fuel-slicked lake through her entire body, surprisingly more excruciating than the agonizing sting of pins and needles she'd felt before. She was going to die. Surely her body couldn't take much more of this.

Her physical pain was paired with a destructive tide of humiliation and sense of betrayal that suffocated her basic will to survive. Her humiliation wasn't caused by her nakedness. Nor was it caused by being strung up like a fish and hung on naked display in front of the man she'd spent the last year and a half hell-bent on destroying. The last year and a half…it had been a complete lie. She'd been so wrong; about everything.

Grant had played her. She'd bought his entire act. The pictures Jauhar showed her were irrefutable. She couldn't see his face, but she would recognize him anywhere. He was there, standing next to Issa's car; gun in hand, right before he pulled the trigger. She'd been such a fool to believe he'd ever wanted her. He'd only wanted the thumb drive. He wasn't good and noble. He was nothing more than the same wicked capitalist he described Jauhar to be. He'd preyed on her weakness, fed her lies and kept her under his control until she told him where she'd hidden it.

It all made sense now. Why he hadn't turned her over to Hamisi's men when they found her on the island, why he wouldn't allow her to make the call to Jauhar, his suspicious behavior the morning after she'd told him where she'd hidden the thumb drive, all those cheesy lines. *You heal my soul.* She'd been a complete fool. She never could understand why he was so determined to help her. Now she knew why. She thought she'd caused him so much trouble. She was no trouble at all as long as he got what he was after. The only thing she couldn't figure out was what part Daniel and Rebecca played. What did they get out of lying to her? Unless Grant was cutting them into whatever deal he'd struck for the data on the thumb drive. Even that wouldn't explain the pictures of her. She guessed they could be faked, but why? Why not kill her and leave them out of it?

Her brain hurt with so many questions. She'd given him everything; her trust, her love, her heart. She'd given him something she'd been unable to give to any other man; her complete surrender. He'd never once blinked at taking it all when he knew all along he was robbing her. He knew the whole time that he'd taken the one thing in her life she could never get back. *Issa, I'm so sorry.*

Her head rocked against the floor of the box as the last wave of chills left her body, the final ounce of fight remaining inside her following in its wake. Her heart ached with sadness and regret as a memory of Grant's awkward, boyish grin floated on a wave of exhaustion through her battered mind before it faded away into nothingness.

CHAPTER TWENTY-FOUR

"Stand down!" Rebecca could hear the order repeating over the ear pieces the men around her wore, the voice of Grant's friend shouting in her other ear as she pulled up a map of Mumbai on the laptop she'd commandeered from her boss, Deputy Director Dax Keller. *Triple D-K.* Her lips twisted in frustration as she studied the map. After Natalie was snatched from the airport in Mozambique and they had confirmed through airport surveillance that it was Hamisi and Jauhar's men who took her, he'd flown in and taken over her entire case. *What an asshole.*

If it wasn't for her suspicion that Natalie would run and using the opportunity to plant the tracking devices, they wouldn't have a damn clue where Jauhar was hiding. She hated thinking of Thalia's circumstances as a lucky break, but her consequential abduction had blown the lid off an international operation. They were now closer than they had ever been to taking down one of the highest ranking traffickers in the bureau's history. And she'd been cut out of the action with a stiff hand shake and nothing else but a nod of appreciation for her efforts.

She didn't get Keller. As a boss he was…efficient. It was about the only adjective she could use considering the man avoided her like the plague. He was good looking, in a brooding *Thinker* sort of way, always deep in thought or too distracted for common niceties such as '*good morning, Danes*' or *'how's your day?'* The dimples that peeked out beneath his perpetual, sexy five o'clock shadow on those rare occasions when he did grace her with a smile, gave him a hint of boyish charm, but before she could fully appreciate them she was staring at his backside as he walked away. *He does have a nice ass.*

When she did manage to wrangle some time from him, or bump into him in their typical comings and goings around the office, he was polite but curt; nothing but a quick nod or a stern hello before he practically sprinted in in the opposite direction of wherever it was she was going.

In the three months she'd worked for him since transferring from Saint Louis to the D.C. headquarters, she could count on one hand the number of times she'd actually had a two-way conversation with him. And always about work. Granted, she liked not being micromanaged, having to report in three times a day, or being treated like a department lackey. He'd never asked her to play mystery shopper for his wife's birthday gifts, or his mistress'…or both like her old boss. She didn't even know if he had a wife or a girlfriend. She'd heard some of the assistants whispering about him a time or two but never paid much attention. She hadn't had time to care about anything but this case. Still, it would be nice to get a '*hey, nice job, Danes'* out of him every once in a while. Now he was inserting himself into her life's work as if he'd been her partner all along, and taking complete control like an egotistical, glory hound.

Having been banished to a surveillance van nearly twenty kilometers away from the exclusive men's club in downtown Navi where they suspected Hamisi had taken Natalie to meet Jauhar, she listened as Diver relayed the information to Keller on Grant's intended destination and what he'd learned from Jauhar's men.

"We're only twenty minutes from that location." Her head snapped up from the map to see the two other men on the surveillance team shaking their heads.

"Not our problem, Ms. Danes." The jerk with the elephant-sized ears looked up from his computer screen, his jaw flapping as he chewed a Texas-sized piece of bubblegum. "Our orders are to maintain a visual and record all traffic moving in and out of the city until we're ordered to locate elsewhere or to stand down."

"What? What if she's not at that club?" Daniel flew from his cramped seat near the double rear doors. "You're going to leave her there?"

Rebecca held up a staying hand, her eyes pleading with Daniel to back down. She'd assured Keller he wouldn't interfere. Ripping this guy's throat out would definitely be considered interfering. "You've got to be kidding me! We're twenty kilometers away from the primary target and it's almost midnight! What could you possibly pick up from here?"

"Yeah, well, that's what you get when you pull babysitting duty."

Rebecca's gaze snapped over to the second member of the geek squad she'd been stuck with. "Excuse me?"

"Nothing," he whispered, shaking his head.

"Oh, fuck you, Larry. Grow some balls." Dumbo whipped his pen at the other man's chest. "We all know the only reason we're out here tagging minivans and mopeds is because Keller doesn't want her anywhere near this take down."

What? "No, we do not *all* know that! Why the hell not?" How was she supposed to do her job if her boss wouldn't let her? First he moves in and takes over the case she'd spent the last five years of her life building. Now he was banishing her to the fringes of the universe to be guarded by the geek brigade while he got all the credit and glory for taking out Jauhar? Not to mention he was putting Natalie's life at risk by not using every resource available to make sure she was located and extracted safely. *Screw this!*

"Hold on," she barked at Diver, nodding at Larry. "Take my phone and give me yours. Have Diver patch his video feed of the secondary location into your network drives so we know what's going on." She tossed her cellphone to Larry and held her hand out for his. When he didn't immediately give it up, Daniel grabbed him by the hair and pulled him from his seat.

"That's my daughter you're leaving out there to die!" Rebecca's gasp of alarm filled the small interior. When she thought Daniel was about to snap the guy's neck he leaned in close and growled in his hear. "You may think this is a babysitting job, but the most dangerous place for you to be right now is exactly where you are. I will not hesitate to end your miserable excuse of a life if it means saving my daughter's. Hand. Her. Your. Phone."

Larry reached into his pocket and pulled out his cellphone, hurriedly handing it to Rebecca. Dumbo jumped to attention and grabbed Rebecca's cell from Larry before it fell from his trembling hand. *Yeah, who needs to grow a set now?*

"When Diver completes the uplink, don't disconnect the call. We don't want to take the chance of not being able to get him back." Rebecca left lovely Larry to Daniel's mercy, dialing Keller as she unlocked the passenger door and hopped out onto the street. Let Daniel tear them apart. Hell if she cared. They might be following orders, but they weren't her orders.

"Yeah, Larry. What's your status? Why are you calling my cell?" Keller's deep voice rumbled over the line.

"His status is neck deep in shit and sinking fast, Director. Like my job apparently."

"Goddammit!" Dax Keller's voice trailed off into a colorful rant.

"Why do you have me out here under lock and key being guarded by the geek boutique? This was my case, sir. I should be the one—"

"This isn't the time, Danes. We're on strategic stand down and I'm not—"

"You're not using your best resources, sir. We're twenty minutes from the secondary location. If Diver is correct then we have to cover it."

"You are not cleared to go to Mumbai, Danes! You hear me? You're staying where I put you and that's final! Dammit! I knew I should have sent you home."

"Excuse me?" Sent her home? What the hell had she done to this guy to make him treat her with such blatant disrespect? "Why are you doing this, Director? I've worked my ass off on this case!"

"No, Danes. And that's fin—"

"If you want the recognition for the capture you can have it sir, but you can't take a chance like this and let that girl—"

"Do not—!" She cringed when she heard his growl, followed by another long string of inaudible curses. "Listen to me carefully, Danes. This isn't the only intel we have coming in. You don't know everything we're dealing with here."

"And whose fault is that, sir? You won't—"

"Rebecca."

Her steps faltered, her frantic pacing back and forth in front of the van snapping to a screeching halt. He'd never called her Rebecca. She didn't think he even knew her first name. As strange as it was to hear him say it, it was the sudden change in his voice, the silky command in his tone that had the fine hairs at the base of her skull prickling against her neck. *What the hell?* A funny sort of tumble tickled her insides at the sound of her name being spoken with such intensity. They had exchanged more words in the last five minutes than they had the entire time she'd worked for him, and still, the familiarity in his voice felt… astonishingly intimate.

"Rebecca?"

Holy hell, he did it again. This time she could hear a hint of laughter in his tone. A superior sort of chuckle that said he knew exactly what he was doing to her. She leaned against the front of the van, ignoring the flush of embarrassment that colored her face. "Uh, yes sir. I'm here."

"I need you to trust me." His whispered plea pulled at something buried deep inside her and shredded her will to argue, obliterating every cold, indifferent image she'd ever had of him. *Trust him?* It made no sense, but she wanted to believe him.

"What about the—?"

"Rebecca, I don't…I will not beg you. Get back in the van and stay there. Am I clear?" To her frustration, her mouth snapped shut, another warm wave lapping at her frayed nerves, simultaneously calming and annoying the hell out of her.

"Yes, sir." The line went silent before her reluctant capitulation had been ground out, her jaw aching with the effort it took not to scream the words at him. *Trust him?* She stomped to the side of the van, Larry's cellphone clutched in her hand. *Rebecca.* Even through a haze of dissatisfaction with his request, she could still hear her name in that rich, commanding tone. How could one man, *that* man, forever change the sound of her name?

"We have movement."

Rebecca crashed into the bucket seat next to Larry. He seemed to have survived Daniel's wrath with his head still intact, but she could sense a tangible animosity rolling off him in waves. Believing it would be better for everyone if she ignored it for now, she slipped on a spare headset and plugged into the server, adjusting the mic as Larry pointed at something on the screen.

"There! Movement on the rooftop of the building next to the secondary location."

Rebecca tapped the screen and zoomed it in on the dark figure crouched at the edge of the five story building. "That's Grant Kendal. Diver, do you have a live link to him?"

"I have a primary connection to a mobile he picked off one of Jauhar's men, but I can't run a direct patch to you and keep the secure link. You're going to have to talk through me if you have intel, but I can't guarantee he'll respond. He's not in a real chatty mood."

"We need to see what's going on in that building." There were no lights visible from any of the closed windows. Their intel said it was an apartment building, but she saw no sign of movement, inside or out. "Diver, has Jauhar's signal moved since you ran the trace?"

"No, but…give me a second and I might be able to make all your wishes come true." Unless he had Jauhar in cuffs and a cure for stupidity, she highly doubted it. A series of beeps sounded in the background. Without warning, a blood curdling scream exploded from the speakers, followed by a cocktail of evil male laughter. "I've got it! I'm inside the building." Her head snapped up to see Daniel, his face void of blood as he crumbled to his knees.

"Jesus, what the hell are they doing to her?" Daniel covered his ears, his face twisting in agonizing rage at the horrific sounds they had suddenly been patched into. Larry's hands flew to the keyboard, his fingers frantically typing out a message to who she hoped was Director Keller. They had to go in. Now!

Rebecca reached up and flipped off the external speakers, the van going quiet except for the echo of more screams bleeding through the headsets. "We don't know if that's her."

Turning away, she focused on the monitors. She couldn't let the sheer terror on Daniel's face distract her. "Diver, I need a visual!" She had to be able to see what the hell they were going into. Orders or no orders, there was no way in hell she was going to stand by and do nothing.

"I'm trying!" By the frenzied tone in Diver's voice, he was pushed to his limits. She would push him over the cliff if that's what it took. "They're using a femtocell to boost their signals. I've hacked into the booster to get audio from one of the cellphones inside, but I have to find the exact code to patch into the phone's video application. Even then, it's only for one cellphone. I'm only getting this because someone is accessing the signal. As soon as they hang up I'll lose the feed until someone else dials out. It's like playing cellphone roulette."

"I don't care how you do it. Get me inside that building!" Out of the corner of her eye she caught movement on one of the monitors. "Diver, tell Grant to stand down until we have a visual."

Diver laughed, followed by a series of strained coughs. "Sorry, not happening. You haven't worked with him long, have you?"

"I've got twenty more minutes with her!" The growled objection rumbled through the headsets and everyone inside the van froze. *Who is that?* She mouthed to Larry as if they could somehow hear her if she spoke aloud.

"You're time is up, my friend. The American is here." The blood in Rebecca's veins ran cold as Jauhar's voice echoed in her ears. "Wake up, pet. You have company."

"What's going on?" Daniel pushed his way between her and Larry and held his ear next to hers as they listened for more. She held up one finger and shook her head. One look at the man and she could see he was on the verge of a complete meltdown.

She scrambled for the mic as she pulled away from Daniel. "Diver, did you get that? They're on to Grant. He's walking into a trap!"

"He's hearing the same thing you are. I honestly don't think he cares though. He's going in." Rebecca watched the monitor, her last breath lodged next to her stomach inside her throat as Grant disappeared down a darkened stairwell leading from the rooftop of the target building.

"I'm a bit disappointed, Kafeel." Rebecca listened as the second man clicked his tongue in a mocking gesture. "I think the drug took all the fire out of her. I had hoped for a much more spirited fight."

"Wake her up. I want her ready when the American is shown in." She could hear a woman's voice in the background moaning a weakening plea. "It is time she is reminded of who her true master is. I intend to allow our esteemed friend the pleasure of reminding her."

Esteemed friend? "Who is he talking about, Diver?" What the hell was going on? Surely Jauhar wasn't referring to Grant.

An eerie silence flooded the connection before another series of loud tones and beeps blared through the speakers in her headset, followed by Diver's shouted curse. "Dammit! We lost the connection!"

Rebecca pulled off the headset and threw it at the monitor. "Get it back Diver! I don't care what you have to do! Larry, update Keller on the audio confirmation! Jauhar is in that building and we're going in after him."

"I did, but our orders still stand. We're to maintain radio silence until further notice."

"Bullshit!" They had real time confirmation of Jauhar's location in Mumbai, a screaming girl, Grant on the inside, and Keller was cutting off communications? Something was incredibly wrong. She threaded her fingers through her hair, a sigh of desperation spilling from her lips. He was going to blow this whole assignment and feed her to the wolves when the shit hit the fan. She could feel it. Even if it wasn't Natalie they heard, they couldn't sit back and ignore those screams. It didn't matter what intel Keller had, there was no excuse for this. Someone had to do something!

The van rocked on its axels from the force of Daniel's roar as he tore through the crowded cabin and pushed his way to the driver's seat. Chaos erupted as Larry and Dumbo scrambled to reconnect the cables that had been ripped from their equipment in his wake.

"Where are the keys?" Rebecca turned to see Daniel ripping the console to pieces in a destructive search.

"We can't leave our post!" Larry jumped from his seat and lunged for Daniel. Before she could process the consequences, Rebecca pulled her firearm and leveled it at the coward's head.

"Where are the keys?"

Larry fell back a step, his hands raised by his head. "You're crazy, lady. You know that? Keller is going to have your ass for this."

"He can have whatever's left of me after I take down Jauhar. Now hand over the damn keys!"

"I don't have them."

Behind Larry, Dumbo slipped his hand into his pocket and Rebecca took aim. Her insides trembled with adrenaline, but her finger remained steady on the trigger. “I don’t think so.”

“If you want to come get the key out yourself I won’t complain.”

Jackass. “Hand them over. Slowly.”

Dumbo fished around in his pocket and stepped around Larry, ignoring her warning to stay where he was. With complete disregard for the gun, he took her free hand and slapped the single key into her palm, his fingers wrapped in a tight grip around her wrist. “Wave to the camera, sweetheart.” He jerked his chin toward a dark orb mounted in the corner above her shoulder, a crooked, sarcastic grin displaying his arrogant satisfaction. “You may have Keller’s dick in a knot, but even he won’t be able to save your ass on this one.”

What the hell is that supposed to mean? Before she could ask, he and Larry spilled out onto the street, the van door slamming shut behind them. Daniel yanked the key from her hand and started the engine. “Put the damn gun away if you’re not going use it.” Without warning, he executed a sharp U-turn toward Mumbai and floored the gas pedal, tossing her into one of the bucket seats vacated by the sphincter twins. “Get that map back. I need you to tell me where my daughter is.”

CHAPTER TWENTY-FIVE

Traffic snarled to an agonizingly slow pace as they approached the outlying suburban ghettos of Mumbai. Rebecca sat glued to her seat in front of the monitors and listened as Daniel pounded his fists on the steering wheel in a frustrated rage. “Can you hear *anything*?”

“No.” She tried to mask her disappointment and anxiety for Daniel’s sake, but the closer they got to the city without knowing what was happening, the harder it was not to pull out her gun and blow a hole through one of the infuriatingly silent radios. “Diver says the signals haven’t moved, but unless someone makes a call or sends a text message he can’t access it.”

“What about Grant? Can’t we use the cellphone he has to…to…I don’t how all this shit works, but can’t Diver do *anything* else?”

Rebecca shook her head in disgust. “Just get us there, Daniel. Diver is doing everything he can.”

She couldn’t imagine the horror Daniel was going through. He’d devoted his life to finding Natalie. They didn’t have confirmation that she was even there, but if they could take down Jauhar… maybe, if they didn’t find her, it would give him some comfort to know her killer would see justice.

“I’ve got incoming.” Rebecca jumped at the sound of Diver’s voice. Her hands flew to her head and she pressed the headset tight against her ears.

“You have audio? I’m not hearing anything.”

“Better.” Two seconds later a distorted picture filled one of the monitors in front of her. “Someone is recording and I hacked the application code. As long as the camera is rolling we’ll see what they see.”

Her head tilted from side to side as she tried to make sense of the image on the screen. “What is it?” The van lurched to a screeching halt and she grabbed the edge of her seat to keep from being dumped into the floor. Between the jarring movements of the van and the disorienting picture on the screen, her head began to feel a little fuzzy until the camera stopped moving and she was able to focus in on picture. *Oh, dear God no!* Her heart stopped for a full three beats before jumping into her throat with the force of the adrenaline that fueled her raging pulse.

“Left or right?” Daniel called from the front of the van.

She fought the urge to close her eyes, to shut out the horrid scene being forever burned into her mind. Her trembling hand flew to her mouth instead, covering the scream of terror she somehow managed to suppress into an agonizing moan of despair. She’d seen photographs of tortured slaves, some of them dead, some of them barely living. She’d listened to countless statements from survivors and read thousands of victim files. Never. Not a single thing she’d ever seen or heard could have prepared her to see the true evil being inflicted upon Natalie right in front of her eyes.

Strapped to a wooden table, her pale and lifeless body was covered in deep, swollen bruises. Trails of bright, crimson blood ran from the old wound on her thigh, mixing with the sweat and dirt covering her naked skin. *Oh, God!* The fingers on her left hand were broken and twisted in odd angles, the swelling turning her entire hand an unnatural hue of blue. Her right leg was suspended by a harness, chains from both the ceiling and the table holding it immobile from every direction. Her other leg was cuffed to the table at the ankle and knee. She could see the sharp, metal spikes on the insides of the cuffs digging into Natalie’s skin, tiny rivulets of blood leaking from their wounds. Even if she had the strength to move she couldn’t, lest the spikes dig further into her flesh. She tore her eyes away from the purely medieval scene and focused on her face. Strands of her sweat-soaked hair were matted against her cheeks, her lips chapped and split in several places. Her silver eyes were open but soulless, focused on something beyond her horrid reality that only she could see. Rebecca wanted to vomit. How could someone do this to another human being?

“Rebecca! Right or left?”

She jumped from her seat, placing her body between Daniel and the monitor as she bent down to peer out the front windshield at their location. Sweat had beaded on her forehead, dripping into her eyes and mingling with the tears she couldn't quell. Her lungs seized, her chest tightened against the ache in her heart and no matter how many times she tried, she couldn't get the words past the lump in her throat. *Sweet Jesus, Rebecca. You gotta keep it together.* She swallowed hard, forcing the air from her lungs and the word beyond her lips. "Right," she breathed, gulping in a fresh lungful of air. "And hurry, Daniel. Please."

"Dammit! I'm trying! Can't you find a way around this damn traffic?"

Her pulse was racing too fast. She needed to get a handle on it before she could tell him more. "Stay on this road. I'll see what I can do."

Returning to her seat she tried to grasp what Diver was saying and block out the images on the screen while she studied the GPS maps. It was a wasted effort. When she thought she couldn't possibly deal with another crisis, her cellphone beeped indicating another call was coming in. She glanced at the incoming call notice. *Keller.* If she took the call she could risk losing Diver and that was not going to happen. "Do you have a cellphone, Daniel?"

Daniel shook his head. "No! I had to give it up as part of their agreement not to send me home."

Hell. She would have to add ignoring Keller's call to her growing lists of infractions. Dumbo was right. She probably didn't have a job to worry about anymore so what was the point? "Take a left at the next large intersection. If you keep the buildings on the right, it should lead you to a roundabout. The train station will be on your right. Follow the tracks for about three miles and it will lead you directly behind the building."

"Got it. Are you back inside yet?"

"I'm working on it." It was all she could give him. She couldn't tell him. Not now. Not until they got there and could do something to stop it.

Grasping for anything that could make a difference, she pushed aside as many of the overwhelming emotions as she humanly could and tried to see the scene from an investigator's point of view.

"Diver, look at the wall behind the table. It's concrete block. Do you see any windows?"

"Are you fucking out of your mind? I don't know! I can't watch this shit!"

"Diver, take a deep breath. We need to figure out where she is inside the building! Please, just try to look at the whole picture!"

"I...damn!" She could hear his growled curses and labored breaths as he tried to pull himself together. "I…fuck! Uh, I'm seeing what you are seeing. I don't think so. Is it a basement?"

"Can you enhance the picture at all? Maybe lighten it up a little?

"I can try. Give me a minute."

"We don't—"

"Look at me, pet."

Rebecca's response derailed. Her skin crawled with anger and revulsion as she watched Jauhar lean over Natalie, the person holding the camera moving to the side to keep her face in the frame. *Sick bastard!*

"Look at me, girl." He patted her face, repeatedly trying to rouse a positive response from her. When she didn't so much as blink he wrapped his hand around her throat, choking off her air supply until her body began to convulse against the table. She gagged, coughing and gasping for air when his fingers finally loosened their strangling grip. Tears streamed from the corners of her rapidly blinking eyes, as if just awakening from a terrifying nightmare. *Only this nightmare is real.*

"That's it, pet," he spoke at a near whisper. "For future reference, I do not like to be ignored." His hand cupped her left breast, pinching her nipple. Natalie tried to squirm away, nearly screaming when the spiked cuffs burrowed further beneath her skin. "Remember that the next time I call for your attention."

Rebecca chocked back her own impulse to vomit as Diver's words turned into wave after wave of deep, retching sounds. "Hang on, Diver. We'll get her out of there." She wasn't sure if he could even hear her over his heaves. Hell, it didn't matter if he did. She needed to believe the words were true.

"I am quite flattered your dear *savior* Issa left my mark intact. I suppose he did not have the heart to tell you about it once he discovered your acute loss of memory. That would have been a little difficult to explain once he filled your head with his carefully constructed tale of your little family tragedy. Poor little orphan, Thalia." His wicked chuckle echoed through the room, the hollow sound feeding Rebecca's suspicion of a basement, or bunker of some sort.

"It's a basement, Diver. I'm sure of it!" The electronics on top of the small built-in desk slid to the far side of the van as Daniel hit the roundabout at break-neck speed. The tires hit the curb and Rebecca was bounced from her seat, catching one of the monitors in her lap as she hit the floor. *Ouch!* Daniel offered no apologies, the engine revving to gasket-blowing levels when he hit the straight piece of broken asphalt on the other side.

"You cannot blame him for telling you such lies, pet. He was never quite the same after his lovely daughter took her own life. He was an embarrassment; entirely unreliable and useless. I was within days of finding a more reliable partner when he passed by your beautifully beaten and broken body lying at the bottom of your cage." He laughed when Natalie turned her head away, refusing to look at him. "I was reluctant to give you up, pet, as I had already invested much time and effort into your…training. But sometimes the power to control a person is more valuable than mere flesh. As long as he did my bidding I thought it was a good bargain. It appears as though I was right, at least for a little while." Natalie's nostrils flared with each raging breath when he gripped her chin and forced her to look at him. *That's it Natalie. Fight him. Don't give up. We're almost there!*

"Issa the Savior. That is why you called him Issa, is it not? You think he saved you?" When she didn't acknowledge his question, he clenched his fist into her hair and yanked her head from the table, his raging face inches from hers. "Be very mindful, pet. No one will save you now. And do not expect such foolish affection from me. You are nothing to me. Do you understand?"

Rebecca's cellphone beeped again with another incoming call. Another call from Keller. It was at least the tenth time since the first call she'd ignored. Her stomach in knots, she ignored this one, too. She couldn't deal with him and Jauhar. Her complete focus needed to be on sending this evil animal back to hell.

"Why is she here?" Rebecca's head snapped up, the sound of a new voice causing alarms to go off inside her head. "Don't we have enough problems?" *I know that voice*

"Who is that? I know that voice," Diver asked, the same sense of alarm in his tone.

"Mc, too." *Dammit! Move the camera!*

Jauhar released Natalie, turning away from the table to greet the owner of the familiar voice, stepping outside of the camera's view. *No! No! No! Come back! Who the hell is that?*

"We're almost there!" Daniel called out over his shoulder as her phone beeped again.

"Okay. I think she's in the basement." Rebecca blew out a frantic breath. "Stop about a block away and we'll discuss how we're going in." She punched the ignore button on her phone again and zeroed in on the voices.

"We should be hearing word from Mumbai any moment, Senator. While we wait, I have orchestrated a little demonstration for you. One I know you will be quite pleased with."

"Senator?"

"Mumbai?" She and Diver shouted over one another.

That's not possible! "Diver, I thought you said his signal was coming from Mumbai! What the hell is he talking about?"

"It *is* coming from Mumbai! And that's Senator Collins!" An ominous chill raced down Rebecca's spine, a full color image of the highly esteemed head of the foreign intelligence committee Senator Collins filling her screen as he approached Natalie's prone body. *This is not happening!*

"Son of a bitch! Grant is inside. He found a wireless repeater cell, Ms. Danes! They could be anywhere and bouncing their signal from Mumbai!" She could hear Diver shouting technical gibberish and barking orders to Grant like a well-seasoned drill sergeant. "Get out of there, Lieutenant! Now!"

"Daniel, stop! It's a false signal!" Daniel slammed on the brakes, the van screeching to a halt behind the building. He threw the gearshift in park and climbed to the back of the van.

"What do you mean a false signal?"

The life drained out of Daniel's face, his eyes focused on the monitor behind her. "Daniel, she's not there. We have to go back to Navi."

"Is that...Natalie?"

Rebecca's phone beeped again and when she raised it to look at the number she heard Diver's shouted pleas. "Rebecca! Rebecca! Ms. Danes!"

"Diver I have to take this call. We'll pick up Grant and..."

"It's a bomb! Get away from the building! Do you copy?"

The deafening silence inside Rebecca's head immediately gave way to a spine-numbing ringing sound. Her mouth moved, calling out for Daniel, but she heard nothing. Heat from the flames warmed her exposed skin, the pavement beneath her cool in comparison. *I'm alive.* Daniel had saved her life, pulling her from the van, pushing her down the narrow side street and into the concrete culvert as the building exploded.

Panic laced her veins when she realized the heavy weight covering her body was Daniel. He wasn't moving. "Daniel!" She pushed against the road, tiny shards of rubble and glass from the crumbled building biting into her palms. She ground her teeth against the pain and finally managed to roll him off of her. Freeing her legs from his tangled and bleeding limbs, she clenched his shirt in her fists and pulled herself up to sit beside him. "Daniel! Wake up!"

She let out an exasperated sigh of relief when he opened his eyes and looked at her. His mouth moved but she couldn't hear his words any more than she could her own. She was fluent in eight languages. Unfortunately, sign language wasn't one of them. Her ears suddenly popped, one after the other, and the roar of the blaze filled her head. It sounded so close she flinched away from Daniel and shielded her ears from the thunderous sounds.

"Natalie!" Daniel called out, his hands cupping his head. That's when she noticed a trickle of blood running from one of his ears.

"Daniel, you're bleeding!"

"Natalie!" Daniel pushed to his feet and ran toward the burning building, screaming his daughter's name. She peeled herself from the pavement and ran after him, grasping his shirt in her fists and pulling him away from the flames.

"Daniel she's not there!"

"Natalie, no!"

"Daniel!" Rebecca stood in front of the big burly man she'd known since the day she took over Natalie's investigation. She'd never seen a stronger, more determined man. He never gave up, literally tearing the world apart with desperate hope that he would hold his baby girl again. Her heart crumbled as she looked at the broken man before her. He'd aged a lifetime in mere moments, the last flicker of hope draining from his tearful eyes.

"Daniel!" She cupped his face in her bleeding hands. She had to get through to him. "Daniel, look at me!" His eyes slowly trailed from the burning building to hers. Emptiness was all she saw, the towering flames reflecting in his hopeless tears. "It's okay!" She shook her head to tell him no. "She was not there!"

"What?"

Rebecca's brows furrowed as she focused on his confused expressions. "Can you hear me?"

"Did you say she wasn't in the building?"

"Yes! Remember in the van?" Every word was shouted over the roar of the fire, but at least he could hear her. "It was a trap! She wasn't there!"

Daniel's shoulders fell, his head lulled back and more tears fell from his eyes leaving a reflective trail down his weathered cheeks. "We're too late."

"No!" Rebecca grabbed his arms and shook him. "Keller is in Navi! That's where she has to be. Daniel, we have to go! You can't give up now!"

"Grant." His head shook in disbelief, his voice laden with grief.

Rebecca released her hold and let her forehead fall against Daniel's chest. "I don't think he had time to get out."

"No." Daniel turned her around to see a dark figure stumbling through the rubble on the far side of the street. "Grant."

"Grant!"

CHAPTER TWENTY-SIX

"You may not remember our last time together," Jauhar purred as he wiped something cold and wet over the exposed skin on her elevated thigh. The way he moved around her felt strangely reverent. There was a creepy gentleness to his touch that conflicted with the hard indifference in his eyes. "But I assure you, pet, you will never forget or doubt who owns you after this day."

Thalia tried to close her eyes, to escape back into the dark and painless place he'd forced her from, but he wouldn't let her. Every time she began to feel the pain fall away, Jauhar would make her scream.

A part of her wanted to die. She welcomed the pain and hoped she was close enough to death she could somehow force them to push her over the razor thin line that existed between her life and her nightmares. No matter how much that part of her begged to be heard, she could not deny the rage. It gnawed at her insides, eating a hole in her soul which quickly filled with a dark need for blood. Jauhar's blood. She wanted to live. For no other reason than to kill the monster who had ended her life so long ago; to see him suffer, see them all suffer in such a way they would feel their pain long after their death.

Jauhar leaned in and whispered in her ear, "We are not usually so barbaric these days, pet, but a simple tattoo for you does not please me. I want you to always remember who your master is." He nipped her ear, intending for it to sting, before he rose and turned away. "Senator, you may do the honors." Jauhar nodded to the man who had joined him and Don Lalia in her continued humiliation and torture. He was American from what little she could tell by the few words he spoke. Salty streaks of gray streamed through his darker, wavy hair. Thick lines appeared at the corners of his mouth and eyes when he smiled at her like a boy who had discovered a new toy or fun game. His eyes. When she looked into his eyes she couldn't help but notice the darkness residing in his soul. They held the same potential for the merciless evil Jauhar had inflicted upon her.

She could see the long, metal rod in his hands as he approached the side of the table, a glowing-hot crest the size of her fist attached at the end. His perfect, white teeth appeared from behind his evil smile as he raised the brand to her thigh and the first wave of searing heat kissed her skin.

Noooooo! Her body thrashed against her restraints, every thought and fear burned from her mind. Only the raw, visceral instinct to survive was left behind. She felt nothing, heard nothing , saw nothing but a blind frenzy of light and darkness as every cell in her body waged war against her restraints. When the stench of burning flesh wafted strong in the air she managed to suck in through her tormented screams, she fought harder, struggling against the hands that held her, beating them off with a savage rage she no longer controlled.

~*~*~*~*~

"Go! Go! Go!" Dax Keller gave the order and his men stormed the club. Sounds of gunshots blasted through the building, but he ignored the threat and pushed his way through the chaos. The team's breacher kicked in the door to the basement and he rushed the Senator, taking out the two guards standing in his way. Dodging the hot branding iron Collins wielded like a knife, he caught the man's wrist and held him at bay as he struggled against him. He fought the urge to shoot him. He was under strict orders not to kill the sick fuck or he would have. He was a spry old man, but one punch to the throat and it was game over as he dropped to the floor, the hot end of the iron tumbling across his face and searing Jauhar's mark into his skin as he gasped for air.

Dax lunged for Thalia. In her fight to survive she'd broken through some of her restraints. She struggled against his hold, fighting him as if he were her tormentors as one of his team members freed her legs from the harnesses. "It's okay. I won't hurt you. You're safe." He tried to console her, to break through the madness that consumed her. She fought him as if he were the devil himself, kicking and biting, screaming at the top of her lungs until suddenly the fight drained away and some of his words finally began to filter through her rage. "That's it. It's over, Thalia. You're okay. Shhh, we stopped them. You're safe now."

It had taken him nearly an hour to console her enough to move her without a fight. Dax sat on the floor with Thalia cradled in his lap, a thin blanket covering her naked and beaten body. He would never forget her animalistic cry of fury that filled the dark basement he and his team had secured. Above all else, every case he'd ever worked, every soldier he'd ever watched die on the battlefield, he knew that sound would haunt him for the rest of his life.

He held back his team for as long as he could, waiting for any verbal confirmation from Collins that he knew about or was part of Jauhar's trafficking ring. Intel or no intel, there was simply no way he could sit back and watch as this innocent girl was mutilated by these wicked bastards. Contrary to some of his superiors' beliefs, there was no piece of information worth her life.

They had the Senator on a Christmas list of other charges, but kidnapping and assault with intent was a far cry from international human trafficking and murder. The bureau wanted all of them alivc, so putting a bullet in his head was out of the question no matter how badly he still wanted to do just that.

He stared at Jauhar across the room sitting smugly in a velvet covered armchair, his cuffed hands crossed arrogantly in his lap as he watched him rocking Thalia in his arms. The only consoling thought he could conjure was that he would never see the light of day once they got him extradited to stand trial on American soil. He wished the coward had put up more of a fight. The only thing that would have satisfied him more than a bullet would have been to beat the life out of him then and there.

Collins had given him a bit of surprising fight, but it had ended much too quickly for his liking. Seeing his face meet the hot end of the branding iron he'd been all too eager to use on Thalia didn't come close to satisfying Dax. Thankfully they had gotten there in time to stop him from inflicting more than a superficial wound to Thalia's thigh. He smirked as they dragged Collins from the club, stripped off his prestigious suit and tie, and paraded him naked through the gathering press to a medevac van waiting to take him to the hospital. Old sagging balls weren't pretty in prison. He'd be lucky to last a week before his asshole became nothing but a cum dumpster. That was a very satisfying thought.

"Keller!" His team's intel supervisor jogged up, a stack of photographs a half inch thick in his hand. "You're not going to believe this, sir."

Dax carefully slid his arm from beneath Thalia's trembling body and took the pictures from his hand. "Can you find me an extra blanket to wrap around her? I think she may be going into shock." The supervisor turned, but Dax couldn't wait any longer. He needed to know. "Have you heard from Reb—Ms. Danes yet?"

He had no other choice but to ignore the panic injected into his bloodstream when the man shook his head. He had a scene to process and miles of red tape to unravel before dawn. Don Lalia had managed to escape through the chaos of the initial firefight, but they still had his henchman, Hamisi. He was sure to give them hours, if not days, of pleasurable interrogation. And then there was Thalia. He couldn't leave her with just anyone. She needed Rebecca. Dammit, *he* needed her. And for many more reasons than he should be allowing himself to consider.

They found the surveillance van, or what was left of it, on the side of the road across from the explosion. Emergency response teams weren't as quick or plentiful in India like they were in the States, apparent by the fact Thalia still hadn't received more than a cursory inspection of her wounds. The fire was still raging at the supposed secondary location with no firemen in sight. They had yet to determine if there were any casualties. Dax couldn't bring himself to think of the word *bodies.* They would find her alive. And then he would fire her for disobeying his orders right before he kissed her senseless and spanked her bratty ass until it was as red as her hair.

"This was all I could find, sir." Dax sat the pictures on the floor and grabbed the thick cotton sheet, scolding himself for letting his mind travel down a road he had no business going down. "Everything else is locked down for evidence processing."

"This is fine." He carefully draped it over Thalia's frail shoulders, tucking it in around her shivering frame to hold in what little body heat he was able to give her. "Rest, Thalia. This will all be over soon."

"Water." It was the first raspy sound she'd made since he'd pried her out of those god-awful restraints and battled to reach her through the fog of war she was waging to survive. He'd seen men on the battlefield die with less of a fight in them than she'd displayed. If he were still a soldier he would fight next to her any day.

His intel supervisor returned with a glass of water and he held it to her bleeding lips. The water turned pink as rivulets of blood drained from the corners of her mouth and into the cup. She didn't seem to care. She gulped the water down in a handful of swallows before her head fell against his chest, that small effort depleting her energy.

"Did you look at the pictures, sir?"

He sat the cup on the floor and picked up the stack of pictures. "What am I looking at? *Jesus!*"

"Yes, sir. I'd say he's the only person who will be able to save Collins now, sir."

Dax flipped through the stack of what he could only call child pornography. Photo after photo of small boys. Some naked, some barely clothed. All of them undernourished with obvious signs of physical abuse. His stomach soured when he flipped to the last one and saw a small, naked, red haired child chained to a rusty dog crate. "These were taken at the Senator's condo in D.C?"

"At his estate in Maryland, sir. We've recovered five children from a hidden room in his basement. The D.C. Police and Federal Marshals are combing through his residence there as we speak."

How did this happen? How had an insect like Collins existed, *thriving* in the political spotlight, right under their noses all this time? If it wasn't for this Lieutenant character, they never would have known. When he was first contacted, he thought this guy was off his rocker. It had only taken one call to confirm him as a legitimate source. He still didn't have a clue as to who this guy was but, whoever he was, he had some damn influential friends and mighty powerful enemies.

At the Lieutenant's request, once he'd confirmed the intel on the thumb drive was legit, he copied the contents and had it hand delivered to Collins with a note from the Lieutenant. The note detailed what the drive contained, which was nothing less than an itemized diary of every shipment of slaves Issa had trafficked for Jauhar and Don Lalia over the past fifteen years. They had never suspected Don Lalia of anything but local racketeering. If the Lieutenant's suspicions were correct, as it turned out they were, the Senator would waste no time in contacting Jauhar with the news. He, in fact, had booked a flight to Mumbai the very next day.

He didn't know how this Lieutenant knew the things he did. He wasn't sure he wanted to know. It didn't matter until he was called to appear in front of the investigation review board and give his statement. He would figure out a way to honor this guy's only request, to be kept as a confidential source. No way in hell was he going to blow that deal. Not after seeing these photographs. *If he's even still alive.*

He hated leaving the guy out to dry, but it was impossible to scramble a second team to the Mumbai location in the short amount of time his friend Diver had requested. He sure as hell wasn't sending Rebecca and a couple of techies in there blind. Not that his orders to stand down had done him a shitload of good.

It shouldn't matter, but he couldn't tell her what they were expecting to go down. He'd been sent with the strictest of orders to keep the Senator's possible involvement confidential until they had confirmed it. That meant only essential SCI clearance personnel. In truth, it wasn't her lack of clearance. She would be subjected to the mother of all investigations. He knew it would make her a walking target, like he and his team now were. These things rarely, if ever, stopped at one individual. Once they got down to the dirty details, they would find others who either knew about or participated in this sick way of life that Collins lived. These were powerful people with dangerous connections. When you combine that with desperation, some of them could turn deadly. He didn't want her anywhere near that. He'd gotten his wish, but at what cost?

CHAPTER TWENTY-SEVEN

Blood soaked Grant's shirt and pants. The sticky fabric clung to his skin, the copper stench matching the taste in his mouth. Daniel had given him his shirt to staunch the tide of blood gushing from his head wound, but the cuts to his chest and arms wouldn't be helped by anything less than stitches.

He ran balls to the wall the second Diver had said the word bomb. He'd manage to make it out of the second story room and down to the end of the hall before the blast catapulted him through the window at the end. He wasn't sure how he survived the blast, flying through the glass and crashing to the ground in a pile of concrete and steel, but he wasn't going to look into too deeply. He was alive. He only hoped the same fate was watching over Thalia.

It was strange how being that close to death could bring such clarity to life. He'd been a fool to leave her. He'd been a fool about a lot of things. He should have known better than to trust his own instincts when he knew he couldn't count of them. He was too emotionally involved to think straight.

If Senator Collins had tipped off Jauhar, then he obviously believed he'd already secured the data on that thumb drive. All that was left was killing the messenger. He should have known from the start it was all a set-up. Collins would know he had access to the resources to trace that call. He also knew the tradecraft protocol and that Grant would have no choice but to investigate the source. He only hoped he didn't know about the tracer Rebecca had planted in Thalia's clothes. It was the one ace they had left.

He bit back a groan as the gash on his side was pulled taught by the hard left turn Daniel made. He didn't dare ask him to slow down. If anything he wanted him to speed up. None of them had a cellphone to call Keller. Rebecca's was probably melted to the inside of the charred surveillance van, and the one he'd lifted from Jauhar's man was blown to pieces. He'd give anything for one damn phone call, but no one was voting to stop at a pay phone. The sooner they got to Navi the sooner he would know Thalia's fate. *Hang on, fossa. I'm coming.*

Twenty-five agonizing minutes later, an army of suits surrounded the car when Daniel nosed through the roadblock that had been set up not far from the men's club in Navi. Agents shouted orders, but Daniel ignored them until he reached the front of the building. They spilled out of the car, gun to gun with the other men until Rebecca pushed her way through the crowd of agents and local police to the other side of the car and flashed her bureau identification.

"I don't care who you are, ma'am. You're not cleared to go in."

"Please notify Deputy Director Keller that Rebecca Danes is waiting outside."

"Rebecca!" Grant watched as a rather large man wearing the standard bureau get-up raced through the front entrance and tackled the redhead with a lip-locking embrace. *How nice.* If it had been any other time and place he still wouldn't have given a fuck. He needed to see Thalia *now*.

"Thalia!" His head felt a little light as he followed Daniel, pushing and shoving their way into the club. Someone snagged his arm and he turned to see lover boy barreling down on him.

"Lieutenant?"

"Keller?" Jesus, he didn't have time for this. "Where's Thalia?"

"You know her?" Grant nearly growled at the man. He was still losing blood. He didn't think he had the strength to fight a piss-ant, but in the next three seconds he was going to start throwing punches if he didn't get to Thalia. Luckily lover boy took the hint and showed him through the crowd in the main lobby. "Right this way."

The crowd thinned the deeper inside the club they went until finally they emerged inside a dimly lit room crawling with tactical agents. The first person he saw was Jauhar, sitting comfortably on a plush lounge as if he owned the world. What blood he had left in his body screamed through his veins. He took three giant strides toward the cocksucker, hell bent on complete destruction when he froze, the sound of Thalia's gasp stopping him in his tracks.

"Thalia? Oh, thank Christ! You're alive." He rushed to her side and enfolded her broken body in his arms. *Oh my God.* His heart beat like a drum inside his chest, his entire body responding to her touch as if she were the very thing that gave him life. "I'm so sorry, fossa." He rocked her in his arms, trying desperately not to crush her. "So, so sorry." He couldn't get close enough. His body, his soul, ached to feel her and now that she was finally where she belonged he would never let her go. "I'm so damn sorry. I love you so much. I should have never left you."

She let out a whimper, her body trembling violently against his. Immediately his body recoiled and he loosened his hold. "Oh God. I'm such an idiot. You need a doctor and I'm bleeding all over you."

Her forehead fell against his bare chest, her fingernails digging into his arms like talons as a heart-stopping wail of pain and rage spewed from her lungs. "Get *away* from me!"

In her feeble retreat, she stumbled. Grant reached out to catcher but she slapped at his hands, screaming and kicking like an animal for him to release her. *What the hell is wrong with her?* He'd heard her tormented screams over the cell line. Had they pushed her over the edge? Had she finally been driven mad? "Fossa, don't fight. You're okay. I've got you. I swear, baby, I'll fix this. You don't have to be afraid of me. You know that."

"Don't touch me you bastard!" She was so weak he barely felt the slap to his face.

It was his heart that ached to the point of breaking as Daniel ripped her from his arms and pushed him away. "Get away from her, Grant. I can't take seeing her like this."

She clung to Daniel, a ferocious hatred flaring in her eyes as she watched him through the strands of matted hair that covered her face. *No. This is not happening.* "Thalia, please. I don't understand."

"Did you think I would not tell her?" Jauhar chuckled, a sadistic tone of satisfaction lacing his words. Grant turned to see a matching superior smirk on his face as he stood from his seat. Guards quickly surrounded him, their guns at the ready.

"Tell her what?" His head whipped back around to where Thalia stood, barely able to hold her own weight as she leaned into Daniel's protective embrace. He'd never seen her so broken. "What lies did he tell you, Thalia?"

"It's not a lie!" She coughed on a sob and it took every ounce of strength he had left to hold himself back from her. "You're a murderer!"

Grant's world dropped out from beneath his feet. What was left of his heart exploded inside his chest, shattering into tiny shards and cutting away at his insides like a million razor-sharp blades. She knew. She knew about Issa and the look of disgust on her face was exactly as he imagined it would be. She was right. He was a murderer; a heartless monster. He had no right, no moral ground to stand on, but he needed her to understand. "Thalia, I…I was a coward. I should have told you, but I knew I'd lose you. I didn't know. Not until I found his grave. I only left because I know how much you loved him. I knew you would never understand why I had to kill him. You have every right to—"

"Lies!" Christ, he didn't know if he could take this much longer. Every second that ticked by the pain and hatred in her eyes grew that much deeper. "I meant nothing to you! You hear me? *Nothing!*" Each of her words hit him square in his soul with enough force to make him stumble back several steps. "The only thing you ever wanted was that thumb drive!"

"That's not true!" *How could she believe that?* "Is that what he told you? That I killed Issa for the thumb drive?" No longer able to stand under the weight of her accusations he fell to his knees, for the first time in his life prepared to beg. He didn't give a rat's ass who saw him. He would do whatever it took to make the torment in her eyes disappear. "Thalia, please. You don't have to forgive me, because I don't deserve it. But please, please believe me. I swear to you. I did *not* know about the thumb drive until I met you! I would never betray your trust that way."

In a move so quick no one saw it coming, Thalia snatched Keller's gun from his holster and leveled it at Grant. The room erupted in chaos, guns being drawn as curses flew from every direction. He didn't so much as flinch when she stared down the barrel at him, raw and naked fury blazing in her eyes. He closed his eyes, no longer able to battle the sorrow that filled her soul. If sending him to hell would end her torment then he would gladly let her. She, more than anyone, deserved her revenge. She deserved to live a life free of pain and regret. She deserved someone who could heal the wounds left behind by so, so many; his mark the deepest of them all.

"Why else would you kill Issa?"

He was struck by the tone of doubt in her voice, giving him little hope she would ever believe him. As significant as it would be to some, it wouldn't matter to her. He didn't give a damn about his oath of complete secrecy. It was all bullshit. Secrets had destroyed her life. After nearly dying in that explosion, he'd decided to tell her everything. There were going to be no secrets between them, ever. She deserved to know his enemies. Above all else she deserved the truth.

He raised his head, opening his eyes to see her standing on her own, her shoulders squared back, the strength of a warrior shining through her pain as she stared down at him. At that moment he was in complete awe of her. No matter what this miserable world threw at her, she would never quit fighting. She would never lose the woman he'd come to love beyond all reason. Closing his eyes, he took a deep, satisfied breath. He wanted that image of her to be the last he would see.

"Senator Collins lobbied for and sanctioned the hit on Issa. He signed the request and the executive office approved it. My orders were to kill on sight."

"That's why you wanted the thumb drive delivered to him." Keller's booming voice echoed above the quiet chaos in him mind. "Because he ordered the hit, you suspected he was working with Jauhar and would move to inform him. If the Senator was clean, the intel would be classified and dealt with using standard intel protocol." His eyes remained closed, confirming Keller's assumption only with a nod. "Jauhar ordered his death and Collins used you and the Federal Government to do his bidding."

Grant swallowed hard, knowing he could be speaking his last words. He didn't want them to be about politics or death, but he needed Thalia to know the complete truth. "I don't regret killing him, Thalia. Not then and certainly not now. Not when I know the truth of what he's done to you and so many others. I only regret the pain I've—"

The sound of a single gunshot was quickly followed by two more. The air burst from Grant's lungs in a rush as shock and adrenaline poisoned the depleted blood supply left in his veins. He toppled forward into a heap on the floor, an unfamiliar, icy sensation creeping into his limbs. He heard shouts and curses, felt the vibration of the crush of people as they rushed the room, but he felt strangely disconnected from all the madness. Almost as if he was weightless and somehow floating above them all.

Thalia's sobs finally broke through the haze of his confusion. Grant opened his eyes to see Jauhar lying on the floor across from him, his cold, lifeless eyes ironically accentuated by a single bullet hole between them. *She killed him.* She'd spared his life and killed the monster that had started it all.

Darkness flirted with his vision as he teetered on the edge of consciousness. His hooded gaze darted to Thalia, her unbearable sobs filling his ears as she lay collapsed over Daniel's motionless body.

CHAPTER TWENTY-EIGHT

Grant sat in a rented sedan and watched the sun burn away the morning fog. In a strange sort of way he missed this place, but he didn't think he could ever live on the mainland. As sprawling as the Montana Mountains were, it still felt too crowded, especially in small towns such as this one, with everyone knowing your every move the moment you made it. No thanks. He'd lived in the shadows too long to appreciate that kind of intimacy in his life.

He'd promised himself a million times he wouldn't come here. He'd spent thousands of dollars on plane tickets he never used. Normally he wouldn't get beyond the packing stage before he talked himself out of it and cancelled the flight. Other times he'd sat at the terminal and watched as the other passengers boarded the plane, ignoring the flight attendant's calls for him to board until they finally gave up and closed the boarding ramp. Those were the worst. He would sit and watch the plane take off, wondering what it would feel like to be on it, knowing he was that much closer to the woman who owned his heart and soul.

He didn't know if she was even here or if she would see him if she was. He'd spoken to Daniel only once, a few weeks after he'd been released from the hospital. One of Keller's men had taken his orders to keep Jauhar alive quite seriously and tried to take out Thalia before she fired that fatal shot. Daniel saw it coming and stepped in front of the bullet, a dedicated father protecting his only daughter.

When he spoke to Danicl he'd said she hadn't spoken a word since he'd brought her home from Navi; to Daniel or anyone else. She'd locked herself away in her mind, closing herself off from the world around her. Grant understood the need. Sometimes the only way to figure things out was to silence all the other voices that were shouting the answers so loud you couldn't make sense of any of them. Unlike Daniel, he wasn't worried. His girl was a fighter. He'd seen it that day, and every day since. Any time he closed his eyes she was there, standing over him with the strength of the world at her back.

Nearly six months had passed since that day in Navi. He'd told himself time and again that she didn't deserve him traipsing back into her life, but he needed to know. He couldn't crush the burning need to see for himself that she was alive and happy. To know that, above all else, she knew he loved her. It astonished him that he could feel it so deeply, so definitely, when before he'd met her he had mocked love's existence. He was resigned to the fact it may never be returned. Love, as it turned out, is a more fickle bitch than fate. It haunts your dreams and plays games with your mind, using sleight of hand tricks to make you see the person you love in everything; on every crowded street, in every passing car, beside you in your empty bed. It was enough to make him go mad until he simply couldn't take it anymore and got on that damn plane.

Now he was sitting on the side of the road in the middle of nowhere, staring at a quiet country house where he hoped he would find the answers he sought. A flash of light in his rear view mirror caught his attention. The large, blue pick-up truck slowed as it approached, the tinted passenger window lowering as it came to a stop beside his car.

"Are you going to go in? Or sit out here all day and bake in the sun like a cow pie?"

"Hey, Cade. Nice to see you again. I think." He should have known Cade would make him. He was nothing if not a spook. He might be reaching the start of his golden years, but there was no such thing as a retired spy. If he ever did decide to move here, he would definitely have to buy an English-to-Spook-Hick dictionary.

"Follow me."

Here goes nothing. His palms were sweaty, clenched in a white-knuckled grip on the steering wheel as he approached Cade and Daniel's house from the long gravel drive. He pulled to a stop next to Cade's truck and cut the engine. He sat there a moment, staring out the windshield, still wondering if he was doing the right thing when two young boys ran out the front door and greeted Cade.

"Uncle Cade, look what mom let us bring!" They held up something Grant couldn't see from where he sat in the car. He was astonished at how much the McLendon twins had grown in the year or more since he'd first met them. Judging by the looks of it, Gabby had grown quite a bit, too. Again he was struck by how odd it felt not to call her Claira. She was as beautifully innocent as ever standing on the front porch, her hand shielding her eyes from the early morning sun as she tried to make out who he was.

There was no use in prolonging this disaster. With a deep, anxious breath, he opened the door and pushed to his feet. Gabby's excited, inquisitive expression fell from her face. He didn't miss how her hand instinctively covered her swollen belly, her maternal instincts warning her of danger. He tried not to take it personally, but he couldn't deny that it stung a little.

"Grant?"

He nodded silently, hanging back by the car to give her some space and time to adjust to his unexpected appearance. To his complete and utter shock she let out a squeal and ran down the steps, engulfing him in a hug with more strength than a woman her size should have.

"Grant Kendal, I'm so glad to see you." When Mason McLendon stepped onto the porch, Grant carefully set her on her feet, unsure of how he would be received by her three protective husbands. They hadn't exactly hit it off the last time he was here.

"Matt! Grey! Get your butts out here! We have company." Mason descended the stairs and came to stand by his wife's side. "Grant. Long time no see." He held out his hand and Grant took it, giving it a stiff shake.

"Yeah, I uh…Jesus, is the entire town here?" This was a mistake. He couldn't do this. Not in front of so many people.

"Already? Matt, did you put the wrong time on the invita—?" Grey McLendon's words trailed off when he locked eyes with Grant, his footsteps faltering to a stop at the edge of the first step.

"Nah, not the whole town. Not yet anyway." Mason turned and waved for his brothers to join them. "It's Con and Car's birthday. We're having a pool party here this afternoon because, well, Cade and Daniel's place has the pool. Daniel's out picking up the cake and some other supplies. He should be back around lunchtime."

Grant heard what Mason was saying, but his eyes never left Grey's as he made his way down the steps and stood behind Gabby, slinging a protective arm around her shoulders.

"Grey. Matt."

"Grant, nice to see ya again." Matt shook his hand, but he could still feel Grey's icy stare. "I gotta say I never thought I'd be sayin' that."

He looked back at Grey and nodded. "Never thought I would be hearing it."

"Oh, stop it. Both of you." Gabby shrugged off Grey's arm and took Grant's hand, pulling him into another embrace as she steered him toward the house. "He's still a little over protective, especially since, well, I guess there's no sense in hiding it. The moment we found out I'm carrying twins he's pretty much been impossible. Give him a few minutes. He'll come around."

By the time Daniel handed him a glass of whisky later that night, Grant was ready to find the bottom of the bottle. There must have been a thousand screaming kids in that pool at one point in the afternoon. Between Gabby barking out orders to both the kids and her men, and expecting Grey to corner him at every turn, his nerves were shot. He'd take a sniper rifle and drug lord any day over this chaos.

"You're looking a little fried." He took the glass from his friend's hand and gulped down the amber fire in a single swallow. Daniel laughed and poured him another.

"Gabby has changed. A lot. I didn't expect her to be so…comfortable around me. It's a far cry from the last time I saw her." Christ! They had skirted talking about Thalia all day, but it seemed impolite not to acknowledge the people who had played such an important role in her recovery. The tension in his neck eased only marginally as the alcohol began to burn through his veins. It's not that he didn't care about Daniel and his new family, but he needed to know what the hell was going on with Thalia. No one had even mentioned her and it was driving him mad.

"That she has." Daniel raised his glass in a mock toast before he threw back his head and drained the glass. "I haven't seen the ghosts in her eyes in very long time. Those men keep them pretty spooked."

"I bet they do." Fuck, he sucked at small talk. "What about you? I assume the surgery went well or you wouldn't be standing here."

Daniel chuckled, lifting another glass of whiskey in the air. "To outstanding spinal surgeons and kick-ass physical therapists." He placed the cap back on the bottle and stashed it back inside the cabinet below the bar. "She's been gone for nearly two months."

Grant froze, the glass half way to his lips. Thank fuck they were done ignoring the hell out of the elephant on the room. "What do you mean gone?"

He watched as Daniel paced to the window and peered into the darkness. "She's improved a lot since we last spoke. Started seeing a therapist in Billings once a week. She eventually came out of her shell and began socializing with the family. She and Gabby hit it off immediately."

Grant's heart sang with the news, but he'd always known she would come out of that nightmare stronger than she'd ever been. "Where did she go, Daniel? I have to see her." He felt a sudden, incredible sense of fear. One moment he was holding his breath waiting for Daniel to tell him, the next he was praying he wouldn't, because that meant getting on another plane and starting the process all over again.

"I don't know where she is." Daniel hung his head, turning away from the window. He paced to the large desk that dominated the room and opened a folder lying on top. "I get a postcard from her about once a week. Sometimes twice. They're from places all over the map. Chile, Nicaragua, Spain, Australia." He pulled out one in particular, studying it for a moment before he handed it to Grant. "They stopped about two weeks ago with this one. I haven't tried to find her. She needs to find her own way back."

A painful knot formed in the back of Grant's throat when he looked at the picture on the card. A sandy, white beach surrounded by calm turquoise water. The face of the most annoying monkey he'd ever known smiled back at him. He flipped the card over, feeling his heart beat against his chest for the first time since that day in Navi as he read the words written on the back.

It's not the same without you.

"I take it you know where that was taken."

Grant looked up through a stream of tears and nodded, unable to hold back the smile that pulled at his lips despite them. "Uh…" He cleared his throat and wiped the back of his hand over his eyes, a little shocked when more tears took their place. "Yeah…uh, I do, actually."

His feet were in motion before his brain had reengaged. The sound of Daniel's voice was the only thing that could have stopped his run for the door. "Try to bring her home in time for Christmas."

He turned and nodded to his friend. He wasn't sure how things would turn out but he would do everything he could to honor his request. "I'll do my best."

CHAPTER TWENTY-NINE

"Ouch!" Thalia stuck the tip of her finger in her mouth and sucked away the drop of blood that bubbled from the tiny wound. Who knew that palm fronds had thorns? She grabbed the next one and peeled back the dead leaves, throwing it into the pile at the end of the ramp. It wasn't *shack de Grant,* but she was proud of the progress she'd made on her little hut. In only a couple of weeks she'd managed to construct a raised floor from some of the unused timber Grant had left behind. The framing for the roof was up, and she only had a few feet of open space to cover before she and Winston would have a somewhat dry place to sleep.

She'd nearly shot the damn primate when she first arrived on the beach. She wasn't entirely sure she'd found the right island when she anchored offshore and waded up. Exploring the tree line for signs of life, she heard a rustle in the bushes behind her and turned to see him barreling toward her like a crazed ape. He'd nearly knocked her over when he jumped into her arms, a chastising tone in his cries of joy.

He was still ridiculously annoying, but to her surprise she found herself grateful for his company. The days were long and filled with hard, tedious chores. It was good to have someone, or some*thing,* to listen to her bitch and complain about the bugs while she worked. The work it had taken to make the island habitable again wasn't much like work. In truth, deep down, she loved it. It was a welcome break from the myriad of thoughts that continually plagued her mind.

The nights were the worst. Even before she'd decided to go back to Grant's island, she would lie awake in a lonely bed, staring at the ceiling of whatever hotel room she happen to land in as different times of her life replayed over and over in her mind.

Astonishingly enough, it wasn't the most recent memories that occupied her thoughts. The physical wounds Jauhar had inflicted had all healed, save an irritating ache in the fingers he'd broken. As long as it wasn't her trigger finger, she would survive. Healing the emotional and psychological damage was still a work in process, but she'd already made tremendous strides, or so the doctor in Billings had told her.

With Rebecca Danes and the doctor's help, she'd been able piece together enough information about Issa to at least begin to understand why he'd lied to her. She was astounded at how closely she resembled the daughter he'd lost. The pictures they had found of her still haunted her dreams. He'd even given her the same birthday. It explained why he doted on her and treated her so much like his own family. It was a world apart from what the other children had endured at his and Jauhar's hands.

Her stomach still curdled at the mere thought of the monster he was. It was like looking into the lives of two wholly different people. Issa may not have participated in any of the physical torture of the thousands of children he'd transported for Jauhar, but that didn't make him a lesser evil. As far as she knew he'd never owned a sex slave, or any other slave, but technically he'd still purchased her. Issa robbed her of her life. In the end he'd paid for it with his own.

Apparently the single lump sum he and Jauhar had agreed to at the time of Issa's *purchase* of her hadn't been enough to satisfy Jauhar. She'd spent countless tedious hours combing through Issa's hidden financials and discovered he had paid Jauhar millions for her over the years, well beyond her adolescence. It was a win-win for Jauhar. He basically got his cargo shipped for free by the time Issa paid his latest demand to keep him from *retrieving his property*. When Issa began to refuse payment and Jauhar's threats became benign, Jauhar had him eliminated through his connections with the Senator, using Grant to unwittingly do his bidding.

In the beginning it was nearly impossible to get a grasp on her feelings for Issa and what he'd done to her. How could she have feelings of love and adoration for a man who was so clearly a monster? How could she hate a monster that spent the last years of his life protecting her from a bigger monster like Jauhar? It wasn't until her doctor pointed out that it was okay to feel both love and hatred for him that she could begin to process the other facets of her recovery.

She still had no memory of Daniel or her life before she woke up in Issa's house. Rebecca had suggested hypnotherapy, but her doctor didn't seem hopeful it would help. Thalia had told her she would think about it, but it truly wasn't an option. The more she thought about it the more she knew she didn't want to remember. Maybe one day. Maybe never. Definitely not now. Whatever happened to her during what she now called the missing year, the year Jauhar held her captive before Issa bought her, would remain buried with the memories of her childhood. Knowing what she knew now, there was nothing good to be found in those memories. Nothing that would help her now. Jauhar was dead, and she'd killed him. She hadn't let him defeat her. Now it was time to move on with her life.

She'd tried to do that in Montana. Despite the appreciated efforts of everyone in Daniel's family and their friends, there was always an emptiness inside her that would never ease. She loved Gabby and her husbands. The twins were a little much to take at times, but she still found them adorable. It certainly wasn't Daniel's fault. Over the weeks and months she'd spent with him she'd grown to love him, but she didn't think he could ever fill the hole Issa had left in her heart. He and his friend Cade had been nothing but kind and understanding, never hovering or pressuring her. After months of trying, she found herself growing more restless and agitated. The panic attacks and nightmares resurfaced and were getting worse instead of better. It was difficult to explain, even to herself, but when Gabby had suggested that maybe she was feeling trapped, something clicked. It was as if she was again being forced to live a life that was not her own. She was more than welcomed there, but she didn't belong.

She felt like an ungrateful bitch the night she slipped a note beneath Daniel's door and snuck out of the house on foot. She'd spent the next month moving from town to town, wherever her thoughts took her. Money was of no concern. She'd inherited Issa entire estate. It had dwindled toward the end of his life, but there was still enough for her to live ten lifetimes. She'd thought long and hard about donating it all to a small, private foundation she discovered that fought real, on-the-ground battles against human trafficking. It was literally blood money and it felt wrong to keep it. In the end she decided some of that blood was hers and kept enough to be able to do what she wanted with the rest of her life, donating the rest to the foundation.

It wasn't until she was strolling through a zoo in Spain and saw a group of Macaque monkeys perched in a clump of palm trees that she began to accept what had been nagging at her soul for months. Standing there in the atrium, the empty feeling inside her chest rapidly expanded to an endless abyss creating a physical ache that wouldn't go away. It was her thoughts of Grant that plagued her with sleepless nights.

He'd killed Issa in cold blood. Her feelings and thoughts about that were as jumbled as they were about Issa. How can she love a man who murdered someone else she loved? How could she hate a man who was only obeying orders to destroy the monster that had stolen her life and the lives of so many others? She knew with certainty he hadn't betrayed her as Jauhar had manipulated her into believing. She also understood why he didn't regret killing Issa even though he, too, had been manipulated into doing it. In the end, after all the soul searching and endless lists of impossible questions of how she could love such a man, there was only one answer. It didn't matter how.

She loved him. She loved him beyond any doubts or circumstances that separated them now. She loved his goofy smile, and piercing golden eyes. She loved his confidence and strength and the awkward way he looked at the world. In most ways, to Grant, the world was black or white, good or evil. Yet he walked a razor-thin line with no hesitation between the two worlds that most would call a gray area. He was a complex man and a simple man all wrapped into an enigma. Yet there was one thing in Thalia's mind that defined him; he was the very essence of truth.

No matter how wicked or outrageous the truth was, he faced it head on. He wouldn't lie to her or betray her like so many others had. He would never placate her with false promises and pretty words. If there was one thing she deserved in her life, it was the truth, even from herself. And the truth was she loved him.

There was no way to know if he still loved her. Her clouded memories of his confession of love that night in Navi afforded her little certainty. There were so many things that had been left unsaid. Lying awake at night she would list all the things she wanted to tell him. Imagine all the things he would say to her. In truth, none of them would matter if she had him in her arms. That was all she truly needed. She had to face the probability she may never know for certain how he felt.

She knew better than to search for him. A few months after Navi, Daniel had told her Don Lalia had been found floating dead in a pool at his beach house in Spain. There was no doubt in her mind Grant had killed him. Looking back now, knowing he'd been there was what had drawn her to Spain in the first place. She'd learned through Rebecca he'd officially retired, but only a select few within the intelligence community knew where he was now. Much to her dismay, Rebecca Danes was no longer one of those people.

She'd been suspended from the bureau for a month after the investigation had concluded she acted recklessly by disobeying direct orders and endangered the lives of both a civilian, Daniel, and two others on Keller's team. Once her suspension was over, her request to remain at the bureau headquarters in D.C. was granted, but she'd been transferred to another division. Thalia was relieved Rebecca hadn't lost her job because of her, but it made getting information about Grant next to impossible since she was apparently no longer on speaking terms with Deputy Director Keller. Her only hope was that Grant would one day decide to come back to the island on his own, or that Daniel would do as she requested if he ever called or visited and show him the postcard. There was nothing left to do but wait.

"Shit!" A bubble of red oozed from yet another puncture wound to her poor tortured fingers. Wiping her arm across her forehead, she tossed the frond into the done pile and kicked off her sandals. "Let's go for a swim, Winston." It was the cool season in that part of the world and the water was a bit chilly. Still, a nice cold dunk would wake her up and give her enough energy to put the final fronds in place before the sun set.

Memories of Grant had plagued her thoughts throughout the rest of the day. The sun had set. Dinner had been prepared and consumed. Winston had settled into his little hammock she'd hung between the corner posts of the hut. And still no sign of Grant. *One more day*. It's what she told herself each night before closing her eyes to go to sleep. One more day and he'd come.

One more day turned into three and still she carried on without him. This last day had been particularly grueling. Where normally her work distracted her from her thoughts of Grant, today's task had brought back a tide of memories she could not ignore. Today she had cleared away the charred remains of Grant's old cabin. She salvaged what she could and set the rest adrift, but at every turn she would see him; standing in the doorway, his eagle eyes cutting to the core of her very soul as he sized her up. Sitting on that dreadful cot, assessing her injuries with that annoying sarcasm he wore so well. Laughing at her frantic reactions to Winston the first time she'd seen him. Feeding her the soup he'd made for her. Brooding over her lack of enthusiasm for his freshman efforts at being nice. Grumbling incessantly at poor Winston.

She remembered every moment she'd spent there with him, some of them not so good, but all of them things she never wanted to forget. She'd laughed and even cried, the task itself having an unexpected cleansing effect on her soul. At the end of the day she was exhausted. Her eyes were closed before her head hit the pillow. It was the first time she'd fallen to sleep without the spoken promise of *one more day*.

~*~*~*~*~

The first golden rays of the sun were only beginning to peek through the thick trees. Sweet scents of night jasmine and dianthus still lingered in the air. The birds had started singing nearly an hour before and Winston had long since left for his morning forage, oblivious to Grant's presence. For once he had to hand it to the guy. He'd scampered off without waking Thalia, allowing him time to watch her sleep. *There is a God.*

She couldn't have been more breathtaking. Literally, his chest heaved with the effort it took to breathe as he absorbed the sight of her for what felt like the first time. The thin, cotton t-shirt she wore hid little. Her slender arms were stretched out above her head showcasing her lush breasts beneath it. He could almost feel the fabric graze his tongue as he imagined himself hovering above her, sucking her ripe nipple deep into his mouth through the material. His cock swelled in his shorts. His hand, twitching to feel her smooth skin against his palm, moved to ease the ache in his groin instead.

He stilled when she shifted in her sleep, her legs tangling in the simple white sheet, dragging it further down her perfectly toned form. *Her legs*. Christ, she had the sexiest legs. His favorite spot was showing, peeking above the hem of the sheet. That supple, tender crease at the top of her hip. His mouth watered at the memory of the purred little moan she made when he'd trace that spot with his tongue. That sound had haunted his dreams for the last six months. He couldn't wait to hear it again, but first they had to talk.

There were too many things left unresolved between them. First and foremost, he wanted her to know he loved her, and that she had a choice. He loved her enough to walk away if that's what she wanted. After coming this far it would kill him, but he would leave. He was prepared to give her anything she wanted, any answer to every question, no matter what it cost him or how long it took. Whatever it took.

In a single silent step, he hopped from his perch in the trees to the raised platform she'd constructed. He'd been more than impressed when he'd first snuck onto the beach, the more than ample moonlight and still-glowing embers from her fire showing him the way to her little hut. He'd debated waking her, but the moment he saw her peaceful form curled up on the thick mattress she'd made, he'd been too mesmerized to disturb her.

Slowly he sank to his knees and relaxed into the mattress beside her, gently pulling up the sheet to cover her exposed skin. The morning air had a bit of a nip, but he wasn't bullshitting himself. It was going to be hard as hell as it was to keep his hands to himself while they talked things out. He didn't need any more distraction than he already had.

"Grant?"

A tight knot formed in his chest when he glanced up to see her sleepy, silver eyes staring back at him through her long black-as-coal eyelashes. Christ, she was beautiful. A sudden moment of panic blindsided his thoughts, sending him into a complete tailspin. He shouldn't be here. He was never going to earn her trust and love. How could he? He was as big a monster as those who had tried to destroy her. He couldn't fool himself. No matter where he went or what identity he wore, he would never be more than a killer. Even though he'd retired, that part of him still existed. Still lurked under the surface. How could he expect her to love that? He had no right to even ask it of her.

"Please tell me I'm not dreaming." A firestorm of need and hope burned through his veins when her fingers grazed his jaw, that simple touch like no dream he'd ever had. Against his will his eyes closed, his lungs pumping hard to supply enough oxygen to feed the demands of his racing heart. He swallowed against the growing knot in his throat, nearly choking on all the things he'd wanted to say, but could no longer find the words to say them.

When the soft silk of her lips touched his, the tight-fisted grip he'd thought he had on his control slipped away, sending him over some invisible cliff. Her mouth opened on a sigh, her desperate breaths mingling with his as his tongue stroked deep inside, her familiar taste fueling the blazing fire deep within his bones. *This is where I belong.* An unquenchable thirst raged inside him, forcing him take more. His fists clenched the back of her shirt, the flimsy material offering no resistance as he tore it from her body, exposing her fevered skin to his touch.

"I need you." He didn't know if he'd said the words aloud or merely in his head, but no words had ever been more true. The last six months without her had been like trying to breathe water. He'd been slowly drowning. Only in these last few moments had he taken his first real breath since that horrible night in Navi.

The feel of her in his hands, against his skin, was like finding a part of himself he never knew existed. He pulled her close, crushing her against him when she slid into his lap, her legs hugging his waist like she, too, couldn't get close enough. He would never be close enough. He would spend the rest of his days searching for a closer connection to this incredible woman.

"Grant, please make love to me. I've missed you so much."

Is this truly happening? He almost couldn't bring himself to believe it until she'd spoken those words. The familiar emptiness lifted from his soul and his heart filled with all the love he thought he'd lost. "God, I've missed you, fossa." His hands tangled in her hair, pulling her head back to expose her slender neck. The taste of her salty skin enlivened his senses, sending a tidal wave of primal desire dancing along his spine straight to his cock. In a blinding rush, he flipped her to her back, dragging her cotton panties to the floor along with his shorts. She fought to rid him of his shirt, sending buttons snapping and flying.

With only one arm free, he hovered above her naked body. Her panted, frantic breaths danced along the fine hairs on his neck until she'd freed the other. He breathed her in, clutching her to him with a gentle strength he'd once though was beyond him. Her delicate fingers framed his face and, when he lifted his head, the sight of her tear-filled eyes nearly stopped his heart. A million unspoken words passed between them in that one moment.

"I love you." Her whispered words echoed the truth in her eyes. He knew. He knew if he died right then, right there in her arms, he would do so without a single regret.

"I love you." He wrapped her in his arms, sliding deep inside her with a single thrust. Her aching moan filled his mouth, the heat of her kiss matching the heat of her womb as she welcomed him into her body. Overwhelmed by an onslaught of emotion, his senses scattered. He reined them in one by one, gathering her taste, her scent, the feel of her in his arms and committed each one to a new memory.

Tender thrusts quickly gave way to ravaging heat as they lost themselves to their remembered passion. It had been so long. So long since he'd held her beneath him. So long since he'd tasted the distinct wildness that lived within her. Grant could feel her inner walls tightening around him, gripping his shaft in a frenzied flutter as she cried out beneath him. He chased his own release, his muscles burning with each powerful, claiming thrust. He would live, right here inside her, if he could only hold out for just…one…more.

His shouts of release filled the trees, sending a flock of birds to flight and a cacophony of island sounds erupting from the surrounding brush. A rush of new blood flooded his brain and he collapsed against her, a sudden dizziness overwhelming his senses. As much as he wanted to stay there, to soak in the feel of her beneath him, he knew he was crushing her. Tremors wracked his arms from the effort it took to push himself up, their sweat-slicked skin slowly peeling apart. Her arms banded around him and pulled him back to her as she tightened her legs around his hips.

"Don't go." Her fingers threaded through his sweaty hair, her lips leaving a trail of tender kisses along his neck.

He would never need more than those words. As long as she would have him, he would walk by her side. "I'm not going anywhere, fossa." He rested his forehead against hers and nuzzled her nose, nipping her upper lip as it curled into a perfect smile. "Not without you."

The End

Survivors' Justice Series reading order:
Surviving Redemption
One Defining Second

Grant and Thalia's story continues in One Defining Second

Follow D.L. Roan for insider peeks of her upcoming books and get to know more about her cast of incredible, sexy characters.

www.dlroan.com
Twitter
Facebook
Goodreads

20753330R00144

Printed in Great Britain
by Amazon